Cadomin:
The Adventures of Billy Boy

Charles Wood

Charles
wood

Leon's Basement Publishing
2014

First Printing: 2014

ISBN 978-0-9936640-0-7

Leon's Basement Publishing
#102 30 Cavan Street
Nanaimo, British Columbia, Canada, V9R 6K3

www.thetinfoilhat.ca

For Logan Pump

Cadomin:
The Adventures of Billy Boy

Contents

The Cave

It was a bighorn sheep that first told Billy Boy about the cave. They were standing beside the river that flowed down from the mountains to the west. The boy had come down to the river to think, but when he'd found the sheep there, he knew that he'd have to put off his thinking, for a little while at least. However, since both of them were awkward, they just wound up standing beside the river in awkward silence.

Not knowing what else to do, the boy picked up a long branch from the ground and started playing in the mud beside the river. He drew a picture of a train. He wished that he could draw the sound as well, since that seemed like an important part of being a train. However, when he tried to draw the sound, all he managed to make were what looked like stink lines. When he was done, he was dissatisfied, and he wound up scuffing the picture out with his foot.

Billy was just about to leave. The drawing hadn't worked out, and it was becoming obvious that the sheep wasn't going to go away and let him think. Conversation wasn't really much of an option either. Generally, sheep don't have much of anything to say, and that particular sheep wasn't any different. They're terrible at small talk, and since the boy didn't feel like talking himself, after they had said hello to each other, neither he nor the animal had much of anything to say. The boy decided that he would rather leave himself than stand around waiting for the sheep to do something interesting.

However, like Billy, the sheep was an adventurer, and even

though it didn't say anything, the animal sensed that it was in the company of a kindred spirit and didn't want Billy to go. Also, while it had always been a bit of a loner, it really didn't want to be alone. The animal was separated from his herd, which is a fairly radical thing for a sheep to do.

The sheep hadn't gone very far, though, and the herd was only about thirty feet downstream, grazing at the grasses that grew between the rocks. Most of them were eating, but a couple of the young ones were jumping around and generally making fools of themselves. They would take eating breaks to graze, and then hop around a little. Gradually the eating breaks became longer, and after a while the hopping subsided.

The sheep saw that Billy was about to leave, so, not knowing what else to do, it started talking about the weather. The past week had been unseasonably wet, and the two of them were able to commiserate about it. They talked about some other equally inconsequential things for a while. Billy found that, in spite of what he had expected, once the sheep got going, it was surprisingly good at small talk. However, after a while the conversation ran its course, and then they both sank into silence again.

Once again Billy Boy turned and was just about to leave. In desperation, the sheep brought up the cave, hoping it would be enough to keep the boy there. It hadn't held much interest for the animal. As far as he could tell in the darkness, the cave didn't contain anything to eat, and so wasn't really very interesting. However, even though there was no food in the cave, the sheep still thought it was unique and would probably be interesting to the boy. So, when he couldn't think of anything else to talk about, he decided that he'd bring it up.

Billy had lived in Cadomin his whole life, but in all of his travels, he had never seen the entrance to the cave. When the sheep told him about it, he knew that he had to find it for himself. Billy thought of himself as an adventurer, and so the caves piqued his interest. He found it almost irresistible to think of them sitting up there unexplored for all those years.

The sheep had told him that the cave would be hard to find. The entrance was small and looked like a depression or small hole in the side of the mountain. There were also trees around it, so it was screened from view as well as being small. You wouldn't be able to find the cave unless you knew for sure that it was up there. It wasn't likely at all that you would just stumble on it.

However, the sheep had been lucky. Despite the odds against it, it had managed to come across the cave by accident. It was close to where the herd had been grazing that day. They often grazed in that spot, and the area was getting pretty picked over. The sheep had found it boring and irritating, especially when he was forced to start pulling grass from between rocks to get the little bits of foliage that were left. After a while, he gave up and started looking for another place on the mountain to eat. When he went wandering, he managed to come across the cave entrance.

He had told Billy the important points, and then the sheep noticed how far away his herd was getting, so he left the boy and walked back along the river. By that time, the sheep had found a shallow spot and managed to cross over the branches of the river to the railroad tracks on the other side. While there wasn't much food on the tracks or the man-made ridge that the tracks were built on, the ditches on either side of the ridge were chock full of delicious little plants to eat.

After the sheep left, Billy gazed up at the mountain behind him. The animal couldn't be exact about the location, but it was certain that the cave was up in that general area. Compared to the others, the mountain was fairly small, and only the very top of it was above the tree-line. He wanted to get going right away, but it was already late in the day, and Billy knew he'd have to wait until the next day. He looked longingly up the slope before he picked up his bike and went home.

When he got there, he didn't say anything to his mother. She knew that in the valley, other than locking him up, there wasn't much she could do to keep him from wandering off and exploring. She still worried though, and he knew that she wouldn't be happy about him going to the cave, so he kept quiet.

The next morning as he was leaving the house he just told his mother that he was going out to explore. It was sort of the truth, just not the whole truth. It wasn't a lie, and it seemed like enough information that he wouldn't spend the whole day feeling guilty. He knew it wasn't really good enough, but he felt that it was sufficient for him to be able to continue.

He knew of a trail at the south edge of town that went up the mountain quite a ways. The trail was wide and looked like it might have been a kind of road at some point in time. It was gravelly and as wide as tire tracks. Even if the trail had been a road at one point, it could never have been that good. Only jeeps and 4x4s would ever have been able to use it. It wasn't as steep as some of the foot trails in that area, but it was still quite steep. By the time that Billy was using it, the road was falling apart. The boy wondered if even a jeep could have gotten up it without getting stuck by that point.

After he'd been struggling up the trail for a half hour, he found a turn off that went uphill, toward where he was sure that the cave was located. The foot trail was almost hidden, but there was a slight gap between the trees that he managed to pick out. The main trail continued in a straight line in front of him and beckoned him forward with how visible and easy it was in comparison.

However, the main trail was also heading away from the cave. After some hesitation, he turned onto the barely visible side trail. Compared to the main trail, it was just a rough track, and it was very steep. It wasn't skirting along the edge of the slope, but going straight up it. There were roots criss-crossing it which made it very bumpy and difficult riding. He wanted to stay on his bike, but soon the path became so steep that he wouldn't have been able to pedal up it anymore even if there hadn't been roots across his path. He had to lay the bike down at the side of the path and continue on foot.

After another hour or so of hiking upward and even, in places, getting down and scrambling on all fours over roots and rocks, he finally arrived at the cave entrance. As the sheep had told him, it was just a hole that opened up in the side of the mountain. It was below the tree-line and so the area around it was still forested. However, there was a bit of a clearing, so the entrance wasn't completely hidden.

Billy went slowly into the cave, ducking a little to get his head under the low arch of the entry. Inside, it became dark almost immediately. He knew that he wouldn't be able to go far, since he didn't have any light. The glow from the entrance extended into the front cavern, but Billy could see that the cave kept going far beyond that. There were signs that, at some point in time, a few of the Hinton kids had come out there to drink and tag the walls with spray paint. But there was only a little graffiti, and even drunk teens must have found it exhausting. It was a long way to go for a party, never mind the climb to get to the entrance. It was easier to tag rocks and cliffs beside the highway than climb all the way up to the caves to do it.

There were piles of boulders on the floor and a dripping sound coming from somewhere in the darkness off to the right. He went up to one of the piles and found that there were large gaps between the stones. He stared into one of the gaps, and even though it was too dark to see anything, he felt sure that there was another cavern below him through that hole. He sensed the open air in front of his face.

He found the cave interesting enough at first, but he knew that it would get boring very fast without a source of light. It was just damp, dark and uncomfortable. He was limited to exploring the first cavern, and even that was too large to explore thoroughly. He could only go as far as the light from the entrance penetrated, which was only about two-thirds of the way into the first cavern. After staring into the darkness for a while, Billy turned around and went back outside.

He gasped as he came back out of the caves. He hadn't realized that he'd been holding his breath, but subconsciously, the darkness had made him feel like he was under water. Coming back into the light of day allowed him to breathe properly again. He felt a little disoriented, so, for a few minutes, he sat down beside the entrance. While he was sitting, he decided that if he wanted to explore the caves properly, he'd need to get some special equipment. He had no idea where he'd have to go to get fancy gear, however. None of his other adventures had required anything more than his feet and his bike.

He told himself that he had gotten bored, but the truth was that he was also frightened. The blackness in front of his face had made him nervous and, even though they were invisible, so had all the depths that he had known were in front of him. He thought of all the holes and gaps in the caves, waiting to trip him up or drop him into some pit.

After more consideration, Billy decided that he probably didn't want to explore the cave anyway, and certainly not enough to go out and find special equipment. He was glad that he'd come to find it, but he'd gone inside, and he didn't feel required to do any more. Once he'd made the decision, he was actually relieved about not having to explore any further. Since he didn't have proper equipment to explore them, he had a good excuse to avoid going into them again.

He stood up and started back down the hill. The sky was overcast, but even though it wasn't really that bright out, after the darkness of the cave, it seemed bright. He was still high on the mountain, but the trail was extremely overgrown and because of the thickness of the forest around him, he couldn't see very far. It was only when he reached the little ridge where he had left his bike that the trees opened out and he was able to see properly again.

Fifty feet below him was the main trail. Further down, in the valley, he could also see his mother sitting on the front porch of their house. Even from a distance she was easy to pick out. There weren't many other houses still standing, and she was the only figure that moved. There were a couple of crows flying above him, and, on the other side of the valley, he could see the herd of sheep grazing on the mountain. However, in the valley itself, all he could see moving was his mother drinking iced tea on the front porch of their house.

Besides Billy and his mother, no one else lived in Cadomin. Most of the town was ramshackle and falling over, and the two of them occupied the last house in the valley that was still standing upright. Even the buildings that were still standing were keeled over drunkenly. Roofs tipped awkwardly and many walls had lain down, leaving the insides of the building exposed. Long grass and weeds grew up through windows and around the edges of the walls.

The village was in a wide valley. To the west were mountains, and to the east were foothills. There was a small gap in the hills to the east and the railroad tracks, the road and the river all found an exit from the valley through the gap. Pine forest covered everything on the sides of the hills, but hadn't yet swallowed the remains of the village.

What was left of a pit mine was dug into the side of one of the mountains at the west end of the valley. When the mine had shut down, most of the people had moved away, making Cadomin a ghost town. Without any maintenance, the roads that made terraces around the walls of the pit were falling apart and, instead of ridges, they were gradually reshaping themselves into a slope. The whole pit was slowly being taken over by the pine forest, and there were young pine trees growing on the slopes, helping to speed up the deterioration.

Despite how mountainous the area was, the valley in which Cadomin lay was quite flat. As a result, it had been possible for the village to be laid out in an almost perfect grid. The main road ran east to west through the valley, ending at the old mine pit on the west end of the village and the old highway at the east end. Once it left the valley, the road soon met up with the highway at a ninety degree angle, and the highway went roughly north-south. The south-bound branch crossed the river and the railroad tracks, and the north-bound branch wound through the hills toward the town of Hinton. There was never any traffic, and while the road wasn't exactly closed, it was slowly falling apart. The only vehicles that still used it were occasional logging trucks, and they were so heavy that they were capable of driving on straight gravel and rocks. As a result, repair of the highway wasn't a priority for anyone.

Since there weren't many buildings standing by that point in time, most of the village was made up of foundation pits surrounded by the wreckage of the buildings that had previously stood above them. Even the foundations were beginning to get filled in. Every year more leaves and soil blew into the basements, and every year the pits got closer to becoming level with the rest of the ground.

But it was still just possible to pick out the remains of the simple grid where the streets had been. The streets had been made of gravel, so it had been quick and easy for grasses and weeds to grow on them, and, by that time, the streets were just long, rocky lawns. Nonetheless, they were still barely visible under a blanket of weeds, and, if you were looking, a person could still find the straight lines that divided streets and yards.

And, of course, you couldn't really see the streets or the foundations or anything else under the cover of the long grass and other growing things that had sprung up all over town. The pine forest that grew on the hills surrounding the valley had already swallowed the edges of the ruined village. It wouldn't be long before the forest would fill the valley and absorb the village completely.

But before the forest managed to take over the whole valley, the little plants were having a heyday growing in all the open air and sunlight that they were able to get. They were especially thick beside the river where there was a bit of sand and moisture. Most of the valley was a thin layer of soil over a bed of rocks, so as soon as a plant dug down a few inches, its roots had to either stop or find a way to burrow through rock. But beside the river there was actual soil to hold onto, so it was a particularly lush area.

The river was fairly swift and cold. It only started to meander when it got to the flats around Cadomin. And even around the village where it had more room to spread out, the water still kept up a brisk pace. Generally, rather than detouring, it cut straight through the gravelly soil and between the pines. Even though the water was clear, it looked murky and muddy. Many weeds grew along the bottom. The long strands of weeds looked like tangles of hair caught in the current.

The river ran swiftly south of what was left of the village in three narrow branches. Between the separate parts of the river were low islands of gravel with a few bushes and grasses growing on them. Once it had gotten past the village, the branches of the river came together again, flowed out through the gap in the hills, and then immediately turned south.

On the south side of the river ran railroad tracks that headed west into the mountains, and east through Cadomin and the foothills. The tracks followed the river through the village, but kept heading east when the river turned south. Generally, the train just rumbled past, but occasionally it let loose with its whistle. Then, before it petered out, the mournful sound would bounce around the valley for a while.

Despite what the rest of the town was like, Billy Boy never let his lawn get overgrown or weedy. The boy took pride in the fact that his yard stood out. Once a week he was out with the old lawnmower making sure that the yard was properly trimmed. As a result, even from far up on the ridge, Billy was easily able to pick out the neatly trimmed square of his yard.

It was a struggle to keep the yard tidy. Long grasses from the yards on either side were too tall to stand upright, and often flopped over into his yard. Then he would have to flip the tall grasses back so that he could mow under them. He had decided that no matter how long they got, he wouldn't mow any of the other lawns. He figured that if he started doing other lawns, it would never end. He'd wind up having to mow the whole valley. And, since everything would have grown back by the time he was done, he'd have to start over again when he was finished. So he just concentrated on his own yard, and let everything else in the valley grow wild.

Billy's mom had mowed the lawn until Billy had turned eight, then she'd passed the chore on to him. Besides the lawn, they also tried to keep the garden in good shape. They didn't bother getting annual plants anymore, since it required a trip to Hinton to get them, and it didn't seem worth it. For the vegetables that they wanted to be able to grow every year, they kept some seeds and planted them in the spring. For the rest of the plants, they didn't bother, but, even so, there were perennials that kept coming back every year without any effort on their part at all.

They also had those little pinwheels that were stuck in the grass and would turn in the breeze. His mother thought they looked great and made the house look cared for in spite of its surroundings. Billy had wanted to get gnomes, but his mother thought gnomes were tacky. He couldn't see how they were any tackier than pinwheels, but he didn't argue.

Billy had been resting as he looked down at the valley and his mother. He noticed storm clouds coming over the mountains to the west and decided that he couldn't linger on the mountain any longer if he didn't want to get caught in the rain. He picked up his bike and started pedaling back along the wide trail down the mountain.

In twenty minutes, Billy was back in the valley, and five minutes after that, he was back at his house. He went inside and got some water out of the tap in the kitchen. He still didn't tell his mother where he'd been. She asked what he'd been up to, but he seemed uncomfortable about it, so she left it alone. It was already apparent that Billy Boy could be prickly about his privacy, so she thought it best not to pry too much.

Billy Boy and his mom often sat out in the back yard in the evenings and watched the sun go down over the mountains to the west. On that particular evening, they thought they might have to change their plans to avoid getting rained on. The storm clouds blew away without doing anything, though, and then they were left with clear weather. They were able to follow their usual routine. They went outside, drank iced tea, and sat on the porch in comfortable silence.

Well, most of the time it was comfortable, but that night Billy caught his mom watching what was left of the road going out of town to the east. Occasionally, even though she tried not to, he caught her gazing down that road. She was thinking about Billy's father, and the boy knew that his mother was still hoping that she would see a light blue pickup coming back along that track. It had been a long time since he'd left, but she was still pining.

Billy's father had left eight years earlier, when Billy was only four. He had left in his blue truck one morning to go to Hinton, but he never came back. At first, they thought he had run into car trouble or something, but after a week or so, it was clear that he wasn't coming back. Billy's mom had been really worried, and they started walking along the road to Hinton to see if they could find him. They'd walked all the way to the town, however, and they hadn't found any sign of him.

They'd returned to Cadomin to wait, and they were still waiting. There hadn't been any sign since then, either.

Billy hadn't been too happy about it, of course. No one likes to be abandoned. At first, he'd cried quite a bit, and sometimes his mother would find him on the road trying to walk to Hinton again to see if he could find his father. However, he'd gotten over it by the time he was six or seven. Billy wasn't the type to linger over things. To be fair, by that time, he'd spent almost as much of his life with his father gone than he'd spent with him. He remembered what his father looked like, but didn't remember his voice or personality.

Billy's mother had been desolated, however, and she was taking a very long time to get over it. He didn't know it, but Billy Boy looked almost exactly like his father. Granted, his father's hair had been blond and his own was dark, but he had the same blue eyes and thin lips. He also had the same prominent jaw. As a result, when his mother looked at Billy she would see her husband, and it only made things worse.

And things were already pretty bad with her. She thought that she was keeping her feelings hidden from Billy, but she wasn't. Though she tried to hide it, she still pined for her husband awfully. She knew it was irrational, but she still thought that he was alive and wandering in the forest somewhere. She decided that he was still trying to get back to her. Of course, she knew that she shouldn't believe these things, and that she ought to give up and just get on with other things, but she couldn't do it.

Even though she knew that she didn't have to, she still slept on her own side of the bed. Sometimes in the mornings, she'd wake up in a position that took most of the bed, including the space that her husband had previously occupied, and then she would feel bad about it. Then she would get angry at herself for feeling bad, since she knew that there wasn't any point, and that she didn't need to feel bad anymore. Then she would get up and try to forget about her husband for the rest of the day, but, in spite of herself, she wouldn't be able to get much sleep that night. She worried that inadvertently she'd take over her husband's side of the bed again, and so, instead of sleeping, she would spend the night concentrating and tense about trying to stay on her own side.

Sometimes in the evenings she would tell Billy stories about his father. The boy didn't really believe most of them. In fact, he was completely sick of them and didn't really want to hear the stories, but he knew that his mother wanted to tell them. To humour her, he would sit still and listen.

She often told him the story of how a brown bear had tried to steal his father's food. His father had caught the bear, grabbed hold of it and then they had had a fight about it. The bear kept trying to get away, and it would have been easy to just let him go, but his father just wouldn't let that bear get away. When he finally got the bear down and was holding him there, the bear begged for mercy. But Billy's father didn't have much mercy in him in to start with, and so with the thrashing and struggling, the bear had already used it all up, and so Billy's father killed the bear.

A crow was sitting in a tree nearby, and had watched the whole fight. The crow told Billy's dad that the bear had lots of friends and relatives, and they would all be after him for what he'd done. Billy's father thought about this for a while, and decided that the crow was probably right, but he still wasn't sure what he could do about it, so he thought some more. He came up with an idea, and then he gave the crow some food and asked if the crow could keep a look out, and whenever one of the bear's friends or relatives were coming, give Billy's father some warning. At least then, he could prepare. Either he'd hide or get ready to fight, but at least he'd have some time to prepare.

The crow agreed, but he said that he'd need a lot more food than he'd already gotten. Billy Boy's father handed over more food and then asked the crow if that was enough. It was more than the bear had been trying to steal, and so the whole fight had been pointless. But the deed was done, and the man knew that there was no point in thinking about it. The bear was dead, and the crow was the only one who could help him.

Now the crow wasn't used to anyone trusting him enough to make a deal with him. Most people just assumed that you couldn't trust a crow. So he was more than a little touched by the faith that Billy Boy's father was putting in him. Also, he was pretty happy about getting the food, so he agreed, and after that the crow kept watch over Billy Boy's dad.

Billy didn't like hearing this story, but he knew that it was what kept hope alive in his mother. She might have given up on his father years ago, if she didn't believe that the crow was still watching over him. However, because of the crow, she felt sure that Billy's father wasn't dead. He was just taking a very long time to get home.

When Billy Boy heard the story, he just wanted to say to his mother that maybe the crow did betray his dad, and so maybe the bears had gotten him. Maybe the bears had given the crow more food just to leave so they could sneak up on the man. Maybe all the bad things you hear about crows are true.

Another possibility was that his father had just decided to take off. Maybe the crow had been faithful and was still watching over his father as the man pursued a totally different life. Just because the crow was watching didn't mean his father had to come back. His mother would never accept the possibility that his father had just left them, but Billy didn't see why it couldn't have happened that way. His mother would rather think that he was dead or lost than think that he'd just taken off. So Billy thought those things, but he kept his mouth shut and never mentioned it to his mother.

Besides, what Billy thought was most likely was that the story was completely made up. It sounded made up. Maybe there had never been a bear or a crow. Billy knew that bears were very strong, so no matter how strong his father had been, it seemed unlikely that he could have beat a bear. So he probably didn't have a deal with the crow either. He was probably just wandering around without anyone keeping watch.

If Billy had been a little older, he would have realized that it might be a good thing if he told his mother and made her give up hope. If she had given up hope, then the two of them would have moved away from Cadomin. The only thing that kept them there was her waiting around for her husband to come back. If they moved to another place, then she might meet someone else. Billy wasn't sure how good that would be or how he would feel about it, but he still thought it would be better than waiting for his father to come back.

But Billy wasn't a little older. He was only twelve and didn't know much yet. Well, not much about his mother, anyway. He just figured that he'd let her keep thinking the things that seemed to make her happy. He didn't realize that she wasn't really very happy at all.

So they stayed in Cadomin even after everyone else had left. When Billy's dad had been around, there had still been a few people in the village. Mostly old guys left over from when the coal mine had still been working. There were a few younger couples from the nearby town of Hinton, who wanted to get back to the land. However, after Billy's dad had left, the old guys had moved away, most of them going over the mountains to live by a lake or the ocean. And the young couples had gotten sick of getting back to the land, so they had moved away as well. They had moved to cities and grown vegetable gardens.

Billy had already figured out that he'd also have to leave at some point in time. He knew that when he got to be a little older, he'd have to get going, but he didn't know what his mom would do then. Billy was happy that at least that day was still a fair way off. He didn't want to deal with it yet, so he didn't. He hoped that when he left, his mother would move to Hinton, since Cadomin was no place to be alone. But she didn't seem to like Hinton. She'd told Billy never to go there, so it was doubtful if she'd ever want to move into town herself. Besides, she was very stubborn, so even if she'd liked the place, she might keep waiting for his father and grow old in Cadomin even if she didn't really want to.

The Bike

Billy had just turned twelve when he found the bike. He came across a burnt out shack a few miles from Cadomin while he was out walking. The roof was missing and it didn't seem safe. In addition, the walls were still standing, but they looked ready to fall over any time. Billy wasn't sure he'd even be able to go inside, but then he noticed the bike and got distracted before he could worry too much more about it.

The bike was on the front porch, chained to one of the burnt columns. With a little effort, it was easy enough for the boy to break the column and free it. However, the chain was still whole and attached to the bike, so, after thinking about it for a minute, the boy wrapped it tightly around the frame and hooked it under the seat, so that it wouldn't drag on the ground while he was riding. If he could have, he would have gotten rid of the chain completely, but he had no tools to cut it with, so the chain had to stay wrapped around the bike. However, except when he occasionally had to reach down to re-adjust it, it never gave him any trouble.

Billy loved that bike, despite the fact that it was in terrible shape. It was rusted and decrepit, and it had never been built to ride through the forest in the first place. It was for streets, puddles and maybe the occasional jaunt on a dirt trail, but not the roots and mud of the forest. But Billy Boy happily rode it anyway, forcing it through puddles and between trees, enjoying the freedom. The machine seemed inseparable from the boy and he rode it everywhere that he could.

And since it was old and falling apart, it wouldn't have been great even if it had actually been made for the mountains. The bike didn't have any shocks, so it rattled like crazy whenever it went over a root, which was often. The tires weren't completely flat, but they didn't have as much pressure as they should. The frame was rusty in several places, and the chain needed to be greased, but Billy didn't have any grease, and didn't really know where to get it.

Billy was mechanical enough to know that the bike was in rough shape, but that the only problem that would actually keep the bike from moving was the lack of grease. He figured that he could put up with the rough ride from the tires and live with the rust spots. They didn't really seem to be causing much of a problem. But he knew that if the chain stopped working then the bike wouldn't work either, and so he also knew that eventually he was going to need to get something to put on it. The chain was already squeaking and cracking as he pedaled, and he knew he'd have to do something about it soon.

He figured his only hope was to go to Hinton. He didn't really know how the town worked, but he knew that he would be able to find grease there. The road from Cadomin went to Hinton, and Billy knew of trails through the forest that would shorten the distance quite a bit. So one morning, while his mother was still sleeping, he started off on a journey to town.

She'd already expressed strong disapproval of the town, and he knew she wouldn't be happy about him going, so he kept it to himself and said nothing. He didn't like to have to deceive her, but the thought of the bike quitting on him made him very upset, and so he knew that he had to get some grease for his chain before that happened. He didn't really know anything about the town, but, unlike his mother, he wasn't disturbed by the mere thought of it. The idea of it was faintly threatening, but he was also happy to be going on another adventure.

He knew that he'd need some money, so even though he felt bad about it, he rummaged through his mom's purse before he left the house, and took a ten dollar bill. He didn't know how much grease would cost, but he didn't imagine it would be more than ten dollars. Indeed, even ten dollars seemed exorbitant to him. He couldn't imagine much that really deserved to cost more than ten dollars. He would have been astonished to find out that his bike had cost fifty when it had first been purchased.

By noon he had made it to Hinton. He crossed the railroad tracks and followed the smokestacks sticking out of the forest in front of him. There was a pulp mill in town, which is where the stacks came from, and they emitted a noxious odour caused by the sulphur and chlorine that they used to bleach the wood pulp. He followed a trail from the tracks to the shopping area where he dismounted and started walking the bike. That way, he'd be able to spend more time looking around without having to worry about riding.

He found the place confusing. There was a collection of stores, or at least he assumed they were stores, since they were brightly coloured and box-like. There were many people around, but he didn't want to go up to any of them to find out where they kept the grease. They looked vaguely irritated, and only cheered up when they saw someone they knew, and then they would stop and talk to their acquaintances. Billy figured he wouldn't be welcome to interrupt to ask them questions about grease. So either people looked too mad for him to ask, or else they were in the middle of a conversation and looked like they were too busy to talk. That's how it seemed to Billy, anyway, so he kept to himself.

He wandered around for a couple hours, but he never did figure it out. There were many shops and buildings, and Billy tried to puzzle out the signs, but while he could figure out the words, he couldn't decide which one might have grease. For example, he knew what "Canadian" and "tire" meant, but he didn't know whether they would have grease or not. He also couldn't figure out why a person would care whether their tires were Canadian or not, but he didn't waste much time worrying about that, since it wasn't really important to him.

He only made one attempt to actually go into a store. It was called "King Drugs." Again, he knew what a king was, and what a drug was, but he couldn't figure out why those words were together. Were royal drugs better? He figured they must be, which was why they advertised it on the front of the store. Did kings use grease for anything? He hoped they did, which is why he went inside.

Inside the store, there were rows and rows of stuff, most of which he couldn't figure out at all. There was nail polish, rubbing alcohol and something called Q-tips. Like the signs on the stores themselves, he understood the words on each package, but he couldn't figure out what they meant. Why would you polish your nails? Was it like wax or something? Would it work on a bike chain? And were you supposed to rub the bottle before you drank the alcohol? And what was a Q-tip, anyway? That was one he couldn't make any sense of at all.

After he had been staring at the shelves for a few minutes, a woman came up to him and asked him if there was anything she could help him with. She was trying to hide it, but she was making a face at the same time as she was asking if she could help. Billy got the impression that she hoped that he didn't want anything and would just leave. Lucky for her, Billy didn't want to be there any more than she wanted him there, so he just mumbled that he was all right and left the store.

He felt dejected as he rode home. When he got back to the house, his mother was out touching up some paint around the windows, so he was able to sneak inside and return the ten dollar bill to her purse. She asked him where he had been, since he'd left so early, but he just said he'd been out riding, and she was satisfied with that. He went riding all the time, so she wasn't going to get upset about it.

After that, he still went back to town occasionally to try to figure out which of the stores might have grease. He decided he would be more careful, and he resolved that he wouldn't try to go into any of the stores again, until he was sure which one actually had it. Staying out of the stores wasn't much of a problem, since he never did manage to figure out which store he really wanted.

While Billy liked to think that he'd have been able to go in if he had been able to figure out the right store, deep down he wasn't so sure. Like the cave, Hinton made him nervous. Billy didn't like being confused or overwhelmed, and the town did both. Even if he'd been able to figure out where he needed to go, he wasn't sure that he would be able to go inside. Besides, even if he could figure out the right store, he'd still have to wander around and find the grease on the shelf, and he wasn't sure that he would be up to that. So, while he wouldn't admit it to himself, the expeditions to Hinton became more about satisfying his curiosity about the town, instead of a mission to get grease for the bike.

However, he knew that the bike was getting desperate. The chain was making awful creaking and groaning sounds all the time and he knew he would have to do something. He tried to make grease for the chain from the things he found in the forest. First, he tried to use sap from different trees, but that was just sticky and made the bike hard to peddle until the sap wore out. Then it was easier to peddle, but the chain was also dry and noisy again.

Then he tried making a paste from some leaves, and mixing the paste with water. That didn't work at all. He spread it on the chain, but as soon as he started peddling, he could tell that it hadn't worked. It just made his chain look dirtier, but other than that, it didn't make any difference at all.

He went out to little lake near the house to see if some of the slime near the edges would work on the chain. He used a stick to scoop some slime out of the water, and then laid it on a rock to dry. Once it had dried out, he spread it on the chain. However, it wasn't any more effective than the leaves had been. It made the chain green, but didn't have any other effect.

Since none of his home-made substitutes were working, he decided that sooner or later he'd have to get some grease. He hadn't wanted to bother his mom about it, but the bike was at risk and he was getting desperate, and so he knew that he would have to ask her. He figured that the only solution would inevitably involve going to Hinton, and he knew that she wouldn't want to go, so he felt bad asking her about it. But even though he didn't want to upset her, he didn't know what else to do. When he asked her, she frowned, but after a few minutes, she told him not to worry, and that she would take care of it.

The next day she was gone. She'd left him a little note to tell him what to eat and to remind him that he needed to clean out the gutters on the house. So he spent the day cleaning, and toward evening she returned, while he was eating supper. He fixed her something to eat, and she sat down in the kitchen and pulled a tube of bicycle grease out of her purse and placed it on the table.

"That should do for a while," she said.

"Did you have to go into a store for that?" he asked.

She replied that she did. He looked amazed, and she realized how mystified he was by Hinton. And she also realized that at some point in time she'd have to give him some sort of introduction to the town. He wouldn't be able to get far if he was still awestruck by stores.

Billy grabbed the tube of grease and went straight out to put it on his chain. She followed him to the front of the house and watched as he carefully tended to the chain. She knew that he was working from instinct and he didn't really have any idea of what he was doing, but, except for the tongue sticking out of the side of his mouth while he worked, he looked like an expert. She decided that he was all right for now, and that she still had a little time before it became necessary to show him how to live in the town.

Once he had new grease for the chain, Billy Boy was very happy again and rode his bike even more than he had before. The closest he came to Hinton were the outskirts, however. Now that he had grease, there was no point in any more exploration of the town. The furthest he went was to look down on it from the top of one of the hills that overlooked the town. He would just gaze at the buildings for a few moments and then turn around and go back into the woods.

Instead, he spent most of his time at the lake where he had gotten the slime. In actuality, it was a slough. The small lake had been created by a beaver damming a creek. Most of the water was covered by tall grasses or slime, but there was also a fairly large area of open water that Billy found peaceful to sit beside. The mosquitoes bit him while he sat there, but he didn't care too much. He always tried to leave before the sun started going down and the bugs were at their worst.

When he got tired of the lake, he explored the area around Cadomin as much as he could. The remnants of the open pit coal mine were dug into the side of a mountain at the west end of the valley. He would go to the edge of the village and ride his bike on what was left of the roads in the mine pit.

On the sides of the Cadomin pit were the remnants of the roads where the big trucks had carried the coal. Driving the trucks was one of the most dangerous things about working a pit mine, since the trucks were huge and could be hard to handle on the narrow roads. Not only were they huge, but you also had to worry about driving them off one of the roads and tumbling into the pit.

There was no way a coal truck or even a pickup could have driven on those roads anymore, they were in such bad shape. But there was still enough space for a bike, so Billy would ride on them. There wasn't much to see out at the pit, but he would take his feet off the pedals and hold his feet off to each side of the bike. He rode down the roads really fast and he enjoyed that. He found it both exhilarating and strangely calming.

While he was out exploring, he also followed the railroad tracks further than he had before. Even though the tracks passed close to Cadomin, he'd never followed them very far. He thought that they might lead to thoughts of leaving, and drag him away from his mom, so he tried not to spend too much time around them. But on his bike, and in the spirit of adventure, he followed them a few miles out of town in either direction.

To the west, the tracks just passed through more forest for several miles, and Billy was getting bored and thinking of turning around when suddenly he came to a railroad bridge that was going over a river. There was a sheer drop of about eighty feet to the water, so not too high, but high enough that he couldn't just jump off if he needed to. Also, the river was wide, so the bridge was long. Billy only went a few feet out and stopped. He didn't want to get caught on the bridge with his bike if the train came.

He looked across the bridge at the forest on the other side. He couldn't hear any sound of a train coming, but he also knew that his hearing wasn't perfect, and if he didn't hear it, it might sneak up on him. Besides that, he wasn't sure if he wanted to get to the other side that day anyway. Eventually he decided that he would have to come back on a different day to cross the bridge. It felt like a big step, and he didn't want to do it right then.

So he turned around and headed east. He went past Cadomin, and toward Hinton. When he'd gone to the town before, he had taken a trail and not the tracks, so it was all new to him. When he passed Hinton, he could see the smokestacks rising on his left. A few miles further along, he found a staircase leading downhill, away from the tracks and back toward the town. He couldn't figure out why anyone would put a set of stairs by the railroad tracks, but there they were, heading down from the tracks toward the town in the valley below. The stairs were dug out of the hillside, each step was made of soil held in place by a wide board that made up the front of the stair. Down the middle was a series of posts with a long cable running through holes in the top of the posts to make a crude handrail. Along the sides of the stairs, to hold them all together, were railroad ties set end to end down the side of the hill. The stairs ran seventy or eighty feet from the railroad tracks at the top to a trail at the bottom.

Billy Boy went down the stairs, but when he got to the bottom, he decided not to go further along the trail. It looked like it was heading for Hinton, and he didn't want to go there, so when he got down, he just turned around and went back up. His legs were tired by the time he reached the top again, but at least he hadn't had to drag the bike back up. He had been able to roll it beside him on the railroad ties. So while he was tired, at least he wasn't completely exhausted.

However, even though he wasn't exhausted yet, Billy decided

that it was time to head home anyway. He was winded, and he didn't really feel like going on. After that day, when he went riding, he found himself sticking a little closer to home. Unconsciously, he'd decided that the stairs to the east and the bridge to the west were boundaries that he wouldn't cross. So he really didn't explore very much, and just contented himself with riding around areas that he knew already. When he was feeling antsy he went back to the pit and rode down the old mine roads, to feel the wind blasting past him and that was usually enough to calm his restlessness. If he was feeling meditative, he would go sit by the lake for a few hours.

So in relative peace, Billy Boy managed to keep up his regular existence in Cadomin. Both he and his mother knew that they were just putting off an inevitable day that neither of them was looking forward to. Eventually he'd have to leave, and she knew that sooner or later she'd have to start getting him ready for the outside world. But neither of them were looking forward to it, so they both stayed quiet and pretended that everything was going just fine. And because both of them were very good at pretending, things really did go well, and both of them were content.

Theft

One morning Billy Boy got up and went outside to the front porch, where he thought he'd left his bike the evening before. It wasn't in its normal spot, and he couldn't think of where else he might have put it. He looked all around the outside of the house, but he couldn't see any sign of it. After he looked around the house, he started wracking his brains. He almost always just leaned it against the front porch, and he was sure that he'd done the same thing the previous night. Where else would he have left it?

He had come home the night before from riding the pit roads. Nothing fancy. Since he'd been riding the bike, he knew he must have had it at the pit, and he also knew that he must have had it when he rode home, so he must have left the bike somewhere near the house. He went back inside, and asked his mom if she'd seen the bike.

"Didn't you leave it out by the porch?" she asked.

He explained that it wasn't there, and asked her if she could remember him doing anything else with it. She couldn't however, and she'd even happened to be looking out the window when he came home the previous evening, so she'd seen him lean it against the porch when he got home. She was sure that the bike had been out there the night before, so there wasn't really any possibility that he'd lost it. The only possible answer was that someone had taken it.

However, there wasn't anyone else living anywhere near them, so they couldn't imagine who might have taken it. In fact, Billy didn't entirely accept the idea of someone stealing it at all. Even if there had been someone around to do it, he probably wouldn't have believed it. He'd never been stolen from before, and he wasn't even familiar with the idea of theft. He thought it was much more likely that he had put it down somewhere and forgotten about it, so he kept trying to figure out if he'd left it somewhere else.

Even when he finally did understand and begin to accept the possibility of a theft, he still couldn't understand why they had decided to steal the bike. Why couldn't they have stolen something else? Something he didn't care about? They could have taken the lawn-mower or the stupid little pinwheels from the lawn. Why did they take his bike?

Billy and his mom decided that even if it was gone, the thief might not have taken it very far. Billy was just clinging to any hope he could, but his mom figured that the thief might have stolen the bike without realizing what bad shape it was in. The thief must have figured out that the tires were flat and the frame was rusty, and then he might have decided to just dump the thing close to the house. She didn't say anything like that to Billy, of course. He loved the thing, but she knew that the bike was pretty decrepit, and because of that she was hopeful that it might have been left lying somewhere nearby.

So they went up and down the moldering streets of the village. They started from the west, checking each square in the grid that made up the town. They used the visible remains of the streets to remember which squares they'd already checked. They went around to the ruins of every house to see if the bike was there. If there wasn't anything left except a hole for the foundation, they would look closely in the pit to see if the bike was down there.

In one basement, Billy thought he saw the bike, so he climbed down. When he got to it, he pulled it out of the pile of leaves and dirt that it was buried in, but it turned out to be nothing but the frame of a tricycle. It didn't even have wheels. He'd just seen the metal tubing and gotten excited. His mom had been pretty sure that it wasn't the bike, but she had let him climb down anyway and look for himself.

By the end of the day they had finished checking the town-site, so they went home and Billy's mom made him some soup for supper. It was his favourite, but Billy Boy was feeling depressed and didn't seem to care.

The next day they got up early and went into the forest together to see if the bike was anywhere in the woods near Cadomin. They split up to cover more ground, but, by that point, Billy's mom was beginning to think that it was a lost cause. She had hoped they'd find the bike in town, but she knew that scrabbling around in the forest looking for it wouldn't be of much use. If the thief had taken the bike that far, then he obviously wasn't interested in letting it go. Even if the thief had dropped it, it would be hidden among the fallen trunks and undergrowth, and they could easily walk right past it without even noticing.

They spent a couple of days searching around in the bush, but they couldn't find the bike. Billy wanted to keep going further out, but his mom convinced him that the bike was gone, and no amount of searching was going to bring it back. She knew he was upset and so she tried to think of a way to make it up to him, but other than cooking food he liked, she couldn't think of anything. And since he didn't seem to care about the food anyway, she was at a loss.

For another couple of days Billy moped around the house. He walked out to the pits and climbed to the top, but the view was only okay, and without his bike, he couldn't go down the roads very fast. He tried running down, and while it wasn't bad, it wasn't nearly as good as riding the bike had been. Even going as fast as he could, he only got a little bit of a breeze and no rush at all. Plus, it made his legs tired, which riding had never done.

Billy decided that even if it was hopeless, he needed to go out and find the bike. He'd spent almost a week without it, and he was feeling like he was going crazy. Nothing was as much fun without the bike. Even sitting by the lake didn't help. At the end of the day, it felt like a long walk home, and he couldn't ride quickly away, so the mosquitoes were able to get at him.

He worked himself up to tell his mom that he needed to go. He spent most of a day preparing, and then one night at supper he broke the news to her that he had to leave to go find the bike. He had thought she would be more upset, but she seemed okay with it, or at least to have expected that it was coming.

He told her she should go to Hinton, but she said she couldn't. "Because you're waiting for dad?" he asked wearily.

"Yes, but I'll also be waiting for you to come back. You won't be able to find me if I go live in town."

He thought of how much trouble Hinton had given him when he was looking for grease and realized that his mom was right. If she went to live in the town, he'd never be able to find her again. He could find the shopping area, but he didn't even know where the houses were. And then he felt sad, because he'd wanted his mom to be able to go to town. Not that she probably would have left anyway, but now it was kind of his own fault that she was staying in Cadomin.

The next day she packed him some food, and gave him a hug and sent him on his way. He felt pretty nervous for a few minutes, but it didn't take long for him to start feeling quite good about everything. It was an adventure after all.

He walked east away from the mountains and toward Hinton. It seemed unlikely that the thief would have come from the mountains, so he thought it would be smarter to search for him to the east. For a little while he walked on the road, but soon the road disappeared into grass, which was fine with Billy. The grass was tall and still covered in dew even though the sun was up and there was a bit of a breeze. As he walked, he felt almost as good as he'd felt when he rode the bike. It wasn't a strong breeze, but it was enough to move his hair around a little bit. And since he was nervous and excited about leaving, the experience served as a pale copy of how he'd felt when he was racing down the hills. He was excited enough that he even forgot to turn around while he was walking so he could look back at his mom.

She stood out on the porch for a few minutes watching him walk away. She hoped that he would turn around or at least look behind him. When she couldn't wait for him to look behind him anymore, she went back inside the house. She had thought he would at least hesitate a little, so while she knew it was probably good that he felt so sure of himself, it also made her sad that he hadn't even looked back.

Poplars

Billy Boy kept walking east until he got to the railroad tracks. Then he started following the tracks toward the staircase. Because of his negative experience with the town, he was sure that the dastardly person who would have sunk to stealing his bike could only have come from Hinton. As a result, he was also sure that they would have had to come from the direction of the stairs. He wasn't sure if it would be necessary for him to go into the town. He hoped it wouldn't come to that, but he was prepared to do it, if he had to. He really wanted his bike back.

As he walked, he noticed that the forest had some strange trees in it. Around Cadomin, the trees all had needles instead of leaves. But in this forest, there were tall trees with a bundle of leaves near the top. They barely had any branches or leaves along most of the trunk, but near the top they sprouted. They were quite tall, taller than all the pines and spruce that surrounded them, pushing their leaves into the sunlight above the tops of the other trees. They had white, smooth bark. There were black blemishes in the surface where the branches stuck out, and parts that were slowly closing over after a branch had fallen off. It looked soft, but Billy touched one of the trees and found that even though it looked soft, the bark was hard enough.

After a few more miles of walking, he came to a railroad bridge over a river. While this bridge was basically like the one on the other side of Cadomin, it was shorter and closer to the river below it. The large and high bridges were back in the mountains, and Billy was heading away from the mountains, so there wouldn't be any really long bridges ahead of him.

In spite of its small size, the bridge still made him a little nervous. It was shorter, but still long enough that if a train happened to come along, he could be trapped on it. He hesitated for a moment, but eventually he decided to cross it. He knew if he didn't cross it, he'd have to head back and go to Hinton, so he braced himself and went across. He could see that if a train came and he had to jump out of the way, it wouldn't be much of a fall into the river below. No train came, so it was fine, and when he got to the other side he felt pleased with himself and continued on his way.

Billy Boy kept walking for a couple of days. He kept wondering if he should turn around, but he was determined to keep going, so he forced himself to keep going. However, he was already getting really tired. He'd barely had anything to eat, and he wondered if the berries he was eating were making him feel even more sick and tired. He lay down in the ditch beside the tracks and started to fall asleep, but he was woken up by an odd pain in his arm. He opened his eyes and sat up, and saw that the pain was coming from a tiny tree that was growing out of his forearm. It had dug its roots under his skin, and he could see and feel them pushing their way through his veins.

He grasped the sapling and pulled. It was very painful, but he managed to pull it out and brought the roots with it. He could feel the roots resisting him as he pulled. It felt like they were somehow grasping the sides of his blood vessels and trying to stay inside. Nevertheless, with a great deal of determination, he managed to get the sapling out and when he did, he threw it into the bush behind him.

As he sat in agony, he began to wonder if the sapling that had grown from his arm had something to do with the strange trees. He noticed that around him was not just long grass as he'd thought, but also a large number of saplings. They were a dark red colour, but he was sure that they were the same as the white trees. They had the same sort of leaves, and since they were the only trees besides the tall white ones that had any leaves at all, he felt that they were probably the same thing. They seemed to be growing so fast that he could actually see them unfolding and stretching. All of a sudden the tall trees weren't just vaguely disturbing, but instead, downright sinister.

He stood up, got back on the railroad tracks and started walking fast down the middle of the tracks where he thought he might be safe. On either side of the tracks the strange, white trees were growing. To Billy's eyes, they looked like they were trying to reach over the tracks. When he looked in the ditches, he could see the saplings crowding out the grasses and stretching toward the tracks from below. He began to wonder if even the spot in the middle of the tracks where he was walking would be safe.

Billy Boy wasn't in any condition to be walking so fast and he quickly got tired again. Not knowing what else he could do, he sat down on the tracks, keeping a careful watch on the forest around him, in case one of the tall trees tried to get him while he rested. He saw that there were some trails through the forest heading off from the tracks, but by then he couldn't imagine how he could take a trail through the forest without getting eaten alive by the trees. In fact, he had no idea if he'd ever be able to leave the railroad tracks again, since, as far as he could tell, the tracks were the only safe place. Maybe the trees had placed the trails specifically to tempt him away from the security of the railroad tracks. He knew that there was a long thin bit of sanctuary stretching in front of him and behind him, but that, even if it looked inviting, everything on either side was dangerous.

As he sat there the trees seemed to pull back from the tracks. At first it seemed like it might just be the wind blowing them back, but after a moment, Billy Boy was sure that they'd actually backed off. Even when he looked down at the saplings in the ditches, they looked like they'd moved away from the tracks a little bit. He couldn't figure out why they were moving back, but he decided that it didn't really matter. Maybe he was just having a little bit of luck.

Then he heard the rumbling of the train, and could feel the tracks beginning to shake. The trees were just pulling back to get out of the train's way. Billy knew he needed to get out of the way as well, but he didn't know how he could do that. He'd have to get off the tracks, but he wasn't sure what might happen to him among all those trees. He could imagine them digging their roots into him, as he tried in vain to pull them all out. Then they'd pull him to the ground, and grow all over him until he was nothing but rich, bloody soil.

That's what he imagined, and so he didn't move from the tracks. The train came around a bend and for the first time Billy could actually see it, maybe a half a mile down the tracks from where he was. It was moving fast. He was surprised that it didn't let out a whistle or something to get him off the tracks, but it didn't seem to care that he was there. It was busy going somewhere, and it knew that he would be a very small obstacle, and so it didn't really care whether he moved or not.

Billy Boy readied himself to jump, but he took a look at the greedy trees, and he still couldn't make himself get out of the way. He knew that not jumping meant that he would definitely get hit by the train. He tried to comfort himself by thinking that it was probably better to get hit by a train than eaten by trees.

By that time the train was getting close. Billy had made up his mind that he wouldn't get off the tracks, and so he knew that he was going to get hit. He wished he could send a note or something back to his mom, so that she wouldn't keep waiting for him in Cadomin anymore. She might still wait for his father, but at least she would know that Billy wasn't coming back. The train was less than a mile away. He sat down again to wait for it. A quick look around at the ditches and he knew that he'd made the right choice. Even though the trees were pulling away from the tracks, they still looked sinister and aggressive, and Billy shivered at the thought of getting taken by them. Much better to get hit than become food for the trees.

Billy Boy was intent on watching the train, so he didn't notice when the old man come up from out of the forest. And so it was a surprise when the man picked him up, tossed him roughly over his right shoulder and headed into the forest. The trees parted for the old man as he walked between them. The boy was glad to be alive, but he wasn't sure what was happening. He just kept quiet and let himself be carried into the forest.

Father John

Billy heard the train roar by them, but the man kept up his rapid pace. He wasn't running exactly, but he walked fast, as if he wasn't carrying Billy or anything at all. He still had the boy draped over a shoulder, and Billy soon got a sore stomach from being bounced up and down on the man's shoulder. Nevertheless, the boy stayed limp. He figured that playing possum for a little while might do him more good than struggling and demanding to know what was going on, so he just let himself hang down over the man's back as he was carried through the forest.

Billy Boy couldn't figure out why the trees weren't coming after them. Maybe he'd had been more frightened of the trees than he'd had to be. Maybe they were actually quite timid. The trees kept backing away as they passed. Billy realized that they hadn't been moving back to get away from the train at all. They'd been moving to get away from the man. The trees weren't timid, just afraid of his captor. It was only that fear that kept them at bay and it was only fear that kept them from trying anything.

After the two of them had travelled a mile or so, they came to a clearing and the man lay Billy down in the tall grass. Billy closed his eyes to keep up the illusion that he was unconscious, but in a deep voice, the man told him to forget about it and open his eyes. Billy Boy still kept his eyes closed, but the man shook him a little bit, and Billy knew the jig was up, so he sat forward.

The old man introduced himself as Father John. Though he gave Billy his name, he didn't explain what he was doing in the forest or why he had happened to be by the railroad tracks. After he had shaken Billy's hand, he sat down in the grass. He wasn't very much taller than Billy, but a lot wider and stronger. He had a full head of grey hair and a moustache that was tinged yellow from tobacco smoke. He also had tobacco stains on his teeth and fingers. In spite of the stains, he looked very well groomed.

He wore a white shirt, unbuttoned at the collar, and he wore a brown vest over top of it. He was wearing work pants, and big black boots, and he was also carrying a satchel at his side. He didn't have anything on his head, and his face was a little sunburnt. If he'd had a bald spot, it would have been burnt as well. As it was, his hair was white, but it didn't look like there were even thin spots.

After he had gotten Billy to sit up, Father John apparently had nothing else to say. He just sat down and pulled a pouch of tobacco and some papers out of the satchel, then proceeded to roll himself a cigarette. When he was finished, the cigarette was a little lopsided, but he nonetheless seemed content with it, because he pulled a lighter out of a pocket in his vest and lit it. Billy wanted to ask him questions, but kept his mouth shut.

Once Father John had lit up, he held out the burning cigarette and asked Billy if he wanted one. The boy shook his head, and they sat in silence for a moment. Then, unable to restrain himself anymore, Billy asked Father John who he was.

"I told you. I'm Father John," he said. Then he chuckled and cuffed Billy playfully on the back of the head. "I know that's not what you mean. You mean what am I doing here."

And Father John explained that he had a mission. He had to catalogue everything that grew. He wanted to write it all down. He didn't say anything about where the mission had come from, or who had given him the mission, but Billy took him at his word anyway. Father John had a cabin about a mile away and inside the cabin were stacks and stacks of binders with all of the things that he'd catalogued.

"Whenever something is growing and I don't know about it... well... I don't like it. It makes me angry, that's what. So I try to make sure I have everything written down."

"Aren't you afraid of the trees?" asked Billy.

"These trees?" said Father John gesturing at the forest around them.

"The tall white ones. They tried to grow on me," said Billy.

"The poplars? We don't get along too well. They keep growing all over the place, and for a while I tried to write it all down, but they were determined to mess everything up. Even when I thought I had everything written down, they were determined to mess it up. They put out all those furry little seeds that float around, and they also put out tubers in the ground so they grow up like weeds wherever there's a blank spot for them to shoot up into the sky. I can't keep track of it all. I wound up giving up and just keeping track of everything else."

"But they also convert the other trees. I didn't believe it at first, but there were groves that I was sure had been pine or spruce and they'd suddenly turn poplar. I would catalogue them one day and I'd go back a week later and there'd be nothing but poplars. Now, I know that even the poplars can't grow that fast, so I know that they must have converted the trees that were already there."

"And, like they did with you, when I sat down one afternoon they tried to grow on me. They weren't scared of me yet. I don't know about you, but it was pretty painful when I had to pull those saplings out. So I never let it happen again. And the way I found to make sure it didn't happen was to make them scared of me."

"So, like I said, we don't really get along, but I've managed to keep them scared. Sometimes I burn the saplings, and when I can't I just pull them out of the ground, or cut them off. They don't like me much. Of course, that's just fine with me. They mostly stay out of my way now, but I know if they got half a chance they'd kill me. Every once in a while I can see them scheming and plotting against me. Then I go out and burn a few saplings, and while I know they don't like me any better, I can tell that they've stopped plotting against me. For a while, anyway."

"But remember son," he said, "no matter what, you've got to keep an eye out all the time. They'll try to get you, and they'll be mad they couldn't get you today. That's why you stayed on the tracks, right? I could see you didn't want to jump into those poplars and I can't say I blame you. But even once they're scared of you, you still have to keep your eyes peeled. Those poplars are always ready to try something."

He had finished his cigarette, and he butted it out on the ground and then rubbed it back and forth in the dirt to make sure it was completely out. He stood up again, and then turned, waiting for Billy.

After Billy had stood up, Father John said that he wasn't in the mood to carry him anymore, so the boy would just have to use his own legs and walk for himself. They headed off into the forest together.

As they walked, Billy told Father John his own story, about the bike and his mother and Cadomin. After Father John had heard everything, he told Billy that he hadn't come across any bike while he was walking around on his mission, but that Billy was welcome to stay with him for a while. He could see that the boy was tired and hungry, and he thought it might be good for him to get a decent night's sleep and something to eat.

When they got back to his cabin, Father John went inside and Billy followed him. The cabin itself was ugly, but it looked sturdy, and there didn't seem to be any danger that it would fall down. It was made of logs but the spaces between the logs hadn't been filled properly. Billy could see little cracks between them where the air would come through. It wouldn't be much of a problem during the summer, but Billy wondered how Father John survived the winter with the wind coming through his walls.

There weren't any windows. Father John hadn't seen any point in them when he was building the cabin, since if he wanted to see the forest or if he wanted fresh air, he could just step outside. Also, with the free flow of air through the cracks in the walls, it was almost like having windows anyway. Because it didn't have any windows, the place looked like a wooden fortification. If Father John had been able to bring concrete up there to make the cabin he would have. He would have been happy with a little bunker in the woods.

Father John tidied up his binders a little, making the haphazard stacks tidier. When he was done, he invited Billy into the cabin. Billy wasn't sure he liked the look of the place, especially when he compared it to his neat little house in Cadomin. The floor was made of dirt, and it was almost pitch black inside, except for the little slivers of sunlight that found their way through the cracks in the walls.

Father John lit a lantern and hung it over a wood stove that squatted in the northwest corner. The stove was a jury-rigged contraption. It was made of what looked like an oil barrel laid on its side, with some flat iron plates welded on top of it, and an aluminum chimney running from the stove and out the roof.

Father John got most of his water from a creek that ran nearby, but he had also diverted the run-off from the roof into the cabin. It flowed down through eaves-troughs and pipes to collect in a barrel that sat in the corner. An aluminum downspout entered the cabin near the same spot that the chimney exited, and then ran along the wall and emptied into the barrel.

There had been a great deal of rain lately, and so the barrel was close to full. There was very rarely enough rain to overflow the barrel, so the only time Father John had to worry about having too much water was in the spring when the snow melted. In the spring, he had a big bucket that he kept beside the barrel, to scoop the water out before it overflowed. If both the barrel and the bucket were full, he just tossed the extra water outside the cabin.

On the wall opposite the stove there was a bed. Actually, it was just a mattress lying on top of some pallets that formed a kind of crude box-spring. In the corner at the foot of the bed was a stack of binders. There were actually four stacks of them. Two of the stacks looked like they were ready to fall over in spite of the tidying that Father John had done. The other two towers of binders were carefully stacked so that the spines were opposite each other, and those stacks looked sturdy compared to the other two towers.

Father John opened the stove and placed a couple of logs inside. There was a steel door over the opening that creaked loudly on its metal hinges when it was opened. When Father John had to open the stove, he used a dirty cloth to protect his fingers from the hot metal. After he'd placed the logs inside, Father John put a pot of water on top of the stove. While the cabin wasn't excessively hot yet, it was already very stuffy, and Billy knew it would only get worse with the heat from the stove. After he had closed the door on the stove, Father John fiddled with it a little bit to get it latched, then he went back outside and grunted at Billy Boy to indicate that the boy should follow him.

There were two Adirondack chairs sitting in front of the cabin. The chairs had obviously been outside for too long. The wood was grey and cracked from sunshine and rain, and they looked like they were ready to fall apart. The two of them sat down and the chair that Father John took made some groaning sounds and seemed a little unhappy about having to take his weight. However, in spite of the chair's complaints, it held together. And the chair that Billy sat down in seemed solid enough, and was actually fairly comfortable once he'd drawn his feet up. He sat with his knees under his chin and his arms wrapped around his legs, holding them in place.

Father John made Billy Boy nervous. Not crazy scared or petrified or anything, just slightly uneasy and anxious. Father John made him feel like something bad was going to happen. And while Billy Boy had never been the talkative type, he'd never really been nervous like that before either, so he began asking questions just to fill the empty air. He asked about the poplars, the cabin, and then he asked how Father John had come to the forest in the first place and how he'd decided that he had a mission.

And Father John answered that he was thirty when he came to the forest. In fact, it was not long after his thirtieth birthday. He'd had a revelation when he turned thirty, and not long after he'd gotten the mission.

Before he turned thirty he lived in the big city, and had gone to school and drank himself stupid in the city bars and had what many people would have called a decadent lifestyle. Actually, they hadn't called him decadent, they had just called him a skid, and he heard them do it. It made him angry, but he couldn't really do anything about it. He had gone to school and gotten as smart as he could, but they still called him a skid, and he didn't know how to make them stop.

So he was facing a bit of a crisis when his thirtieth birthday came along. Even before he turned thirty he had already begun to feel like his life was empty and he was angry about how clever he had become. His education just seemed like another burden to him, and one that sapped his strength even while he carried it. Not only was it heavy, but it was making him weaker.

And so, on his birthday, he went out and got really drunk because that's what he was good at and he figured that he would play to his strengths. Most of the evening was black, but Father John remembered the morning.

He woke up in the old freight yard in the middle of the city. At one time, the trains had run through the field, but by that time, it was just a dirt field with lots of weeds and a little slough in one corner where some ducks were living.

When he woke, he sat up, but he didn't bother standing. He just lit a cigarette and stayed where he was. After the trains had stopped running through it, the field had been used as a depot for trucks to load and unload for a while. There was still a long building with lots of garage doors that was left over from when it had been used by trucks. But it had been years since they had used the field for that, and so the building was abandoned and there were weeds growing around it. The sun was coming up over an apartment building in front of him, and in the bright light, Father John sat in the dirt and smoked.

For a few minutes he managed to sustain a comfortable early morning nihilism, feeling so ragged and smoky that he could convince himself that nothing mattered very much anyway. But soon that feeling wore off, and then he felt about as low as he'd ever felt. He knew that there was still a long way to go before he bottomed out, but he could see the trail to the depths going down ahead of him, and he couldn't see any other trail to take.

It was then that a little bird with gray feathers came down and landed on the ground in front of him. It cocked its head a couple of times, and Father John couldn't help feeling like the bird was shaking its head in dismay as it looked at him. And Father John knew that he deserved its dismay and as he started to cry.

"The only time I've ever cried, son. And I wailed. I figure I've gotten it all out of my system by now, because I cried so much that morning. Like a little baby. All because that bird was looking at me with so much disappointment in its eyes."

Then the bird started to speak, and told Father John that he needed to get himself together, since he was sinking fast. Father John asked the bird what he was supposed to do, but the bird wouldn't tell him. Instead, it just told him that he had to get out. Living in the city was bad for him.

So Father John went home and started packing. He felt tired and hung-over, so he easily could have slept for a while instead of doing any packing. But he was so determined to get started on his new life that he wouldn't let himself take any rest before he left the city and he forced himself to pack up.

He only brought enough stuff to fit into his backpack. When he was done packing, he went to the bus station and bought a ticket for the great outdoors. The bus ride took about four hours, and when he got off he was in Hinton. He wandered around the town for a while, and checked into an older brick hotel downwind from the pulp mill. It was cheap because of its age and the rotten egg smell of sulphur and chlorine that surrounded the place.

He was woken up in the middle of the night by a bar fight that had moved out of the hotel and onto the street below his window.

There were a couple of guys, really drunk, duking it out in front of the hotel bar. There were a few minutes of fisticuffs, and then one of them pulled out a knife and stuck it in the other one.

There were a few other drunk guys outside watching the fight, but when the knife came out they ran away. After he'd stabbed his opponent, the guy with the knife hesitated for a moment, looking astonished at the result of his own actions, and then he ran away as well. The fellow who'd been stabbed staggered back to the hotel, clutching his side where the knife had gone in.

Father John kept staring out the window at the street even after everyone had left and there was nothing to see. He hated himself for not yelling. The sound of a siren was approaching, and he figured it was probably the ambulance coming to get the stabbing victim. The front desk must have seen what happened and called. He hated himself for not being the one to call the ambulance. At least he could have called the front desk, instead of just depending on them to see the incident. He hated himself for a lot of things.

Because of the hate, he realized that he still wasn't far enough. He wanted to be away from these kinds of things, but he also wanted to be better than this silent person that he'd become. He couldn't remember when he'd started being so quiet. He often yelled in the bars when he was drunk, but it was always about something stupid, like more drinks or cigarettes or something. He knew he had to change so that he only yelled about things worth yelling about. But he really wanted to be someone who would yell loud when he needed to.

So the next day he took his backpack and walked out of town.

When he came out, he saw a large blood stain on the pavement in front of the hotel. He wished he had a camera so that he could take a picture of the stain, to keep a record of what he was running from and where he was trying to get.

Since Hinton is in the middle of the forest, he didn't have to go far to get out of town. The town is long and skinny, and runs along the river. So if you walk either west or east, it will take you a few hours to get into the forest. But if you walk a mile north or south, you quickly get out of town and into the woods. He went south, away from the river. He found the stairs and went up them. When he got to the top, he followed the train tracks east for a while. They seemed to know where they were going. As he was walking along, he saw a little clearing on his left, so he thought he'd stop for a bit. He didn't yet know about the poplars, so he just jumped off the tracks and walked carelessly through the forest to the clearing. Then he sat down and lay back. He put the backpack behind his head and stared at the sky.

Of course, he didn't mean to, but he fell asleep, and it was only the pain in his stomach that woke him up. He sat up and saw that there was a poplar sapling growing out of his shirt. He froze for a minute, not knowing what was happening, and then he grabbed the sapling and pulled.

He could only get the sapling about halfway out, and even pulling it out that far was very painful. There was blood everywhere, staining his shirt and pants. He let go for a minute, and could feel the sapling scrambling to get back into him. So he grasped it hard again, and then he pulled out his lighter, flicked it on, and held the flame against the sapling.

It took a few minutes, but the lighter managed to burn through the sapling, and Father John could feel it getting weaker as he burnt it. When the sapling was burnt through, he snapped the top off, and it became even weaker. He imagined that he could hear it yelling and snarling, though when he thought about it later, he decided that it was his own shouts that had been in his ears, and that the plant itself had stayed silent.

After that, he was able to pull the plant out completely. He looked at his stomach, and though the sapling had caused a lot of pain, it didn't seem like there was all that much damage. There was a little hole in his skin, and the shock and loss of blood made him feel very weak, but otherwise everything seemed to be fine.

He stayed standing up and looked around the clearing at the forest. It was basically the same—mostly pines and a few spruce—but he saw that there were also a few tall, white trees that he hadn't noticed before. He didn't know what they were or even their connection to the sapling that had just tried to grow out of him, but, like Billy Boy, he had decided that they looked sinister.

And then he realized that he didn't know much about the forest, so he thought he would start writing it all down. Then he would know all about the forest and the trees wouldn't be able to sneak up on him like that. At the time, he didn't know how big a task he was taking on, but even when it became apparent that it was more than he could deal with, he kept it up. By that time, he had decided that it was his mission to catalogue everything in the forest, and he became committed to it.

So it really was just a self-imposed mission and Billy Boy wondered why Father John hadn't just given it up. The man knew that he'd never be able to write down everything, but Billy did understand the desire to keep track of things. The boy had mentally done something like it around Cadomin. Things you know about aren't as much of a threat, so he would keep an inventory of things that he knew around his home, and sometimes when he was riding past on his bike, he would stop and check just to make sure that things hadn't changed. He hadn't written it down or anything, though. And if he forgot about stuff, he didn't really get too worried about it. But, he understood the man's desire to make the world familiar. He just felt that Father John was taking it too far.

Father John stayed in the clearing and built himself the cabin. He made the clearing bigger so that no branches would touch it. He didn't like having any branches on his roof, since he knew that if he grew used to the sound of branches then the poplars would be able to sneak up during the night and start clawing at the place, and he wouldn't even notice the sound they would be making.

"It's kind of a hard life, but I actually get a lot of thinking done when I'm out writing everything down. You would think I'd be distracted, trying to keep track of everything, but I still manage to think about other things. And now that I've been out here so long, I can't imagine going back, so I don't bother. Trying to imagine it, I mean. I go into town to get paper and things for the inventory. I also usually pick up some gasoline and matches while I'm in there. But that's the only reason to go in."

"I know those people in town just think I'm that crazy guy from the woods, and they wonder why I buy so much paper and gas. But let them wonder. There's a bunch of things to know in the world, and they know their stuff, and I know mine. And whatever they say, what I know is harder to figure out. There are millions of people who know their stuff, but only me that knows what I know. That's what I figure anyway."

With that he was silent again. He'd finished a cigarette, so he rolled another one and lit it, and then sat back happily in the chair again. Then he gestured into the cabin with his thumb and he said, "Go inside and see if that water's hot yet."

Forgetfulness

Billy Boy stayed with Father John longer than he thought he would. At first, the desire to find his bike weighed heavily on him, and it was only fear of the poplars that made him keep coming back to the cabin. After a while though, there really wasn't any need for Billy to stay close. Father John had made it clear that Billy was with him, and so the poplars left the boy alone. Billy figured he probably could have left if he'd wanted. But by that point in time, the boy had gotten comfortable. And besides, he didn't really have a plan. Sticking around the cabin seemed like a better thing to do than wandering aimlessly around the forest.

Also, it didn't seem like Father John wanted Billy to leave. Whenever the boy wandered too far or for too long, Father John would come after him, find him and bring him back to the cabin. Billy found this kind of irritating, but since he didn't have anywhere else he wanted to go, it didn't bother him too much or otherwise motivate him to leave.

So summer became fall, and fall became winter and Billy Boy was still living with Father John. He'd have been disappointed if he'd known how close he was to Cadomin. He'd have felt bad about leaving his mother behind just so that he could go live in a separate, very crappy little cabin that was only forty miles from her. But he felt like he'd gone much further so he didn't know how close to his mother he still was. He knew he had to get going, but by then winter was coming and he knew that whatever happened, he'd at least have to wait until spring before he could leave.

During this time Father John was teaching Billy Boy about all the things that he knew. Father John was a scientist, a philosopher and a theologian, and so he had a great many pieces of knowledge to give to the boy.

"They talk about natural law, son," he said one day while the two of them were walking past a wide clearing in the forest. The clearing was covered in yellow flowers that shone beautifully in the sun. "What they mean is that animals and plants have to follow natural laws. So the way those flowers grow and how they reproduce and everything about them is natural law. When you find an animal or a plant that doesn't follow the natural law, then it's the law that goes. If it's not going to get followed all the time, it's not a law anymore."

"Human laws don't work that way. Whenever you break a human law, the law stays and they punish you for breaking it. They try to get you to follow it. They fail a lot of the time, but they keep trying, anyway. People will hold onto those laws forever, no matter how many times they get broken."

"That's what separates us from the animals, son," he said. "Humans are always thinking about how they should be acting before they actually act. Human laws aren't what people do, it's what they think they ought to be doing. Plants and animals don't care how they should act. They don't know there are any laws, and even if they did, they would just act however they wanted to act and the laws be damned."

"That's why I'm trying to write everything down. So I can see which natural laws are being broken."

"Then the poplars are just following their own law," said Billy Boy.

"They are, and they need to be stopped."

"I thought you said..."

"I didn't say that it was good that wild things don't give a damn about laws. Maybe you're missing my point," said Father John. "There needs to be middle ground, not chaos. On the whole, I think the wild things might know something we don't, but there should be limits. Take the poplars. When something decides that it's in its nature to grow out of my chest or my leg, I figure I just need to make it understand that it has a different nature."

"But, didn't you just say...?"

"I also said there have to be limits. Aren't you listening, son?"

By that time they were almost back to the cabin, and Father John rolled himself a cigarette and sank into silence. Billy Boy was still confused, but he decided it would be best to keep quiet about it.

Eventually the snow started falling, and the poplars died, and then Billy was able to walk around more freely than he had been able to during the summer. When he was by himself, the boy was still cautious. The poplars seemed to know that he was with Father John, but they still made him nervous. However, when the leaves had turned yellow, the poplars seemed to get sluggish. Once all the leaves had fallen and the temperature dropped below zero, they stopped completely. Once they'd frozen, Billy knew he had nothing to fear from them, and he became more bold.

He was able to take longer walks in the forest. He got cold, but he was enjoying the relative freedom, so he suffered with the low temperatures. One day while he was out walking, he tripped on a root buried in the snow and he fell forward, sprawling out on the ground. Automatically thinking that the poplars must have caused it, he quickly flipped over, assuming that they had only been playing possum in the cold weather so that he'd go too far into the forest with Father John. However, there was no sign that the poplars were trying to get him. At first, he was going to spring to his feet and start running, but when there was no attack forthcoming, he relaxed and began to think that perhaps he'd just legitimately tripped over a root. The trees still looked dead, so he just stayed on his back and looked up at the sky.

His vision, as he looked up, was framed by the tall black shapes of the spruce, pine and the dead poplars. He watched for a while, and as he watched all the trees at the periphery of his view disappeared one at a time and he was left looking at the clear blue sky and nothing else. He blinked a couple of times to try to correct his vision, but it stayed the way it was. After the blinking didn't seem to do anything, he turned his head right and left to see if he could see the forest around him, but all he could see was more pale blue. He was tempted to try standing up, but he wasn't even sure if the ground was still there. If there was nothing but more blue sky underneath him, if he found himself standing on thin air, he didn't know what he would do about it. Besides, he felt strangely happy lying there, so while he knew he should be feeling nervous and upset, standing up seemed like more effort than it would be worth.

As he lay there a cold wind came up. If he hadn't been lying down, it would have blown him over. As it was, the wind still felt like it was trying to peel his clothes off, and it was strong and cold enough to make his face feel like it was frozen. After a minute or so, the wind calmed down and the trees came back. Unlike when they had disappeared, they came back all at once. He blinked, and they all reappeared. He looked around and the forest surrounded him again. He felt contented, and even though he was still feeling very cold, he also had a smile on his face as he stood up. Since he was a bit drowsy, he decided that he would head back to the cabin.

After he'd gotten back inside and warmed up a little, he told Father John about what had happened.

"You've seen the blank slate, son," said Father John, "It's a good thing to happen. You'll never get anything done without getting rid of the old things, so it's not a bad idea to clear your mind every once in a while."

"So what do you think it means?" asked Billy.

"Means? It doesn't mean anything. It's not a message or a vision or anything. Believe me, I know. It's just a friendly knife cutting away all the crap in your head."

"I don't feel any different."

"You don't feel lighter and happier?" asked Father John.

"I suppose I do. But I still remember everything."

"But do those memories still give you pain?"

Billy concentrated on how he'd felt the last time his mother told him the story about his father. Usually that made him sad and angry, but as Father John had said, even though he remembered the moment, he didn't feel much of anything about it.

"They don't," said Billy with a confused smile.

"I told you," said Father John. "The bad feelings come back soon, and then you'll wish you could see the blank slate again. I've seen it myself a few times. I've tried to figure out how I could get it to come, since its good when it happens. I can't figure it out though, so I just have to wait for it to come in its own good time."

"As far as I can tell, it isn't related to anything. It's just random and so you just have to wait for it. At first, I thought it had something to do with the train, so I would try to be out by the tracks whenever the train was going by, but that didn't seem to do anything. Then I thought it might be only in particular places, and once you found those places then you might be able to bring it on. But after years of searching, I still can't find the right places, and now I don't think it even has anything to do with where you are. You can't make it show up, no matter what you do. You just have to wait for it to happen."

Cabin Fever

After the blank slate, the winter was still long and hard. The snow fell heavily, and soon the cabin was half-buried. Father John only went out a few times to get wood and find food, and Billy Boy stayed inside. Since the door was closed all the time, the place was getting really stuffy. Between the two of them, they really managed to stink the place up. It was mostly Father John's fault, but Billy also had to suffer with it.

There came a day when Billy couldn't take it anymore so he bundled up and went outside for some fresh air. Father John had gone out, so he wasn't around to tell Billy that he had to go back inside. The forest was covered in snow and looked pristine and perfect. Everything was untouched except for a set of footprints that led away from the cabin. Father John had left them that morning when he had left to find food. The pines carried a heavy burden of snow, but the poplars had very little snow on them. They were dead, so they had no leaves for the snow to cling to.

Billy started walking toward the tracks, hoping that a train would come by to relieve the monotony of the forest. Eventually he made it, though he took much longer getting there than he thought he should have. Wading through the deep snow had slowed him down quite a bit. When he arrived, he could hear the rumble of a train coming, and he knelt down facing the tracks. As the train got closer and closer he began to feel a little nervous since he was only kneeling a few feet from the tracks. The sky had been overcast before, but it had only started snowing at that point. It started coming down heavily, and it was only a few minutes before his legs and knees were buried. He looked up at the sky, breathed deeply and then tried to calm down so he would be ready for the train when it came past.

It seemed to take forever, but finally it arrived. It was heading east, away from the mountains. Billy had seen many trains, but he'd never before been so close to the tracks when they went by. It felt as if the train was twenty feet tall and going at least a thousand miles an hour. As it went it was not only rumbling and groaning loudly, but also screaming and squealing, and Billy wondered if the noise was going to burst his eardrums. He put his hands over his ears, and thought about moving back from the tracks, but he had been so starved for stimulation that even though he was nervous, he also kind of enjoyed the onslaught of sensation. He forced himself not to stay put, and just let the train blur past him.

After he had closed his eyes for a minute, he opened them, but he didn't even try to actually focus on the train. It was too close for him to be able to see it properly, and so he let it just blast past his vision. All the different colours from the cars and the graffiti blurred in front of him. He found it soothing.

As the last car went past where he was kneeling he heard someone calling his name. At first he thought he was just hearing things. Between the noise of the train, and his hands covering his ears, he couldn't be sure that his ears weren't playing tricks on him. But then he heard his name again, and so he turned his head and saw his mother clinging to the back of the train. She waved to him and he stood up and stepped onto the tracks while she kept waving and waving. The snow billowed around her and she disappeared into it as the train pulled out of sight into the trees.

He stood up to wave back to her, and for a long time he just stood there. He felt bad for a while, but he knew that it was probably a good thing. He'd been waiting for his mom to leave Cadomin for years, and she had finally done it. He'd never expected that even if she left she would go any further than Hinton. They were well past the town, and he wasn't sure if he should believe his eyes. He was feeling pretty odd, and he wouldn't have been too surprised if he was having hallucinations. Seeing his mother had made him remember all of the things that he felt bad about and he realized that the blank slate had worn off. But even though he couldn't figure it out, and he was feeling bad about seeing her, he was glad that she had decided to leave Cadomin and was taking the train to somewhere else.

Billy was smiling, but he was also feeling really exhausted. After a minute, he lay down in the snow. He knew that he shouldn't, because he might not get up again, but he couldn't help himself. He didn't want to go back to the hot, gloomy cabin. It was such a relief to be outside, even if it was really cold. And since the train had passed, it seemed so quiet and peaceful. He lay back and the snow started falling more heavily, burying him even more quickly.

He didn't hear Father John coming. He looked down at Billy, and shook his head. "You've got holes in your head, son, and they're there for a reason. If you let them fill with snow, it'll be a hard, white world to live in. So stand up, give yourself a shake and come with me."

Billy Boy tried to stand but was feeling too weak, so Father John picked him up. The boy was stiff from the cold so Father John threw him over his shoulder again, and took him away from the train tracks and back to the cabin.

Hair

After that, Billy didn't venture out much. He still found himself longing for the outdoors, but since he'd had an emotionally exhausting experience the last time he had gone out, and it had almost resulted in him falling asleep in the snow and freezing to death, he decided that it wasn't worth the risk. So he mostly stayed inside, even though he really didn't like the inside of the cabin by that point. When he did go outside, he didn't go far, and he was careful to stay away from the tracks.

Soon, the happiness about his mom leaving Cadomin had worn off, and he had begun feeling sad and angry that there was no longer any home to go back to. Then he sat down and thought about it some more, and decided that seeing his mom must have been a dream or hallucination, and that her leaving was just wishful thinking on his part. She was probably still in Cadomin and he felt glad that she was still there, even though he knew that it wasn't actually a good thing for her.

Billy wasn't sure how they managed, but he and Father John made it through the winter. By the spring, the cabin had been shut up for six months with the stove going almost non-stop, and so the smell was unpleasant to say the least. Also, they had been surviving on nothing but dried meat. Father John seemed to have an endless supply of the stuff, so even though it was nasty, when everything else ran out, they had no choice but to eat it. It didn't taste very good and it nearly tore your teeth out when you tried to bite into it. Also, Billy didn't know where it had come from, and so he didn't really know what he was eating.

One miserable day in March, after he had been gnawing on the mystery jerky for a while, he made the decision that whatever happened he wasn't going to spend another winter in the cabin. He was sure that Father John would try to stop him, but he was determined to leave. He had forgotten all about the bike by that point, except when he thought about his mother and was reminded of why he'd left in the first place. He decided that the bike wasn't worth this much trouble, so even though he hadn't had any luck finding it, he knew it was still time for him to head back.

So one day not long after spring came, Billy set out again while Father John was off burning poplars. Reluctantly, he took a little of the dried meat with him. It was a long walk home, and he didn't want to starve on the journey. He'd been close to starving on his way to the cabin, and he didn't want to be forced to eat berries again before he could get back to Cadomin, even if it meant that he'd have to eat the mystery jerky.

It was still early enough in the year to be kind of chilly in the shade, but once he got to the tracks, the sun shone on him, and he was warm enough. He started following the tracks west toward Cadomin and the mountains. The little house would be much more comfortable than the cabin had been, and while he knew that there would still come a time when he would want to leave Cadomin again, he knew that it wouldn't be any time soon. He'd had enough of wandering for the time being, and he knew that it would be a while before he wanted to leave the valley again.

He hadn't gone far when he started noticing that the poplars were crowding around the tracks. He had thought that they would still be afraid of him because of Father John, but when they saw him alone and heading away from the cabin, they figured that he wasn't under Father John's protection anymore. They hoped that they might be able to get him. Billy started getting nervous, but he figured that as long as he stayed on the tracks he would be all right. He also knew that after a while there wouldn't be any more poplars, and then he'd just have to walk through friendly pines back to Cadomin.

While he was looking around at the poplars he took another step and his feet were pulled out from under him as if someone had yanked on the tracks. He fell backwards and immediately curled into a little ball to try to cover up. He didn't know what had happened, but again, he was sure it must have had something to do with the poplars. He was a little surprised, because they'd never shoved or tripped him before. They had seemed too sneaky for something so blatant. Nevertheless, he was sure it was them, and he was already frantically trying to figure out how he'd be able to get away from them and back to Father John's cabin.

He was on his back and had pulled his arms and legs into a ball above him so that he looked like a beetle that had been flipped over. He froze in that position, but after a few minutes it became clear that the poplars weren't going to do anything to him. He laid his head back on the tracks so that he could see. Though the poplars were still crowding around the tracks, Billy was too far away for them to try anything. They couldn't have reached him in the middle of the tracks, so they definitely couldn't have tripped him up. After a few more seconds, Billy could feel something sliding past him along the tracks and brushing against his back as it moved. It made a quiet slithering sound as it went past.

Billy uncurled and sat up so that he could see it clearly. In front of him, a thick bundle of brown hair was slithering over the railroad ties. It ran along the tracks in both directions. Billy couldn't see any start or end to it, and he wondered how long he'd been walking along beside it without noticing. He must have been concentrating on the poplars so completely that he had never noticed the hair.

He sat down on one of the tracks and watched for a while. All the time he was looking at it, the hair kept slithering past him over the ties, and even though he was expecting to see the end of it, he never did. It looked blonde in the sunlight, but he knew that it wasn't. It wasn't a dark colour either, just not blonde. It was more of a light brown colour, so when it caught light from the sun, it looked bright, but then, in the shade, it looked very dark.

He'd gotten pretty curious by that point, and, since it seemed to be heading the same direction that he was, Billy Boy started following the hair. It was moving pretty fast, and he had to walk quicker to keep up. It didn't speed up or slow down, it just kept sliding over the ties and gravel at the same steady pace. Since the hair was running between the rails, he kept outside the right-hand rail and went from tie to tie so that he wouldn't step on it again by accident. However, the poplars were close enough that they were able to brush against him while he walked, so, to get away from them, he moved back between the rails. He decided that, for safety, he would have to stay between the rails, and he'd just have to be careful where he stepped to avoid the hair.

The further Billy walked, the closer the forest got to the tracks. There were a few poplars at the front, but even the pines seemed to be crowding the tracks and trying to get to him. Billy figured that they were probably just following along, and didn't really mean him any harm. The poplars were the ringleaders and had just convinced the pines to crowd around the tracks. Nevertheless, even if the pines didn't mean any harm, the forest kept closing in and blocking his path. Soon Billy couldn't stand up straight anymore, and to continue he had to hunch and lumber along.

Eventually, even hunched over he couldn't walk any further. The trees had gotten so close to the tracks that he had to get down and crawl. He thought about taking one of trails that led away from the tracks, since it couldn't be much worse. But there were still enough poplars around to make a trail dangerous. Besides, he couldn't see any trails, in any case. So even though it was getting impossible to keep going, he forced his way through.

The hair passed between his hands and knees. Luckily, while there were still poplars reaching out sinister branches at him, most of the trees close to him were pines. They crowded the tracks, but they didn't seem to know what else to do. If there had been many poplars in the crowd, then they would have gone after him, and Billy would have had to turn around right there. As it was, he got scratched, but none of the trees was trying to grow on him or anything.

Nevertheless, he thought he might have to give up. He was getting cut up very badly from trying to crawl forward. He was trailing blood from the palms of his hands and his knees. When he looked behind him, he could see poplars stretching down to dip their leaves in the bloody trails he'd left behind, getting a little taste of him. With a grimace, he again forced himself to continue. Because there weren't very many poplars, he thought he might be getting away from them and so getting close to Cadomin. Also, in spite of the ordeal that it was putting him through, he was still curious about the hair.

He managed to keep going forward for a little way, but soon the tracks disappeared completely and he was forced to stop. He could still see where the tracks ran under the trees, but the track itself seemed to be covered by a heavy thicket of pine. The hair just kept on moving, rustling through the grass and around the pine branches. It got caught a few times on the needles, but it kept moving, either freeing itself, or tearing the needles away from the branches as it moved.

He couldn't follow it, so he couldn't see any way to go forward. At that point he figured he'd have to give up and head back to the cabin. But when he turned around in the narrow space and started to crawl out the way he had come, he could see that a dozen poplar saplings had taken over the tracks behind him. They had sprouted up in the little puddles of blood that he'd left behind and now they were blocking him in, growing perceptibly while he watched.

Tubers shot up between the ties, each one a little closer to where Billy sat hunched up under the pines that were blocking his way. He was feeling very anxious. He had tears on his face and when he tried to wipe them away, he left blood stains on his cheeks. He was sore all over from crawling and the poplars were sprouting up behind him like a little army.

Seeing no other choice, he decided that he'd have to try to go on. Since he couldn't see any way to force his way through, he grabbed hold of the hair, which was still moving easily past the pines, and wrapped a loop of it around his waist. He just tried to relax as it dragged him over the gravel and railroad ties, and through the pine boughs that were covering the tracks.

It was a nasty, dirty trip, but he'd known that it would be. The needles from the pines scratched him, and he started bleeding from the places where he hadn't been bleeding previously. It was still better than getting pulled apart by the poplars, however. Ten feet into the thicket, he realized that he didn't have to hold on to the hair anymore. He was tangled up in it so completely that it was pulling him along without any effort on his part. The hair had wrapped around him like a net. It didn't provide any protection, so he still felt every snag and bump, and as the trip went on he began to worry that he'd made a mistake and that he'd wind up in worse shape than if he'd just stayed and let the poplars have him.

But after a hundred yards or so, he broke out of the forest and into the open. Even though he was still getting dragged over the railroad ties, there were no more branches tearing at him, and that was quite a relief.

Almost immediately, he saw that he was being pulled over the railroad bridge that he'd crossed to get to Father John's cabin in the first place. The river underneath it was wide and brown. The way he was held by the hair he could look down through the gaps in the metal work to the river. As he'd noticed before, the bridge was only about forty feet above the water, which was lucky, because the hair took a sharp right turn, around the edge of a girder and then dove into the river. He got hung up on the girder for a minute and the inexorable pull of the hair nearly crushed him against the metal, but he managed to push himself away and between the girders, and then he fell and was carried down into the river.

That was a relief. He settled into the water like it was a pillow. After the bumping and scraping that he'd been through, the river was quite nice. The water was cold, but not icy as he'd worried it might be, so he was quite comfortable. The hair was still pulling him, but was barely going faster than the current, so it just felt like he was on a raft. The sun shone down and he managed to push his head out through the cocoon of wet hair that he had become wrapped up in. He laid his head back in the sun and the rest of his body slid through the water just below the surface.

He lost track of time. He knew that at some point, he'd need to free himself, but it didn't seem very pressing at that moment. He was very comfortable in the cocoon of hair. The sun started going down and he closed his eyes. Everything was working out quite well, and, even though it had given him a lot of trouble, he was glad he'd followed the hair. He regretted that he'd even considered stopping at the thicket of pine trees, especially now that all his scrapes and cuts were being soothed by the river. He began to doze a little, waking up every few minutes. He only woke up completely after the sun had gone down. He started watching the stars and the black outline of the forest at the edge of the river. Then he closed his eyes again and fell fast asleep.

When Billy woke up, the sun was high and he was hooked on a logjam at the edge of the river. He scrambled to free himself by pushing away from the logs, like he had done with the girder on the bridge, but he just got himself more thoroughly tangled in the hair and more securely wrapped around the logs that were holding him. The hair kept pulling on him, and no matter how hard he struggled, he couldn't get free. The way he was hooked, his right arm was being pulled forward by the hair but his lower body was stuck in the logjam so he was being stretched as if he was on the rack. It felt like his right shoulder was being pulled out of its socket, and he shouted with pain. The logjam creaked and moved a tiny bit, but then stopped again and held. The hair kept pulling on him, never slackening. Up ahead, it was growing tighter and tighter, since it was trying to keep going forward even though it was attached to him, and he wasn't moving. The tension lifted it out of the water. As it pulled on him, it got higher and higher. He screamed and cried and he was sure he could hear his bones cracking.

Father John bounded out of the woods, pulling out his knife as he came. He came down to where Billy was stuck and leapt up on the logs. Then he gathered the hair into a bundle and with one movement, cut through it. Billy slumped over, sobbing, his right arm dangling in the water. Father John cut him free of what hair was left around him, then broke through branches until Billy was free of the logs as well. Billy was still shuddering and convulsing when Father John lifted him up and carried him over his shoulder through the forest. He looked back from where he dangled on Father John's shoulder and saw the hair floating on top of the water. The end that Father John had made by cutting the hair was moving down stream, but the rest of the hair just seemed to float around aimlessly, slowly following the other hair on the current and drifting around the logs which still held it.

Sarah

Father John took Billy Boy back to the cabin and wrapped his arm up in dirty cotton. After that, the boy wasn't allowed out much, but it wasn't a problem because he didn't really want to go out. He had nearly died twice when he had gone walking. Once in the snow, and then he'd nearly been pulled apart by the hair. So for a few weeks, he was content to rest at the cabin. After his right arm and shoulder healed up, he did start wanting to get outside, but Father John was dictatorial about it, and whenever he could he forced Billy to stay inside.

"You don't listen, son," he would say. "If you did listen then I could trust you to wander around a bit, but since you don't, you'll just have to stay around the cabin."

Billy was allowed to sit in the chairs outside, and when Father John was out cataloguing or fighting poplars, the boy sometimes went for little walks around the forest. He avoided going too far though, since he didn't want Father John to have to rescue him again.

Nonetheless, when he felt better, Billy began planning another escape. Despite the disastrous way that his previous attempt had ended, he still didn't want to be in the cabin when the snow started falling again, so he knew he had to try to escape before that happened. Also, Father John was seriously curtailing his freedom, and he figured that even without the bike, he would still have a lot more freedom at home in Cadomin than he had around Father John.

He knew that it wasn't worth making things any worse before he made his escape. For that reason he didn't push the boundaries by going too far from the cabin or sneaking around behind Father John's back too much. When he did go for walks, he kept them really short so that he knew he'd be back in the cabin well before Father John could return and find out about them.

It was early in July before Billy felt ready to try again. Father John had been keeping an eye on him, but unless Father John was willing to give up on cataloguing — and the boy knew that he wasn't — then Billy Boy figured he'd still get opportunities to escape. So since Father John was still going out quite a bit, Billy just planned his escape for a Friday when he knew Father John would have to go on a fairly long excursion that would keep him away from the cabin for most of the day.

On Friday, Billy left the cabin not long after Father John had gone for the day. Again he followed the tracks west toward Cadomin, though this time he was determined not to let anything distract him. He also knew what to expect from the poplars, so he steeled himself for that as well. A train had gone through just the night before, and so he knew that the tracks would have been cleared of any thickets, whether poplar or pine, that might get in his way. He was hopeful that the train hadn't left the trees in any shape to crowd the tracks. All in all, he felt more confident that he'd be able to handle whatever happened this time around. He knew the forest was against him, but he didn't figure it would be able to stop him and he felt certain that he'd be able to get all the way back to Cadomin.

He walked along the tracks for several hours. Without even realizing that he was getting close, he came to the bridge again. The trees had been cleared away by the train, as he'd knew that they would, and while the poplars still tried to come close, they were far from the tracks, and so he just stayed in the middle and they couldn't get to him. He listened intently before he crossed and couldn't hear the rumbling of a train, but, just to be sure, he still sprinted across. As he ran, he could see that there were still a few strands of the hair tangled around the beam where the hair had plunged downward into the river below. However, he didn't stop to investigate further, and so he didn't look to see if there was still any hair left down below in the water.

When he got to the other side, there were hardly any poplars, and when he'd gone another mile or so beyond the bridge, there weren't any left at all. He knew he was getting close to home and he was watching for landmarks to tell him he was near. Because he was watching he was able to see the top of the staircase when it came into view even though it was hidden in the trees.

He was happy to see the stairs, and he had the urge to go down them. The stairs reminded Billy of being at home when he had thought that the staircase was the most significant thing east of Cadomin and he wouldn't go past it. He already felt free of Father John, since he was across the bridge and had gotten away from the poplars. They hated each other, but the poplars and Father John seemed to go together. Billy decided that he could leave the tracks to go down the stairs. As usual, he was curious, and since he was sure he was free, it seemed all right. He knew he'd have to come back up the stairs so that he could follow the tracks, but he really wanted to see what was at the bottom of the stairs, so he started down.

It had been getting progressively more overcast for most of the day, but the clouds hadn't done anything other than make it darker and muggier. When he was about a quarter of the way down, the clouds finally opened up and started pelting the forest with rain. Even then, it only came down in fits and starts. The drops were fat and seemed to be descending lazily, so instead of trying to get under cover, Billy sat down on a stair and started catching the drops on his tongue.

It started raining harder, and Billy was getting quite wet. He thought about heading back to the tracks. Better to get soaked on his way home than on some little diversion. Soon it was coming down even harder, and so he got off the stairs and hid under a large pine tree that kept most of the rain out. But the storm only lasted a few minutes, and then the rain started tapering off, so he came out from under the tree and decided that he would keep going down the stairs.

When he got to the bottom, he looked around him. There was a wide trail heading off into the woods toward Hinton. He didn't want to go to the town and he had satisfied his desire to see the staircase, so he was about to turn around and head back up when he noticed that there was a woman lying face down in the bushes to the right of the trail.

She was wearing blue jeans and a red T-shirt that was riding up so that the skin on her back was visible. A little black leatherette purse lay beside her left hand. He picked up the purse to see if there was anything in it that said who she was. However, the purse was empty, and so he just put it back on the ground beside her.

She was soaked by the rain. Where her shirt rode up her skin was red-brown. Water collected in a pool in the small of her back. He kept his eyes on that pool for a while. He could see she was breathing and he tried breathing at the same pace, but he soon stopped because it was so slow that it hurt his lungs.

The rain started again, and he kept his eye on that pool in the small of her back. The water spread out over her back and poured over the side of her onto the ground. Other than the movements caused by breathing, she didn't move at all.

He sat down beside her and tried to figure out what he should do. He thought about just going on and telling his mother when he got home, but that didn't seem like a very good option. It seemed like there might be enough to talk about without talking about the girl at the bottom of the stairs.

He felt terrible for thinking it, but for a few minutes he was a little angry with the woman for messing up his day. It was going so well, and then she appeared. Then he was mad at himself for leaving the tracks and coming down the stairs. Then he was really mad for being a disappointment to himself and being mad about the situation when he should have been thinking about how to help this woman. If she needed any help. Maybe she was just taking a nap. The boy wasn't sure.

He was just about to poke her to try to wake her up, but as he leaned forward, Father John suddenly spoke behind him and said, "Don't be an idiot, son." Billy Boy had thought that he had really escaped this time, so he felt like crying when he heard Father John's voice. He managed to hold it in, though. He didn't know if Father John would take any satisfaction from seeing him cry, but nevertheless he was determined not to do it. He took a deep breath and then turned back toward where Father John's voice had come from.

Father John gave no indication that he was disturbed. He was determined not to let Billy know that he had been worried. However, when he spoke, it became pretty obvious that he was quite angry. His tone was very dark. "Don't be stupid," he said. "You think it's just chance that you found her out here, but it's not luck at all. She looks quiet, doesn't she, but that woman has worked her way up through dirt and roots and mouldy leaves and now she's resting quiet. I know where she comes from, and she isn't here for our good, I'll tell you that. Mark my words, son, women found in the woods are nothing but trouble."

So at Father John's insistence, they left her where she lay. Father John told Billy that she was a spy, an interloper that the poplars had sent to destroy them. It enraged him that they would stoop so low and try to exploit their weakest spot, which, apparently, was Billy's decency.

The boy considered just making a run for it, but even if he got away he really didn't want Father John to follow him to his mother's house. Billy knew his mother would probably fight him, and though he had confidence in his mother's abilities, Billy was beginning to think that Father John would probably win.

So Billy went back to Father John's cabin again. He didn't want to, and he was pretty sure that he wouldn't get another chance to leave that summer, but he didn't know what else he could do.

The Siege

It was a long walk to the cabin and Father John barely spoke. It was after dark when they got back. Billy went to bed immediately, but Father John sat outside watching the sky and smoking.

When Billy woke up the next morning, Father John was already disappeared, causing him to think about taking off again. But he decided that Father John must have spies planted throughout the forest who told him when Billy Boy left. That's why his attempts to escape hadn't worked, because there were birds or squirrels reporting back to Father John on Billy's movements. So it wouldn't have been very helpful to start running again. Father John would know about it right away and come find him again.

So Billy stayed put, and a few hours later Father John returned to the cabin. He still wasn't talking much, so Billy went inside, and Father John sat down outside again.

Within a few hours it was clear that something had gone terribly wrong. The poplars crowded in around the cabin, and for the first time, Billy could hear them scratching on the roof. Father John came back inside. Billy noticed that, whatever the man had been up to that morning, he was wounded and there was blood on his hands.

"We're going to have a little fun," said Father John. "I think I might have made them mad, and now they may be trying to get back at me."

"What did you do?" asked Billy.

"I don't want to talk about it."

Billy knew that it must have been a really bad thing that Father John had done. If he hadn't felt ashamed, then he wouldn't have had any problem telling the boy. If he didn't want to talk about it, what he'd done must have been awful. And Father John must have known how bad his actions had been, which was why he was keeping things to himself.

Billy could hear the poplars crowd around the cabin, but they couldn't get inside. A few tendrils snaked inside, between the logs that made up the walls, but Father John cut them off as soon as he saw them, and soon they stopped trying to come through. They seemed to have given up, so Father John bent down and looked through one of the cracks to see what the trees were up to.

"They've surrounded the place," he said. "It looks like we're under siege. They'll give up eventually. They haven't got it in them. They're impatient and they won't wait."

But they did wait. Billy Boy and Father John were stuck inside, while the poplars crowded around the cabin. Since they hadn't been expecting a siege, the two of them didn't have much food stored. They still had the mystery meat, but after a couple of weeks, even that got low, and both of them were getting skinny and desperate. They couldn't go out to get their hands on any more food, and Billy wondered how they could hold out, but Father John seemed determined.

After three weeks, all of the food was gone, even the meat, and so they both spent most of their time sitting down because they didn't have much energy to spare. However, Father John still went to the effort of going around and checking the cracks for poplars trying to get inside. It was rare, but the trees still tried to push into the cabin occasionally, and Father John would cut any branch that he found that had gotten through.

By the time another month had passed, Billy Boy had begun wishing that he could make his own separate peace with the poplars. He still didn't know what the siege was about or why it had happened, but he knew that he hadn't had anything to do with it. He wanted to run away, but he knew he wouldn't be able to get very far between starvation and the poplars. The poplars would kill him as quickly as they'd kill Father John. He might not have had anything to do with it, but the boy knew that they thought of him as an enemy anyway.

The two of them barely moved anymore. Luckily, the poplars had entirely stopped trying to get any saplings inside. Father John hardly ever checked by that point, so if the poplars had tried to get in they probably would have been successful.

This was the situation when the woman who had been at the bottom of the stairs dug her way up through the floor into the cabin. At first, they saw only her right hand as it came out of the ground. After another twenty minutes her left hand followed. In another hour, she had pulled herself up far enough that her face was out of the ground, which was when both Billy and Father John recognized her. Billy would have helped her if he could, and Father John would have tried to stop her, but neither of them were even capable of standing by that point.

It took her the better part of the day to get her whole body free from the ground. When she was fully above ground, she stood up, brushed the dirt off of herself and immediately started peeling strips of wood from the logs of the cabin. Billy looked over and could see from the expression on Father John's face that he wasn't happy about her being there, but he was so starved that he didn't have the energy to fight about it.

Billy and Father John had been sipping water from a pot that was still left on the stove. The two of them had nothing to cook, so there wasn't much point in having water on the stove, but neither of them had been able to summon the energy required to remove the pot. Occasionally it rained, so they still had some water left in the barrel. It hadn't been much, however, so they had been rationing water very closely and only drinking when they absolutely felt that they had to.

Once the woman had gathered a few strips of wood, she put them into the pot of water. There were still several logs left near the stove for fuel, so she put a couple in. Because it was summer, they hadn't felt the need to burn much to keep warm. With the fire going, the cabin got hot again, and it took a while, but the water began to boil. She moved it to the back of the stove to let it simmer. While it was simmering, she sat down beside Billy Boy and introduced herself.

"My name is Sarah," she said.

"Were you at the bottom of the stairs?" he asked in a voice that was barely a croak. He was fairly certain it was the same woman. However, she looked much healthier than the woman at the bottom of the stairs had looked, so Billy couldn't be sure that it was the same person.

"At the bottom of which stairs?" she asked. She looked friendly but genuinely confused by what he had said.

"The stairs by the railroad tracks," he said. He was confused himself. He had been sure that she would know what he was talking about.

"I'm sorry," she said, "but I don't know those stairs."

He decided that it didn't really matter, since they were starving and wherever she had come from, they needed her help. However, just for a second, a slight, knowing smile crossed her face which made him fairly certain that he had been right and that, for some reason, she was trying to hide her identity.

When the wood had simmered long enough, she pulled it out and placed the strips on a couple of plates. She handed a plate to Billy and then walked across the room to Father John. Billy snatched up one of the strips and began eating it, but Father John didn't seem to have enough strength left to do even that much, so Sarah began feeding him.

He still didn't look happy about her presence, but Father John was obviously relieved to get something to eat. The strips of wood weren't tasty or anything, but they did the job. After a week both Billy and Father John were feeling better.

After he was up and about, Father John and Sarah began to get along better. He seemed to lose his suspicions and they had long chats about the forest and they began laughing together about trees that they both knew.

She asked about his binders, and while he seemed a little hesitant to tell her about it at first, he eventually showed her what was in them.

He wasn't used to anyone taking an interest, so he seemed pretty happy that someone had finally asked about them. When Billy Boy had first arrived, he had tried to feign curiosity about them for a while, but soon he had stopped trying and now he never showed any interest in them at all.

Actually, the boy was kind of surprised that Sarah was interested in them. Father John's project just seemed kind of crazy to Billy, and definitely not something that he'd want to waste any time with. It was this odd interest that first got Billy's suspicions up, at the same time as Father John's suspicions were disappearing.

They still had to stay in the cabin since they were still surrounded by poplars. However, once they could eat the walls, it wasn't much of a hardship. They still had to be careful with the water, but it kept raining regularly enough that they could make do. If they could have gotten a whiff of fresh air, they would have known that the inside of the cabin smelled awful. But since they were all immersed in it anyway, they had gotten used to the smell, and it didn't really bother anyone too much. Well, it might have bothered Sarah, since she was new to the smell, but she never said anything.

Billy began to have bad dreams. He would often dream that the poplars were growing on him and that he was swiftly rotting away to become part of the soil. Sarah kept him company and tried to comfort him when he woke up shouting from a nightmare.

After one particularly bad dream, when he sat up, it was terribly cold and Sarah wrapped him in a blanket. She held his shoulders while he shivered from fear and cold. He looked at her after she had wrapped him up. She was staring across the cabin at the sleeping form of Father John. She looked a little hungry as she watched him, and Billy thought he understood why she had shown such an inexplicable interest in Father John and his cataloguing project.

"Are you with the poplars?" Billy asked.

She quickly turned to look at him. For a second she just looked at him blankly, and then she smiled and nodded. She stood up then, with a gesture, she silently invited him to do the same.

"Do you want to go for a walk?" she asked, and of course he did. He'd been cooped up in the cabin for weeks, and he was aching to stretch his legs. She looked over at Father John again, and when she was sure that he was deeply asleep, she opened the door and then she and Billy went outside.

Of course, the first thing he noticed was how fresh the air was. He breathed in deeply and the blast of air hitting his lungs made him cough. He smiled when he saw the moon. It had been weeks, and he felt himself hoping that she was just going to let him go. The walk back to Cadomin would be a nice jaunt after being forced to stay in the cabin for weeks.

Sarah was a spy working for the poplars, as Father John had thought, but Billy was still astonished at how easily she was able to pass between the trees. As they walked, the poplars let her through without any trouble, which only made sense, but Billy had spent so long in fear of the trees, that it still seemed amazing to him. As they walked into the forest, she started talking to him.

"Are you going to tell Father John?" she asked.

"I'm not sure," he replied. "I don't like him anymore than you do, but it still seems wrong to keep this from him."

"He's awful," she said.

"I know, but he's still a friend. And he's saved me a few times. Sometimes from you poplars. Why haven't you just killed him?"

"If we'd caught him in the first few weeks, we would have. After that, calmer heads prevailed and we decided to find out more about him before we killed him. We've lived in fear of him for a while, and we wanted to know what he was like. From what we've found out, he's kind of a disappointing enemy. Just vicious and odd. Did you ask him what he did? Why we started going after him?"

"I did, but he wouldn't tell me."

"That's because he knew you'd be disgusted."

"What did he do?"

"He went down by the river and peeled strips of bark off of some of the poplars down there. He pulled off complete circles around the trunks. He was torturing them. He went slowly, and he knew that it would take some time for them to die. But they'll die eventually. There's nothing we can do except wait."

"He's done terrible things before."

"But only when we try to get new territory. I won't lie, he was right to see us as an enemy. We saw him as ours, so it was fair enough that it would go both ways, but we never thought he'd sink so low. It was just revenge, there wasn't any other point to it. Those poplars down by the river weren't doing him any harm. They were old and they had taken over that area a long time ago."

Billy wasn't sure if he understood why peeling bark off old trees was worse than burning saplings. He just figured that he didn't get it because he was still an outsider. There were obviously rules of conduct between Father John and the poplars that Billy didn't understand. No matter what, though, the poplars were mad about it, so even if Billy couldn't see why, in some way it must have been worse. So, even though he really didn't get it, the boy tried to make himself see it from Sarah's point of view. He tried to make himself mad, even though he mostly just felt confused.

"I don't like him either," said Billy. That was one thing he was sure of, regardless of what he'd done. "Actually, I've tried getting away from him a couple of times, but it didn't work."

"We knew about that," she said. "Would it be better if you didn't have to worry about the poplars?"

"Yeah, of course. I mean, they try to eat me every time I get away. It'd be a lot easier if I could just walk away and not have to worry about them."

"That's no problem," she said. "As long as you don't tell him about me. Let me get some more information."

Billy thought about it for a few minutes. Despite what Sarah had told him, he felt conflicted about it. He was tired of the cabin and Father John, but he'd been saved by Father John many times. However, he also knew that he'd never be able to get back to Cadomin and his mother unless he made peace with the poplars and Father John wasn't after him. So after hesitating for a few minutes because he still felt funny about it, he said that he would keep quiet.

She turned toward the forest around her and addressed the trees. "You heard that," she said to the forest. "He'll keep my secret, and we'll let him go where he wants." Then she turned to Billy and said, "We should head back to the cabin now. He might wake up and wonder where we are. As far as he knows, we shouldn't be able to go outside at all."

They turned around and went back the way they had come. There was a funny smell in the air, but from being stuck inside for so long, Billy's nose was messed up, and he couldn't figure out what the smell was. When they got back to the cabin, they could see that Father John had woken up and was standing in the doorway. The cabin was on fire, and the weird smell in the air was smoke. Before he even saw the two of them, Father John had known exactly what was going on. He looked very sad. Billy expected him to look angry, but he didn't.

When Father John woke up and the two of them weren't there, he was worried. Then he decided that there was no way that the poplars would have taken the two of them, and left him alone. Also, there was no evidence that the poplars had breached the cabin, and so it seemed like the two of them must have left the cabin willingly. After he realized that, his old fears about Sarah came back, and he knew that they were plotting against him.

When he figured that out, he had set fire to the cabin. Father John knew that if the two of them were working together, then it was only a matter of time before the poplars got him. The thought was very disturbing, so he decided that it was better to burn everything down. So when the two of them returned, and confirmed his suspicions, he felt glad that he'd done it. And even though the cabin was on fire, Father John just stood and watched Billy and Sarah standing together at the edge of the clearing. Flashes of flame appeared behind him and in the gaps between logs.

There were flames licking around the walls and eating the roof. The poplars were shrinking away from the cabin to avoid getting burned. A brave poplar tried to reach out and grab Father John where he stood in the door, but Father John stepped back into the burning cabin before he could be taken.

After Father John disappeared into the burning cabin he didn't come out into the doorway again. Billy could see that he was sitting down on the dirt floor just inside. There was nothing that Billy or Sarah could do, so they just watched as the cabin burned. Soon the roof caught fire and it wasn't long after that the roof cracked and roared and then collapsed on top of the man inside.

Billy thought he heard a shout of surprise as the timbers came crashing down. However, he couldn't be sure that he had heard anything through the noise. When there was silence again, Billy figured that Father John must be dead. Billy had been expecting some sort of unmistakable, tortured shout or something, not the hint of a surprised yell that he couldn't even be sure that he had heard. However, except for the crackle of the flames, there wasn't any sound, until the walls started falling as well. They came down one at a time. Three fell outward, onto the grass of the clearing, but the back wall fell forward on top of the wreck of the collapsed roof.

Billy didn't know how to feel. He had known that he was leaving

Father John to die, but it had been remote and abstract. He hadn't expected to have to watch his benefactor die. He had expected to be far away from the cabin before things came to a head. Father John would never have given in, and the poplars wouldn't have given up until he was dead. After Sarah had gotten whatever information she was looking for, the poplars would have killed Father John. And that had been the fate that Billy Boy was going to leave him to. He felt awful, but he also knew that there wasn't any other way that things could have ended. He hoped that it would be good enough. He was also hoping that he'd find the blank slate on the way home, so that at least for a little while, he wouldn't have to feel bad about it.

Sarah and Billy stood and watched until the building collapsed completely. A few hours after the roof fell, the cabin was just a burning heap. It was hot enough that it looked like it might catch the grass on fire and spread to the trees at the edge of the clearing. Luckily, they'd had rain recently, so the grass was damp enough not to burn and the forest was safe from the fire.

Eventually, when the sun started coming up, the heap had stopped producing flames, and was just really hot. Billy could feel the heat from where he was standing. However, it didn't look like it was going to catch anything else on fire. Even if it had, they didn't have any water to douse it, so there wasn't anything that Billy or Sarah could have done in any case. Not knowing what else to do, they turned and started walking away.

Home

Billy had gotten so used to thinking of the trees as dangerous, that he took for granted that he'd need company to get through them. They walked together to the railroad tracks before he remembered that he would be able to go by himself without any trouble from the poplars. He looked around at the forest, and then up at her and said, "Can I go on my own now? The poplars won't try to eat me?"

"No, they won't," she said. "Obviously, you didn't have to keep my secret, but we'll honour our end of the bargain anyway. You can go anywhere you like and we won't bother you."

"I'm just going to go back along the tracks to Cadomin. That's where I'm from," he said and started walking.

She watched him go for a minute. To her he looked forlorn, even though he thought of himself as very capable. Now that Father John wasn't around the poplars wouldn't need her for anything, and so she knew that she could also leave if she wanted to. There was something about watching Billy Boy's back as he walked away that got to her, so she started following him. When she caught up to him, she said, "I'll take you."

"You don't have to."

"I'll take you anyway," she said.

So as the sun came up, they started heading back along the tracks toward Cadomin. As they passed, the poplars kept to themselves.

They didn't move away from them, as they had done with Father John, but they didn't bother them either. They walked for a few days, and Billy was feeling almost as good as he'd felt when he'd first left the valley. A great deal more exhausted, but very happy after the end of the ordeal. The weather was beautiful, and fresh breezes blew over the two of them as they went.

They passed by the top of the stairs, and a couple of hours later they crested the hill overlooking Cadomin. Billy could see his neat little house standing amongst the tall grass and ruined buildings. Even from a distance, though, he could see that it was in rougher shape than when he had left. The yard was looking a little overgrown, for one thing.

After they'd walked for another hour, they arrived at the house, and Billy rushed inside to find his mother, leaving Sarah standing on the front porch. He shouted out, but there was no trace of his mother. He went around to the different rooms, in case she was there and just hadn't heard him come home. The house wasn't very big and he knew that there really wasn't much chance of that happening, but he wanted to make sure.

After he'd checked the other rooms he let himself be convinced that she wasn't there. Not knowing what else to do, he went into the kitchen and sat down at the table. Feeling confused and worried, he glanced over at the fridge and saw a note stuck to it with a magnet shaped like the letter T. He got up and pulled the note off the fridge and then sat down at the table again before he began to read it.

Dear Billy,

I'm not sure where you are right now, but I suppose if you're reading this, you must have made it back all right. So, I hope you are well, but if you're home, you are probably okay, so I'll stop worrying.

However, I've left. I know I said I'd stay here, but I just couldn't take it anymore, being alone all the time. So I decided I would go looking for your father. I'm going to town first, but after that I'll probably head west over the mountains. I don't know why I think he went that way, but I do.

So if you get back and wonder where I am, I've gone over the mountains. I don't know when I'll be back.

If you're reading this, I'm sorry. Part of the reason I left was because I didn't think you would ever be coming back, so I would be surprised if you're reading this note. And if you are back, then probably you'll be sad to find me gone. And if I knew that you were reading this, then I'd feel sad too.

But the truth is, Billy, I don't know any of that. All I know is that I wander around this deserted town by myself and wonder what's happening. And so I needed to get going. I hope you understand.

Love,

Mom

Billy Boy put down the note on the table and began to cry. Sarah had been standing out on the front porch the whole time, but when she heard him crying she came inside. She came into the kitchen, and sat down beside him at the table, then put her arm around him, and asked him what was wrong.

He passed the note to her, and she read it, and realized that Billy Boy was on his own, at least for the time being. It didn't sound like his mother was coming back, either, or at least she didn't expect to. Sarah wanted to cry about it, but she forced herself not to for Billy's sake. She figured he didn't need her to start bawling as well.

Sarah handed the note back to him, and he folded it up and put it in his pocket. Then he started crying loudly again. Sarah hadn't really thought of Billy as a child. In the cabin, he had been an enemy, and a cleverer one than Father John. After that, they'd briefly been partners in trying to bring down Father John, and since they'd been travelling together, it had become clear that Billy knew his way around the forest, and didn't really need any help. He seemed very capable most of the time. However, at that time in the kitchen he was wailing and clutching her back and shoulders.

She wasn't really a motherly type of person, and she felt a little unqualified for the kind of comfort that she was being asked to give, but she did her best anyway, and, if she was doing it wrong, Billy didn't seem to notice. It took him a half hour or so before he finally calmed down. He still had tears in his eyes when he stood up from the table, but at least he wasn't making anguished sounds any more.

He just wanted to go to bed, even though it was still light out. He thought about showing Sarah to his mother's bedroom, but he felt odd about having her sleep there, and so he decided that Sarah would just have to sleep on the couch that night. She seemed fine with that. He asked her if she needed any extra blankets or anything, but she said she was fine. She went back out onto the front porch to sit and wait for darkness, since she couldn't fall asleep while it was still light out.

Billy went to his bedroom and shut the drapes so that they were overlapping each other. He left them open a tiny bit in the middle near the top, so that a little bit of light was able to come in, but otherwise the room was completely dark. He lay staring at the ceiling for quite a while, trying to think of what he ought to do next.

He briefly considered staying in Cadomin. He didn't really want to go travelling again, and there was a chance that his mother would return. It was a small chance, no doubt. In fact, there wasn't really much of any chance at all. She thought he'd left for good, so it seemed likely that she'd done the same. And Cadomin would be a dismal place without her, so he decided that staying wasn't really much of an option.

He also briefly considered going back to the cabin even though it was burnt. At least the area was familiar. He could live around there with a minimum of effort and wouldn't have to explore. Given some time, he could rebuild the cabin, and this time he'd put windows in it, and he wouldn't have that huge pile of binders. Father John hadn't really been very happy there, which was ironic, since he'd only left the city and gone out to the woods in order to make his life better. But Billy Boy was sure that he could make it enjoyable, since he didn't have Father John's weird obsessions.

However, it didn't take him long to dismiss that plan as well. He knew he wouldn't really be happy, and he wondered how long the truce with the poplars would last. He didn't think he could be nasty enough to make the poplars scared of him, and, even if he could, he was fairly sure that he didn't want to become that nasty a person. Besides, he figured that if he was going to have to go to the effort of rebuilding the cabin, he might make the effort to go after his mother. It would probably be less work than rebuilding would be.

So then he thought about following his mother over the mountains. He hadn't even been able to find the bike, and so it didn't seem likely that he'd be able to find his mother. Hopefully she was on the move, since if she was stopped somewhere, it was probably because she was dead. He didn't want to think about that, and he really didn't want to think about finding her that way.

But he also knew that it was his only real choice. He wanted to find her, and there wasn't even a chance of that happening if he stuck around Cadomin or went back to the burnt cabin. He really hadn't wanted to be going again, so it was strange that the decision made him feel better. However, at least he wasn't confused anymore, and the confusion was what had made him feel the most sad and angry.

After he'd made the decision he managed to go to sleep. Sarah stayed up on the porch for an hour or so after sunset to watch the stars come out. It started getting cold, so she went back inside, and prepared the couch for sleeping. But even after she lay down, she couldn't fall asleep, so she wound up staring at the ceiling for a while. It wasn't that the couch was uncomfortable. The upholstery was fine and soft, and Sarah was fairly short, so she was able to stretch out. However, she had a number of things going around in her head, and she couldn't get them to stop.

She was having the same problem deciding what to do that Billy had had. After she had seen Billy safely returned to his home, she had been planning on going back to the poplars. However, his mother had left and he was all alone, so she wasn't sure if that was what she still wanted to do. She was confused, and she was thinking about just going with him wherever he wound up going.

However, she didn't know if he was actually going to go at all. Of course, she didn't know how useful she would be even if she accompanied him on his journey. She figured that if he did go, then he would probably head west into the mountains, and she didn't know anything about the forests in that direction. The only thing she knew was that there weren't many poplars to the west, and none at all once the mountains got high enough.

And if he decided not to leave, she wasn't sure that she wanted to just plant herself in Cadomin. She hadn't seen many poplars past the railroad bridge, let alone around the village itself. There were a few poplars along the river, but most of the mountainsides seemed to be covered in pines. She felt out of place amongst pines, and so she felt like she would be just as uncomfortable in the valley as she would be in the mountains. And while she wasn't sure she'd be of any help to him as he travelled, she thought she might be even less useful trying to play house for him in Cadomin.

She decided that if he wanted to stay where he was, then she was going to head back. She decided that there wasn't any point in her staying. She wouldn't be much use anyway, and she would just be unhappy hanging around the dismal valley with nothing but pine trees. She also decided that if he wanted to go west, then she would go with him. She still didn't know how much help she could be, but she couldn't stand the thought of him wandering around in the forest by himself.

She still didn't know what Billy was going to do, so making the decision wasn't that much of a relief, but at least she could just put it all away for the night, and try to get some sleep. She still tossed and turned for a few hours, but finally, around three, she managed to fall asleep.

On The Road

The next day, over breakfast, Billy told Sarah that he'd decided to try to follow his mother. She had kind of hoped that he was going to stay in Cadomin, so that she would be free to go back to the poplars, but nervously she proclaimed that she would go with him. He was a little surprised since he hadn't considered the possibility that she would want to come along. However, he quickly decided that it was probably a good idea, and that her company would make the journey more bearable.

So they packed some food and got ready to go. They left the house around ten in the morning. At first, they followed the train tracks again. After they'd walked for a few hours, however, the tracks passed over the highway. Both headed west into the mountains, the highway running along beside the tracks a few hundred yards to the left. Since the road was going in the same direction as the tracks, if they followed it instead, it would still be no trouble for them to head west into the mountains. The road would be easier to walk on than the tracks and besides, if they travelled on the road, then they wouldn't have to worry about getting hit by trains. So they struggled down to the road from the hill that the tracks were on, and started following the highway instead.

The highway was a great deal busier than the tracks had been. Cars and trucks rushed by regularly. They both jumped the first time a car went by, and even after several had passed them they still found it disturbing.

However, it was nothing compared to the big trucks. When one went by, Billy was reminded of the train that he had kneeled beside that first winter at Father John's. However, unlike the trains, the trucks went by fairly regularly. Also, instead of making a low rumble for several miles before they passed, they seemed to sneak up on the travellers. It seemed like one of the huge trucks would hurtle past them totally unexpectedly.

Also, there hadn't been any road kill by the train tracks, so they weren't ready for the corpses of dead animals that lined the highway. Every twenty feet or so, they seemed to be stepping past another bundle of fur and blood. Neither of them stopped long enough to find out what had been hit, since they knew that they wouldn't like it if they found out too much. Occasionally, there was a deer on the side of the road, and no matter how hard they tried not to notice, the animal was too big for them not to see some of the injuries that had killed it. They just hurried past with their eyes averted and tried to ignore the dead animal. Despite their best efforts, they almost always got a glimpse. But they tried to put it out of their heads as soon as they'd passed. Billy found it unpleasant, but Sarah was more upset by it than he was. She really didn't like the sight of that much blood.

After they had walked another five miles or so, there was a dead moose lying in the middle of the road. The car that had hit it had skidded off the road and into the ditch another hundred yards ahead. They both stopped walking and looked at each other. The moose was on its side in the middle of a lane. Admittedly, they didn't investigate too closely, but other than mangled legs, it really didn't look that bad. The car had pushed its legs out from under it, and then the animal had smashed into the windshield and flipped over the top of the car until it had landed on the highway behind the vehicle. No doubt its innards had been badly damaged, but the outside of the moose looked fine, at least from the side of the road where Sarah and Billy were looking at it.

Then they looked down the road at the car where it had come to a stop in the ditch. Most of the damage was on the front of the vehicle, but even from behind, they could see that it had been badly smashed up. Obviously, from where they were, they couldn't see the broken windshield, but they could see the huge dents the moose had left in the roof when it had rolled over the car. There were skid marks on the pavement where the car had tried to stop before it hit the animal, but none heading into the ditch where the car was. The driver had been unconscious after he hit the moose and so he hadn't hit the brakes, or even steered away from the side of the road.

Sarah started walking toward the car. Billy Boy sat down and asked her if she really wanted to do that.

"Of course I don't want to," she replied, "but I have to take a look."

When she got close, she could see that the damage was worse than she had thought. Not only was the roof dented in and the windshield smashed, the front of the car had been damaged when it hit the moose, and then completely crushed when the car had hurtled off the road and hit the hill on the other side of the ditch. Obviously, it had still been going at a fairly good speed when it had gone into the ditch, and when it had ploughed into the bank, the front end had crumpled up.

It was an older car. It was quite long and was painted brown. It was kind of boxy, or had been before the accident had forced it into a twisted shape. The antenna looked very odd, because it was undamaged. It stood above the wreckage, pointing straight into the air.

Sarah hesitated when she saw the damage. She knew that there wasn't much chance anyone had survived, and so she also knew that there really wasn't much point in forcing herself to look inside. But she decided that, even though she really didn't want to and even though it was probably pointless, she had to at least check. So, reluctantly, she kept walking until she got close and then looked inside the car.

Because it was an older car there weren't any airbags. The driver was propped up against the steering wheel. He was facing away from her, and all she could see was the back of his head. It just looked like he was taking a little nap. There were shards of glass everywhere from the broken windshield. The driver side window had been rolled down, and there wasn't any glass between the two of them, so Sarah was able to reach in and give him a poke. When she did so, she could see the puddle of blood that had collected on his lap and on the seat between his legs.

He didn't move when she poked him, and so she took hold of his shoulder gently and gave him a little shake. He still didn't move. Then he shifted slightly and she could see that there was a great deal of blood coming out of his mouth and nose. His nose had been crushed against his face when the moose had come through the windshield. Above this wreckage, she could see that his eyes were still open. She had been thinking that he might just be unconscious, but when she saw that his eyes were still open, she felt sure that he was dead.

She took a step back from the car and, like she had done with the animals, she looked away from him. She took several deep breaths and tried not to panic or throw up. After a few minutes she calmed down, and she looked back to where Billy was standing by the side of the road watching her. He looked like he was about to start walking over, but she held up a hand and he stopped. Then she turned back to the car and the driver.

She knew she wasn't up to pulling the body out of the car. Besides, even if she could have gotten him out, she didn't know how to give a full examination. And even if he was still alive, which didn't seem likely anyway, he obviously needed more medical help than she was capable of providing. Reluctantly, she looked full in his ruined face again, and when she did, she decided she was just going to go with her gut instinct. He didn't look like he was breathing, and his staring eyes convinced her that he was dead.

After she had decided to give up, she turned around and walked back to Billy Boy sitting on the pavement.

"We need to get back to the train tracks," she said as she approached.

"What did you see?" he asked.

"We need to get back to the tracks," she said.

"All right. When we get close again."

"Now," she said, and he stood up.

"We don't even know which direction to go," he said.

"Billy, I don't want to spend another minute on this road," she said, "so I'm going to find the tracks, even if I have to spend the rest of the day doing it."

It didn't seem like he really had a choice, so he agreed, and they crossed the ditch beside the road and started climbing the hill on the other side. They hoped that the tracks were still running just on the other side of the hill. That was the direction that they had originally come from and they hadn't seen the tracks cross the highway again, so they were hopeful that they were right.

The Swamp

It was a tough climb, but eventually they made it to the top of the hill. The trail was quite muddy, and both of them found it hard to keep their footing walking between the trees. In spite of the roots tripping them, the large trees were a help, because they could grab hold of them and pull themselves up while they climbed so that they didn't slide back down the hill.

When they made it to the top, they were able to look down the other side, but they couldn't see any sign of the tracks. Nevertheless, they started down the slope, hoping that the tracks would appear when they got closer to the bottom. Halfway down, Billy noticed a glint of light, and thought that maybe it was the sun glinting off the metal tracks, so he told Sarah about it. She stopped and looked for a second and saw it herself, but it looked like water to her, not rails.

She was right, and when they got to the bottom, instead of the railroad tracks, they found themselves face to face with a slough. On the other side, about a half mile away, they could see a large dike that had obviously been built for the tracks, so they knew that they were close, but in the meantime, they had to figure out how to get to the other side of the swamp.

At first, Billy just wanted to try to walk across it. It didn't look very deep, so he figured that if they were careful, it wouldn't be any problem to just walk across. However, he took a couple of steps and sank into the mud. If Sarah hadn't been there to pull him out, he would have gone under and drowned.

After that, they knew that they would need to be more careful. They started walking along the edge of the swamp, trying to find some way around it. It was a hard hike, since often they would step on what looked like dry land, and realize too late that there was water below a thin covering of grass and mud floating on top. Even where the dry land was real, it was hard going between tangles of dead trees and mud. After an hour or so, they came to the conclusion that while the swamp must end somewhere, they weren't going to be able to find the end, so they needed to come up with another plan to get across unless they wanted to keep trekking along the edge of it forever.

The swamp was full of sticks and dead trees. Sarah figured that even though they hadn't seen a lodge, the swamp was probably a lake created by a beaver dam. There were many dead trees sticking out of the water, so it had obviously been a forest at some point. It must have been flooded fairly recently, probably just in the past few years.

Along the edge of the swamp there were many large dead trees that were still standing upright. She convinced Billy to help her try to break the trunk of one of these trees. At first, they tried to break a fairly large tree, but even though it was dead, there was still enough good wood in the middle of the trunk that it was impossible to break. So they found themselves a smaller tree and tried to break it instead. Billy jumped on one side of it, while Sarah tried to pull it over. It eventually toppled, but it didn't break. Instead, the roots just came away from the mud and the whole thing fell over.

The lower part of the tree didn't float because it was waterlogged. However, most of the trunk that had been above water was still dry, so it still floated. They pulled the tree out of the water so that it wouldn't float away, and then they found another tree that they could knock over. Once they had two trunks, they set out across the swamp, each grasping a tree trunk under one arm. In places where they could touch the bottom, they were able to use the trunks to balance themselves, and where the water was too deep for them to reach the bottom, they had to go slower, but they were able to use the trunks to keep them above the surface.

They had to be careful, and so it was a long, hard journey through the swamp. It was slowest in the parts where they couldn't touch the bottom since they found it hard to propel themselves forward without being able to push off from the bottom. Billy had this problem more often, since he was shorter, and Sarah sometimes had to wait for him to catch up.

The sun was starting to go down by the time they got to the far bank. When they got there, they climbed up the dike and found, as they had hoped, that there were tracks running along the top of it. Sarah had put it out of her mind, but the whole time they were struggling across the swamp, they hadn't been entirely sure that the tracks were actually on top of the dike in front of them. If the tracks hadn't been there, the whole journey through the swamp would have been for nothing. Sarah was very relieved that they had found their way back to the tracks, both because she was happy to be away from the highway, but also because it had made the swamp worth crossing. Billy, while he still wondered whether they should have left the highway, was also happy to see the tracks again. He was tired of the swamp and just happy to be on dry land again.

The sun was going down behind the mountains, and they decided they'd have to find a place to stop for the night. They didn't want to stop right on the tracks, but they couldn't find any other place to rest. On one side of the tracks was a sheer cliff where, unless they had been mountain sheep, they'd never have been able to find a place to camp. Below them there was a short slope and then the swamp started. They couldn't see any place on that hill to camp where they wouldn't run the risk of rolling back down into the swamp while they slept.

So they had to walk along the tracks looking for a safe place to stop for the night. The sun had gone behind the mountains, and they were still searching around in the twilight before they managed to find a suitable place. A rock shelf stuck out of the side of the hill below the tracks, and a few thin trees grew below the shelf. The two travellers scrambled down to it, even though it wasn't a great spot. It was getting dark and they knew that it was as good a spot as they would be able to find. They hoped that if the shelf didn't hold them up, then at least the trees below the shelf might stop them from rolling too far toward the swamp.

There weren't any incidents during the night. Despite their fears, neither of them had had to cling desperately to a tree to avoid sliding down into the swamp. A train passed them at about two in the morning, so of course they both woke up. However, the train had been noisy and had woken them up long before it arrived, so neither of them had been particularly startled by it. It took a little while, but they both managed to get back to sleep after it had passed.

They got up in the morning happily. Billy Boy stood, stretched and smiled. They were both looking forward to a day without any roadkill or surprise trucks passing them. Sarah couldn't help thinking that, however awful the highway had been, at least the horror of the road had made them a great deal more thankful for the tracks, and so, at least temporarily happier about the uncertain journey in front of them.

After they had eaten breakfast, they started walking west along the tracks again. The swamp disappeared and the ground on the left rose almost to their level. The cliff on the opposite side went further away from them for a few miles, but then came close again, until it was hugging the right side of the tracks.

In the afternoon they came to a bend where it seemed like the tracks had been cut into the side of a mountain. On their left, where the swamp had been, there was now a sheer drop into a heavily forested chasm below. On the right side was a cliff rising straight above them. There were only a few feet on either side, so if they kept following the tracks and got caught by a train they would be in trouble since they wouldn't be able to get off and out of the way. They would have the same problem as they'd had on bridges, but they wouldn't even have the option to jump into the river. Furthermore, they couldn't see around the bend, so they didn't know how far the tracks went on like that.

For a few minutes, they didn't know what to do, but then they decided to risk it. They walked quickly along the tracks far enough to be able to see where the narrow spot ended. Luckily, it wasn't very long, because just after they'd passed the half way point they heard the rumble of the train coming behind them. They both started running forward.

The train's rumble had given them ample warning, but they still were just barely able to get to past the cliff. Before they were overtaken by the train, they managed to reach a point where the mountain side was at least a few feet away from the tracks. As the train roared past, they threw themselves up against the mountain, and even though they were squeezing against it as hard as they could, it was still much too close for comfort.

"Maybe we should find the highway again," Billy said.

Sarah said nothing. She knew he was right, but she really didn't like the idea. Also, by this time they'd climbed far enough into the mountains that they couldn't even see the highway anymore. She didn't know where they were, and so she had no idea which direction the highway was in. Even if they were to try, she wasn't sure that they'd be able to get back to the road.

"Would your mother have taken the highway?" she asked.

Billy thought about this for a moment, and then shook his head, resigned. "No, she wouldn't have liked the roadkill any more than you did. She would have taken the tracks," he replied.

"Then we need to stay on the tracks," said Sarah.

They continued walking along the tracks, though they were both more cautious now, listening for the rumble of a train coming behind them. They walked on for another day, but early the next morning they came to another narrow spot, where there was just room for a train and nothing else between the mountainside and a cliff. They ran along the tracks around the bend. It was much longer than the one the day before, so they were much more worried, but there was no train, and they made it to the end of the narrow part without any problem.

However, when they had made it, Billy Boy shook his head and said, "We have to get off the tracks." After they got around the bend, they had sat down in the grass beside the tracks. They were both quite tired from the fast pace they'd set around the curve, and both were also fatigued from having to be nervous the whole time.

"I thought you had said that your mother..."

"I was wrong," he said. "This is stupid. My mother would have seen it was stupid, and gone back to the road. We need to get off of these tracks. We're going to get killed."

"All right," said Sarah, "but I don't know if we can find the highway again."

"We don't have to get back to the highway. It would be good if we could, but we don't even know where it is anymore. In the meantime, we can just take a trail. There aren't that many here, and we can figure out if we're going west. At least it'll get us off the tracks."

"We'll get lost."

"As long as we're heading in the right direction, we should be okay. And even being lost will be a lot better than getting hit by a train."

They still had to walk another mile or so before they were able to find a trail that went away from the tracks. They took the first trail that they came upon, even though they weren't sure if it was heading where they wanted to go. It climbed steeply up onto the mountain on their right, so they had a bit of a scramble before they could rest. However, when they reached the top, they sat and looked down on the train tracks below them. They could see that, despite how it had looked like at the beginning, the trail was heading in generally the right direction.

After they had rested for a while, they went on and for several miles they were able to keep the tracks in sight. The railroad ran at the base of the mountain they were on, and since the trail ran along the top of the ridge, they were high enough to be able to look down and see the tracks through the trees. Eventually, they lost sight of them when they went around a corner and began hugging the side of the mountain. It seemed possible that the tracks were hidden because they were at another narrow part, and it seemed to be quite a long stretch. Neither of them said anything, but they both felt glad that they were passing above the narrow part and that they didn't have to run between ties to get past it.

They still couldn't see the tracks when the trail finally left the ridge and started gently running down the northern side of the mountain. It seemed like a fairly extreme change in altitude, since they were suddenly plunged into deep forest, and they couldn't see much either above or below them. However, in reality, the trail was only about fifty feet below the level of the ridge, so they hadn't actually gone down very much.

Eventually, they came to a small clearing with what looked to be the remains of a fire and some orange peels scattered around. Sarah thought it might be a sign of Billy's mother, but he didn't think so. His mother had never really liked oranges, and even when she did eat them, she preferred cutting them into sections rather than peeling them. Billy knew that it probably hadn't been his mother, since the scattered orange peels were jagged rather than triangular.

Which left them wondering why this fire had been made, and who else was out there. Sarah found some traces of them, and wanted to follow, but Billy was sure that it wasn't his mother, and he didn't want to waste time following someone else.

"You can't be completely sure it wasn't her," said Sarah.

"I'm sure enough," he said, and started walking down the trail on the other side of the clearing. Sarah shrugged her shoulders, and followed him. She figured that Billy knew his mother best, so if he didn't believe that it was her, then Sarah wasn't about to tell him he was wrong.

When the trail continued, it went downhill again, this time it fell deeply into a valley between high ridges that towered above it on both sides. After a few hours, they came to another abandoned fire pit in another small clearing. Sarah didn't say anything, she just looked over at Billy. He investigated the fire pit and then he scratched his head.

"I still don't think it's her," he said.

"All right," said Sarah and they continued on.

Beyond the second fire pit, the trail started to climb once more, this time up the ridge to the right of them, away from the tracks, or where Sarah assumed that the tracks were still running. It was a long climb, but gentle, so they never got out of breath. As they went up, the forest thinned out, and they were able to see the remains of the third fire before they reached it.

It was hardly worth calling the area a clearing since the forest around it was already thin. There were a few less trees than the surrounding area, but it was barely noticeable. A pile of ashes was all that was left of the fire. There wasn't any smoke, but from the look of it, the fire hadn't been out for very long and the ashes were still warm.

"All right, I guess we should look around," said Billy.

"I don't think we need to." Sarah replied. "Somebody obviously uses this trail, so we'll just keep following it, and we should come across them sooner or later."

"I still don't think it'll be mom," he said.

"I believe you, but like I say, we'll come across them anyway."

Billy took a quick look around the fire pit, but he didn't spend that much time on it. There wasn't anything else to do but follow the trail they'd been on. So that's what they did. The trail kept climbing, and became quite steep. There were a few spots where they had to go on all fours to get up the trail. They were getting above the tree line, and were surrounded by rocks covered in lichen. What trees still managed to grow were stunted pines no more than four feet tall and widely spaced from each other.

From the top of this ridge, they could look down on the ridge that the tracks had followed, and beyond that a wide river that spread itself out in the wide flat area beyond the ridge, in front of another set of mountains far away to the left of them. The sun was just above the mountains, so even if they hadn't yet found the mysterious person in front of them on the trail, the travellers knew they'd have to stop soon.

Without the forest to hold it together, the trail had spread out and almost disappeared on the bare rocks. There was a vague indication that a particular path across the hard ground had been used a bit more, but there wasn't much else. There was a large outcropping of rock standing out above the ridge that seemed to be in the way of the trail, so they continued around it, and when they got to the other side they found the person who had been on the trail in front of them all day.

Jacob

He was crouched in front of another fire. He was a young man, but he had a thick, long beard that made him look older. He looked up at them as they approached as though he'd been expecting to see them. He had nervous brown eyes, and he seemed to look at you longer than he should.

Without hesitation, Sarah walked up to the fire and sat down. "Hello," she said. "I'm Sarah and this is Billy."

"I'm Jacob," said the young man.

Billy sat down, and they all felt at home with each other very quickly. Jacob was new to the forest, and even newer to the mountains. He had left a forestry tower. Jacob had been working in a liquor store, and decided that he needed a change. He had gotten a job in a watchtower with the forestry department. He made sure that when forest fires started, he told his superiors quickly, so that they could get fire fighters out before it became a catastrophe.

After a few months, they decided he was losing his mind. He had left his radio on and some of the other people had heard him talking to himself. Not that it was terribly uncommon for people to talk to themselves when they were living alone in a watchtower, but people were troubled by the kinds of things that he was talking about.

When they tried to convince him that he was going crazy they were very gentle, and told him that it wasn't uncommon. Many people get a little crazy from the loneliness of working on the towers. That's why they generally try to hire couples for the watchtowers, so there's at least a little bit of human interaction. They hadn't been able to find any couples, which was why he'd been hired in the first place.

He tried to explain that it had just been an accident that he had left his radio on. While it might have sounded like he was going nuts, talking to himself was just a good way to get things out and think things through. He tried to explain that that was why he had wanted to leave the city. He was surrounded by people, and so when he talked to himself, everyone could see him, and they thought he was nuts. He was looking for someplace where he could talk freely, and he had figured that a forest watch tower was the best place to do that. Apparently, he had been wrong.

They fired him, and tried to take him back into the world, but the night that they were supposed to leave, Jacob had slipped out of camp into the forest. He was kind of sad not to have any job at all anymore, because he'd been brought up to believe you should always work, but he also realized that if even the forest service couldn't handle him, the only choice he had left was to escape to the woods.

So he had headed for the hills. He thought they might still be after him, and he warned Sarah and Billy Boy that if they wanted to stay, they should watch out for helicopters and sniffer dogs. Billy wanted to tell him that since it had been a few months, they probably weren't looking for him anymore, but he liked Jacob and decided that Jacob would probably be unhappy if he didn't believe that anyone was looking for him.

Then Billy told Jacob his story, and asked about his mother, but Jacob hadn't seen her. Then it was Sarah's turn. She didn't say much however, just told Jacob the same things that Billy already knew. She asked Jacob if there were any poplars around, and he told her that he didn't know of any. He'd seen a few while he was still watching the forest for fires, but that was lower down in the foothills, and he hadn't seen any since he'd headed up into the mountains.

They kept talking after the sun went down. Mostly, Jacob stayed up on the ridge. For one thing, it reminded him of the watch tower because it had grand views, so he was able to just sit and talk to himself while he watched things going on. Also, when he wanted silence occasionally, it was nice to be able to just sit with the view and be quiet. Finally, because of the valley, there was deep forest nearby, and so he would be able to escape the helicopters on short notice if he needed to.

When there was no light left in the sky, they went to bed. Summer had arrived, but that high up it was only hot during the day, and it was still cold at night. In the morning, when they woke up they were shivering. Billy Boy and Sarah were just about to leave, but Jacob stopped them, and asked if they wouldn't stay for a couple more nights.

Billy was anxious to get going, but Sarah was happy to stick around. She didn't relish further climbs chasing after a woman she was pretty sure that they wouldn't find. She had hung her hopes on Jacob. Even though Billy had been sure that it wasn't his mother, Sarah had still secretly thought it might be her ahead of them. When it turned out that it wasn't, Sarah had felt kind of let down and tired.

So when Jacob asked them to stay, she was ready for a rest and had no problem agreeing. Billy Boy looked a little surprised, but he didn't make any fuss.

They wound up staying with Jacob for the better part of a week. They quickly discovered why the forestry people had decided Jacob was crazy. They both still liked him, but he did talk to himself quite a bit. Even when one of them was around. Occasionally they would have to get him to clarify who he was talking to, since even while he was eating lunch with them, he still might be talking to himself. It was a little nerve wracking.

Also, he really did say some crazy things. Granted, he only addressed the really questionable stuff to himself, but they heard it. So when he claimed that the pines were plotting against him, Sarah heard him. She tried to reassure him by telling him that pines were terribly good natured and would never do any harm to anyone, but he wouldn't have any of it. In fact, he seemed a little defensive about it. He told Sarah that it was just what the pines wanted her to believe, and, in reality, they were the puppet masters of the whole forest. He'd heard some bad things said about poplars, but he knew that it was really the pines at the root of it. She was glad to hear him defending poplars, but she really wanted to straighten him out about the pines. In the end, however, she decided it wouldn't be worth it, and that he didn't want to be straightened out anyway.

And when Billy told him about the orange peels at the fire pit down below, Jacob decided that it was further evidence that he was being followed, since he couldn't remember eating an orange himself at any time. He described in detail the orange eating agents of the forest service, combing the woods in their black suits and tossing their peels around carelessly. Billy didn't know much about men in black suits, but it did seem odd that they would wander around the forest snacking on oranges while they were looking for Jacob.

Jacob told Billy that there'd been several groups after him, even before he'd left the city. It all revolved around the conversations he had with himself. Apparently one of the times that they'd heard him talking, they'd decided that he knew too much and that's when they moved in to try to take him.

Jacob had thought he might be safe from them in the forest, but after the forest service decided he was crazy, they'd started acting more and more like the men from the city who'd been trying to get him. Soon it was clear that the same black suits that had chased him out of the city had completely infiltrated the forest service and were the ones that were really trying to get Jacob.

Billy found all of this very unlikely, and he wanted to tell Jacob so, but even if it were the truth, it didn't seem like Jacob would want to hear it. In spite of his odd fears, Jacob was quite nice, and Billy didn't want to upset him.

Most evenings they all gathered around the fire, but one night Jacob just wasn't there. Billy and Sarah called for him, and went off in opposite directions to look for him, but he was nowhere to be found. When they came back to the fire, and were both sitting down again, they tried to figure out what had happened to him. Billy held out the possibility that he might show up again, but Sarah figured he'd seen something that spooked him and taken off. They both briefly and silently considered the possibility that the forestry department had come and taken him away like he'd claimed they would. However, neither of them said anything out loud.

They both wished that they could have convinced Jacob to relax and stop worrying, especially if it would have kept him from disappearing. They knew that it might have been anything that had set him off and caused him to run away, and they also knew that there wasn't anything that they could have done about it. They decided that, no matter what, they would have to leave if he didn't show up by the next morning.

Sliding

However, Jacob still hadn't shown up by the morning, so Billy and Sarah knew that they'd have to leave and just let him do whatever he was doing. Sarah still took a quick look around to see if she could find any trace of him, but, Billy Boy was waiting. She wondered what had happened to Jacob, but she also knew that they had to go find the boy's mom and didn't have time to start a search for Jacob as well. They packed up and continued walking down the trail. Just beyond the campsite it plunged down the side of the ridge into another valley.

After they had walked several miles, they suddenly arrived at an area that had been burnt in the recent past. The burnt trees were right against the healthy forest and there was no obvious reason why the fire had stopped instead of eating through the healthy trees as well. The trail went straight through the burnt area, but Billy and Sarah hesitated before entering. However, unless they wanted to go back to the campsite and continue looking for Jacob, they had no choice except to go forward.

The trees were just as tall as they had been in the healthy forest, but they were black and devoid of any needles or branches, just pillars of soot that rose to the sky. There were areas where all the trees were lying down. One tree had fallen over and it had taken several more trees down with it, and each of those several had taken several more, so what had started with one tree falling over, wound up bringing down an acre or more.

The undergrowth was very happy. For one thing, it had all the rich ashes to grow in. Also, since the branches and needles of the forest were no longer blocking the forest floor from the sunlight, the small plants had access to light for the first time in a very long time. Finally, the undergrowth didn't have to struggle against the blanket of acidic needles that the pines always dropped around them. The heat of the fire had burnt off the needles, and the burnt pines weren't putting down any more to replace them. The pine needles killed most of the little plants, and so the healthy forest actually had very little growth on the forest floor, but the burnt area was vibrant with the happy green of the burgeoning undergrowth.

In fact, Billy and Sarah had difficulty following the trail because the undergrowth was thick and had absorbed part of the path. Everywhere they looked there were black pillars and green shrubbery and the trail itself seemed to have disappeared. Billy wandered around unabashed, but Sarah tried her best to search without stepping on the new growth. She knew that it wouldn't work since there was too much greenery, but she still didn't like crushing the little plants beneath her feet.

For another twenty minutes or so, the travellers tried to continue on their way, but it soon became clear that they didn't really know where they were going anymore. They stopped, but they didn't want to sit down, because the ground was covered in soot. Neither of them was that concerned about cleanliness, but they knew that getting soot out would be very difficult. So even though they didn't care that much, they still wanted to be careful. Also, they couldn't lean because the trees were as sooty as the ground. Besides, the trees that were still standing were terribly weak, so if either of the travellers had leaned on them, they would have pushed them over. As a result, they wound up looking like they were at a party where they didn't know anyone, standing awkwardly in the middle of the forest.

Since neither of them really liked the burnt forest, both of them were pretty anxious to get going. However, they didn't know which direction they needed to go in to escape it. It was around noon, and the sun was directly above them, so they couldn't even use its position to make a rough guess of the direction they ought to go.

They wandered around in circles for a while, and then, having accomplished nothing, they returned to stand in the middle of the forest. Billy noticed black clouds gathering on one side of the sky, and the wind had picked up slightly. All of a sudden, there were creaking sounds all around them.

Sarah frowned, but she'd become hopelessly turned around, and she didn't have any idea which way was back anymore. So she just said, "Come on," and started walking. Billy stood still for a moment, looking confused, and then he followed her. She was walking very quickly however, and he couldn't keep up. He asked her to slow down, but she just turned back to him and told him to hurry up. She wasn't trying to be mean, she just knew that when the wind and rain hit the burnt forest, it was going to be disastrous.

The wind started picking up some more, and the clouds were advancing over them. Off to the right they suddenly heard a scream and a crunch, and one of the burnt trees broke and fell over. Luckily, it didn't seem to hit anything else on the way down. However, the boy understood Sarah's hurry when he saw the tree fall over, and he immediately picked up his pace.

They were walking downhill through the undergrowth. Of course, they didn't know whether they were actually even going the right way, but it was the easiest direction to go. It was downhill and wasn't as overgrown, so they could move quicker. Sarah hoped that it would be enough to let them reach the end of the burnt area before the storm that was coming really let loose.

Unfortunately, she was wrong. The burnt forest seemed to stretch on before them while they trotted downhill, and the storm was almost upon them. In fact, the wind was already threading through the forest, pushing down some more of the burnt trees. Off to their right there was already a large area that was falling down. Sarah kept an eye on it as the trees kept crashing into each other, and pushing each other down like dominoes.

Suddenly there was a loud groan just to the left of them, and a burnt tree came crashing down right beside where they were walking. Without a word, they both began running as another couple of trees came down nearby.

The wind actually calmed down a little as the rain started pelting down. They kept running, but the soot under their feet got slippery very quickly in the rain, so they had to slow down to avoid falling over. There weren't as many trees falling anymore, but they could still hear the occasional groan of a trunk breaking and a tree falling to the ground.

By that point, the area they were walking through had steep hills sloping up and away from them on both sides. Sarah looked up to the left when she heard a cracking sound from above her. Another tree had broken and was falling. It hadn't taken any other trees with it, but because the ground was slippery and the slope was steep, it half rolled, half slid down the slope toward them. Soon, it stopped rolling and was just sliding down the slope, pointed toward them like a spear.

They were able to move out of its way fairly easily, and when it reached the bottom, it just ran into the opposite slope and stopped. So while it hadn't really been much of a threat, they knew they'd have to keep careful track of breaking sounds above them.

The trail started to go downhill more steeply, and they found it difficult to keep their footing on the wet leaves of the undergrowth and soot that blanketed the ground. However, Billy thought he could see the end of the burnt area ahead. He was sure that he glimpsed a flash of green pine needles, and so he told Sarah, and she looked in the direction he was pointing. She thought she could see something as well, and they both started walking faster.

In their excitement, they didn't notice that the slope they were on was getting even steeper and harder to walk on. Billy slipped and fell, and before he could get to his feet again, he began sliding down the hill toward the edge of the burnt forest. He thought about trying to get up again, even after he'd started sliding, but he was going the right direction, and since he was already on his bum, he didn't have to worry about slipping and falling over, so he decided to just stay down and let himself go.

Sarah tried to catch him, but then she also slipped. Unlike Billy, she struggled to get up again. She managed to get upright, but then she had to sit down to get over a ledge, and when she tried to put her feet down on the opposite side, they went out from under her. She again tried to struggle to an upright position, but she wasn't able to, and she saw that Billy wasn't even trying, she just let go, like the boy, and she started sliding down the hill as well.

Obviously, the sliding around wasn't what they'd had planned. They were both quickly covered in soot. Neither of them was very concerned about staying clean, but the greasy, wet soot was more unpleasant than regular filth. It was both gritty and slimy on their skin. Also, Sarah felt very out of control. Billy didn't seem to mind, but she didn't like the reckless pace of their slide.

Nevertheless, it seemed like they'd make it out without further incident. But then there was a loud cracking sound above them on their right. Another tree had fallen over, and it had taken three more with it when it fell. All four of them were hurtling down the slope. Sarah could see where the trees would hit the bottom, and she could also see that she was still behind that point. Since she was moving at just the right speed, she'd be beneath the trees when they hit. She wasn't sure if she could do anything about it since she was a little out of control, but she immediately started struggling to get to her feet again. She managed to slow down a little, but she still couldn't get back on her feet.

Billy kept on sliding, and even let out a happy little yelp as he neared the healthy forest. He hadn't been paying attention or looking behind him at all, and so he hadn't seen or heard the falling trees. He slid into the healthy pines and his feet hit a root. With the momentum, he hurt himself a little bit, but he was able to get to his feet. Then he turned and looked back toward Sarah.

She was still sliding, and even though she'd managed to slow down, it was clear that she was still on a collision course with the tree trunks that were coming down the slope. She had stopped trying to get up, and she was just digging her heels into the ground to try to slow herself down. However, she could see that she was still going to be in the wrong place at the wrong time when the trees came to rest. So she grabbed one of the burnt stumps beside her and held onto it. She came to an immediate stop, though Billy thought that she must have pulled her arms out of their sockets. The trees came crashing down just in front of where she was holding on to the stump. They roared and cracked and then settled down in a tangle of black trunks.

She was able to get back to her feet. She stood up but she just stayed still for a moment. She took a deep breath, and then she slowly started walking. She climbed over the tangle of tree trunks in front of her, and walked the last twenty feet or so to where Billy was waiting in the greenery.

The Grinners

It turned out that while Sarah's arms were indeed sore, they hadn't actually been pulled out of their sockets. Billy insisted on having her sit down, and then he proceeded to give her a kind of check-up. He didn't know what he was doing, but after a quick inspection, he gave her the all clear. He gently patted her on the shoulder wearing a grim smile, and then they stood and went on again.

There wasn't a trail visible where they had come out. There were a few bare patches that looked like they might be trails, but they couldn't know for sure. It was late enough in the day now to see the sun going down, so at least they knew which direction they had to walk in. They improvised their route, following the phantom trails, but generally just weaving between the trees in the direction of the sunset.

Still, it was pretty miserable. Both of them were covered in wet soot. While Billy had enjoyed the sliding, he was beginning to think it hadn't been worth it to get covered in soot. Also, though Sarah was trying to act cheerful, it was apparent that her shoulders were hurting her and it was causing her to be in a bad mood.

The sun went down and they wandered in the twilight for a while. They still hadn't found a trail, so they had to stop soon after sundown. They knew they would only get more lost if they wandered around in the dark.

They settled down with their backs to trees trunks. Because they were on a steep slope, they still had to worry about rolling down the hill, so they had to find something to prop themselves against during the night.

In the morning, they continued walking down the hill. They headed away from the sunrise, so they knew that they would, in general, be going west. With relief they found what looked like a trail and began following it. It was still hard going, since they were still heading steeply downhill, but they were following a trail, so at least they weren't quite as lost as they had imagined.

After they'd been on the trail for a few hours, they came back to the railroad tracks in a wide flat area. After some discussion, they decided to follow the tracks again. For one thing, after wandering around the forest without a trail most of the time, the railroad tracks seemed very certain and secure. Also, there were wide spaces on either side of the tracks, so they didn't have to worry about the train coming and running them down. They couldn't be sure that it would stay that way, but it did look like the area was opening up, and so they had some reason to hope that the tracks would keep running through the open for a little while.

Their hopes were justified. After a few miles, the tracks started running along beside a wide, milky looking river. It was shallow and very wide. At that point, in fact, it looked almost like a lake instead of a river. They both scrambled down from the tracks to the water and dove in. The soot clung to their clothes in spite of their best efforts to scrub it out. At best, the pitch black stains turned charcoal coloured, and generally the water made no difference at all. However, they did manage to wash away the black marks on their hands and faces. So when they got out of the water, even though their clothes still had large black stains on them, at least their skin was clean.

Far away, on the other side of the river, Billy could see a large truck speeding along the highway. He knew that the highway would be better than the railroad tracks. Sooner or later, the tracks would go through a narrow spot again. Since he hadn't really understood why they'd left the road in the first place, he started trying to convince Sarah that they should try to get across the river and back to the highway. Sarah still didn't want to go back to the road, however. She thought that they should stick with the tracks, at least while they were on the wide flat area. Besides, she couldn't see any way of getting across the river. Granted, the water was only a couple feet deep by the shore, and maybe most of the way across, but she knew that somewhere in the middle of the river there must be a deeper channel hidden.

So she convinced him to come back up to the tracks, and they kept walking along them. Eventually, the river got a little narrower and made a wide curve around a large flat area. The flats were on their side of the river, below the tracks, and there were many leafy trees. The area looked inviting, so they left the tracks and went down off the ridge that the tracks were running on. As they walked between the trees, it occurred to them both that it had been quite a while since either of them had seen any trees with leaves instead of needles. For Billy, who had spent years growing up in the pine forest, it hadn't been that big a deal, but for Sarah, seeing leafy trees again was important. She had felt uncomfortable among the conifers even though she knew they were friendly and meant her no harm. Nonetheless, she hadn't known how tense the pine trees had been making her until she saw all those leafy trees.

Also, once they had gotten down onto the flats and were walking between them, Sarah noticed that the trees were exerting a strange influence over her. Though not the kind of poplars she was used to, they were poplars. They were gray instead of white, they didn't grow as tall, and they were quite bushy all over. Nevertheless, she could tell that they were definitely poplars.

Billy didn't have any idea what they were. He'd only ever seen the tall, white poplars, and so he assumed that these must be a completely different kind of tree. They grew far apart on the flat area, and between them there was long yellow grass. It was more like a park than a forest.

He sat down with his back to a tree, feeling terribly calm. He couldn't remember feeling so calm since he'd been able to sit out on the porch with his mother. He closed his eyes and after only a few minutes he'd fallen asleep.

She sensed the familiar yet alien presence of the poplars. The initial sense of relief that Sarah had felt when she had seen the trees was gone. Since she couldn't relax, she just continued exploring the area. She had only walked for a few more minutes when she saw in front of her a large house squatting beneath the trees. It was two stories, with windows peeking from above the garage and a wide window on the front of the house beside the front door. There wasn't any road that Sarah could see, and no vehicle could have gotten close enough to the house to park, but nevertheless, the house had a large, two-vehicle garage on the front of it.

She went up to the house, and just stared at the front of it for a while before she walked around to the back. There were windows on the side of the house, and at the back there was a deck off of what looked like the kitchen. She came back around to the front, and then went up to the front door and looked inside through the big window. Inside, there was a wide expanse of hardwood floors with a leather sofa and chair, as well as a coffee table. The living room was open to the back of the house, and she could see another sitting area around a fireplace, and then the back doors onto the deck.

Sarah jumped a little as, without any warning, the front door opened and a friendly looking woman poked her head out, and said, "Come on in." Sarah stepped back from the door, and tried to pretend that she hadn't been looking inside. However, the woman didn't seem to care particularly, so Sarah's embarrassment was for nothing. "My name is Lisa," she said and gave Sarah a quick hug. Lisa was blond and quite thin. When she hugged her, Sarah could feel how delicate the other woman was.

After Lisa had closed the door, she led Sarah through the living room and back to the kitchen where a pot was bubbling on the stove. The back of the house was open and had huge, floor-to-ceiling windows along the back wall and a glass door that opened onto the porch that was at the back of the house. On the north wall was a fireplace with a sitting area around it, consisting of leather couches and an armchair gathered in a circle around the hearth. On the other side was the kitchen, with black cupboards and stainless steel appliances. In the middle of the room there was an island and a few tall stools. "Have a seat," said Lisa, and then dished some soup from the pot and gave the bowl to Sarah. Sarah sat down on one of the stools at the island and waited patiently while Lisa got her a spoon from one of the drawers in the island.

"So did they mention the problem I'm having?" asked Lisa. Sarah slurped her soup and shook her head. Obviously, Sarah didn't know what the woman was talking about, but she was enjoying the welcome she'd gotten so far and wasn't about to jeopardize it.

"No problem. I'll show you when you've finished your soup," said Lisa. Sarah had been very hungry, and had almost finished the bowl of soup already. She picked up the bowl and drank the last of the broth.

When she was finished, Lisa put her bowl in the sink, and then started walking back toward the front of the house. Sarah followed her to the front landing, and then up the staircase to the top floor.

On the landing at the top of the stairs was a tall man with light brown hair standing still in one corner with a huge grin on his face. He was wearing a light brown suit and a red tie. He wasn't moving, and after a moment, Sarah realized that he was actually leaned against the wall so that he wouldn't tip over.

"They've made it out here," said Lisa. "It's only a matter of time before they get downstairs."

Then she showed Sarah into the guest bedroom, and not only was there a short man standing in one corner, there were two women in the bed. All of them were grinning. They all seemed terribly happy about the situation.

In another bedroom there were another two grinners, and the master bedroom held three more. One was lying on the floor beside the bed, facing the wall.

"He was in my bed last night, so I had to push him out. That's why he's down there."

"All right," said Sarah. "But I'm not sure what you'd like me to do."

"I just need some help moving them. I can't do anything with them by myself, but if you could help me, then we could get them outside at least."

So Sarah went back downstairs and opened the front door. Then she came back upstairs, and the two of them struggled to pick up the tall man standing on the landing. First they tipped him over and then gently lowered him to the floor. Then Sarah took his feet, Lisa took the shoulders and, with a great deal of effort, they managed to get him downstairs and out the door. They carried him past the garage and lay him down in the grass. Then they went back upstairs and picked up the one that was lying on the floor in the master bedroom.

When they took him outside, Sarah realized why it might be very difficult to get rid of these people. The tall grinner had somehow managed to stand up and was leaning against the garage staring at the front door. He wasn't moving at all just then, in fact, he still looked like he was paralyzed, but obviously he must have had some way of moving himself toward the door of the house.

Lisa gestured at him in frustration, "You see what they do. The agency sent someone out months ago to get rid of them, but they just keep coming back."

So after they had lain the stocky one down in the grass, they went back and grabbed the tall one again. Sarah took his feet and they tipped him backward, so that they could carry him. They moved him back onto the grass, taking him further away from the front door this time.

Then they went back upstairs and grabbed another from the master bedroom. This time, when they came downstairs and out into the yard, both the tall grinner and the stocky one from the floor of the master bedroom were leaning against the garage. They were both still grinning, but Sarah thought that it looked like they were staring with longing at the front door of the house. When she saw them, Lisa made a little sound of frustration.

Sarah suddenly thought of Billy Boy under the tree. She had thought this would be quick, but it didn't look like it would be, so she decided that she'd better go and get him. She told Lisa to stay outside and watch the grinners, and then she walked back to where Billy was sleeping at the base of one of the trees.

When she got back, Billy was still asleep and the tree was starting to consume him. He had roots and limbs draped over him, and she bent down and started trying to pull the parts of the tree off of him. They weren't as quick as the white poplars, but the trees were still poplars, and if Sarah hadn't thought to return, it would have absorbed Billy completely. Even as it was, when she tried to pull the roots off of him, the tree resisted her. She put a hand on its bark and spoke softly to it, hoping that the kinds of things that the white poplars had responded to would work for these strange trees as well.

She was right, and after she spoke to the tree, it seemed to realize who she was, and it let her free Billy. Then, without waking him up, she stood up again and looked around. There was a light breeze rustling the leaves of the poplars above her, and the sun was starting to go down over the mountains. She felt comfortably warm. She had stopped noticing, but she had been feeling anxious all day, so when she started feeling relaxed and calm, she noticed the sense of relief in her shoulders.

Sarah had the beginnings of an idea. Now that she had an understanding with the trees, she knew that the poplar wouldn't do anything to Billy. She left him lying where he was and headed back to the house, knowing that the trees wouldn't try anything. When she got there, Lisa opened the front door for her. Lisa was a bit surprised to see Sarah without the boy, but Sarah told her that Billy was still sleeping and looked so peaceful that she couldn't bear to wake him up. She said she was going to leave Billy to sleep for another couple of hours before she went to get him. Lisa thought this was odd, but she took it in stride.

The grinners were still in the same places where they had left them, so the two women went back inside to get another one. Sarah convinced Lisa to carry their load out to the nearest poplar tree instead of just dumping it in front of the house. The tree was more than a hundred feet away, and so it was a bit of a trek carrying the grinner to it, but between them, they made it. When they got him there, they struggled with him until they could lean him up against the tree.

Then they returned to the garage and picked up the tall fellow.

They brought him out to the same tree, and leaned him against the trunk beside the other grinner. Finally, they returned to the garage again and picked up the stocky fellow. They brought him out to the tree as well and leaned him against the trunk in the last open space that was available, so that the grinners made a kind of triangle around the trunk. Once this was done, the two women returned to the house and went back inside.

The next time they came down with another grinner, there wasn't anyone leaning against the garage waiting for them. The three grinners they'd stacked against the poplar were still under the poplar. They took the next one to another tree. That tree fit three more, and then they had to use another tree for the last of them. By the time they were done they could see that the first grinners had roots growing over their legs.

That's what Sarah had thought would happen. Even though the grey trees weren't as overtly aggressive as the white poplars, they were still poplars, and after seeing Billy, she had been betting that they would act like it. The grinners had tried to get back to the house when no one was looking, but the poplars had stopped them, holding them tight.

Lisa made a show of wiping her hands and then her brow, and said, "Thanks."

"No problem at all," replied Sarah.

"Where are you staying?" asked Lisa. "You're welcome to stay here if you'd like."

Sarah agreed that she would go and get Billy Boy and that they would stay with Lisa for the night. Lisa invited her inside for a drink before she went to get Billy. She asked Sarah what she felt like drinking. Sarah thought for a minute and then said that, if it was possible, she'd like a gin and tonic. Luckily, Lisa loved gin and tonics, and so she had the fixings on hand and was able to make one for each of them.

Sarah had quite a tolerance, so even though they drank the same amount, Lisa was getting drunk, while Sarah was just getting warmed up. Also, Sarah was being careful and pacing herself, so the drinks would never make her feel more than a little bit warm. For every drink that Sarah actually finished, Lisa had at least two, and after a few hours of chatting and drinking, Lisa was quite drunk. She had been sitting on one of the tall stools, but she fell off, and couldn't figure out how to get back on again. She just stayed seated on the floor instead.

While they had been moving the grinners, Sarah had sensed that the poplars were resentful and angry. She thought it might have something to do with her and Billy, but the more she concentrated on the trees, it seemed clear that they didn't particularly care about the two travellers. They only seemed to really care about Lisa. Sarah got the feeling that they didn't like her at all and that they would be happy to see Lisa disappear completely. It had given Sarah another idea.

"Let's go out for a walk," Sarah suggested. "You'll feel better if you walk it off for a while."

Lisa protested, but Sarah picked her up and draped her over one of her shoulders. Then she helped Lisa toward the glass doors to the porch, and slid them open. Once they were out on the deck, Lisa began to get her feet under her again, and while she still clung tightly to Sarah, she managed to walk down the stairs into the backyard.

It was dark out by that time. The wind was blowing at a fair clip and the leaves were roaring above her. She could hear waves being created by the wind on the river. Lisa looked up and saw the stars between huge black blobs created by the poplar leaves. By the light of the enormous moon, she could see that the sky was clear except for one little cloud blowing quickly across it.

It felt like they had been walking forever. Lisa told Sarah that she was tired and wanted to lie down, so Sarah brought her over to one of the trees and laid her down at the foot of it. She sat down beside Lisa while the other woman quickly fell asleep. Lisa was leaning against her, and had started snoring. When she was sure Lisa was completely passed out and wouldn't wake up again, Sarah stood up carefully and lowered Lisa so that she lay on the ground at the foot of the tree. She fished in the other woman's pockets until she found the keys to the house, then she went back to the tree where Billy Boy was still asleep.

Sarah scooped the boy up in her arms and started carrying him back to the house. He woke up while she was carrying him, and asked her what she was doing. "Taking you to my house," she said. And while he was confused, he just thought he'd heard wrong, and he fell back to sleep right away.

When they got back to the house, Sarah took him in, up the stairs to one of the guest rooms, and laid him down on top of the covers. Then she went to the master bedroom and found a clean nightgown that she could change into. With a sigh of relief and a vague feeling of apprehension, she slipped between the clean sheets of the queen sized bed and quickly fell asleep.

In the morning, she woke up before Billy but she didn't feel like moving, so she just stayed in bed. When Billy poked his head into the master bedroom she sensed it. She turned her head toward him and opened her eyes.

"This is a really nice place," he said. "Who lives here?"

She got out of bed, and grabbed a robe from the back of the door. "We do," she said, smiling. "Go downstairs and we'll get some breakfast."

He did as he was told, and soon she joined him after looking in the mirror in the on-suite bathroom, and giving her face a quick wash. She was still quite grimy from the burnt forest, and she knew that they would need a better wash later. The worst of the soot had come off when they had taken their dip in the river, but there was still a lot of grime to get rid of. And she knew that Billy would be in even worse shape than she was. She also knew that, even though they had tried to clean them in the river, their clothes could use a wash. They still wouldn't be able to get the soot out, but it would be nice to get them as clean as they could, anyway.

She prepared breakfast for Billy, and as they sat eating, he asked her how she had gotten the house.

"There was nobody here, so I just thought we would take it," she said. She was a little nervous saying it, but she was good at hiding her anxiety, and so he believed her.

After breakfast, they looked around for the laundry machines. They were in a small room near the garage and when they found them, they cleaned Billy's clothes. She didn't bother with her clothes. They looked to be ruined, and Lisa had had a large wardrobe, so there were plenty of other things for Sarah to wear. Sarah wasn't all that interested in the dresses and things like that, but Lisa had also owned at least a few items that were more practical, like jeans and sweaters that Sarah could wear. Some of the jeans were way too tight, but there were also four pairs of bigger ones that she could wear. Most of the sweaters were big and loose enough that it wasn't any problem.

However, there weren't any boy's clothes around the house, and so Billy still had only the one set that he'd been wearing all the way from Cadomin. He wrapped himself in one of Lisa's bathrobes while he did laundry. Even when they were done, his clothes were still pretty badly blackened from the soot. The stains had faded a little, but they still looked like black dye. But even though the stains from the soot would never come out, at least after a wash they were dry and cleaner than they'd been.

While Billy was doing his laundry, Sarah went outside to check on Lisa and the grinners. The grinners seemed to have disappeared without a trace. She couldn't find any sign of them around the trees where she'd placed them. She smiled and went to the back of the house to see about Lisa.

Most of Lisa's body had sunk into the soil at the foot of the tree, but her legs were still stretched out in the grass. Sarah wondered if she'd put up any struggle when the poplar pulled her under, or if she'd been out of it enough to just accept her fate willingly. Sarah wondered for a moment if she should cover up the legs, but then she decided that if she did, it would only draw more attention to them, and Billy Boy's natural curiosity would make it more likely that he would find them. So she left them where they were, hoping that Billy wouldn't notice them before the tree pulled them under the soil.

When she returned to the house, Billy was in the sitting area beside the kitchen, relaxing on one of the sofas facing the fireplace. Sarah had thought he might have more questions, but it was clear that he was enjoying the place, and he wasn't one to ask too many questions about things that he liked.

Another week went by. Sarah checked daily on Lisa, and after a few days, she was barely visible and her legs had been pulled almost completely under. Only her feet were still sticking out, and the tall grass hid them so that you'd have to be standing right beside the tree to even notice them.

Soon the day came when Billy Boy was ready to set off again. Sarah sat him down in one of the big couches to talk to him. However, she wasn't actually able to say anything, and all she could do was give him a concerned look. After a minute of this, he let out an impatient sigh, and she forced herself to start talking.

"I've decided that I like it here," she said. "I'm not sure that I want to go any further. Actually, I am sure. I don't want to go. I know you still need to find your mother, and I'm sorry to leave you. But I haven't liked this travelling, and I'm comfortable here."

Billy Boy looked shocked. Sarah's decision had really come out of nowhere for him. He hadn't been expecting it at all. He'd kind of figured that maybe Sarah wasn't really happy to be travelling, but then again, neither was he. Nevertheless, he wasn't ready to stop, so he hadn't imagined that she was either.

"This is as far as I've ever gone in my life," she said. "I never imagined trying to go anywhere, and I only came, because you didn't have anyone to go with you. I couldn't stand the idea of you struggling through the forest by yourself. But it seems clear that you don't struggle as much as I do."

"I don't like travelling either," he said.

"But I really hate it. I know that it's hard to understand, but I'm nervous all the time."

"There's always bad stuff happening. Of course you're nervous."

"It's not that. I'm nervous even when everything is fine. This is the first place we've come to where I feel at home. I'd like to go back across the mountains to my forest again, but I don't even know if I could find my way back. And at least here I would be close to you."

"Well, I'm not going either," he said.

"Okay," she said. "I would love to have you stay. But I think that at some point, you'll probably want to keep going. I would be happy if you really wanted to stay here, but I don't think you do."

They were both quiet for a few minutes. Billy sat and scowled at the fireplace, and Sarah looked down at her hands. She thought for a minute about going on, but she knew that she had already said what she needed to say. She didn't know if any more talking would help, so in spite of the temptation to continue, she kept her mouth shut. She looked over at him and she couldn't help but remember how he'd wailed when he'd discovered that his mother had left, but she also forced herself to remember that he'd be just fine on his own. She had wondered if she'd be any use on the road, and she knew that she hadn't done much that he wouldn't be able to do for himself.

After a few minutes of silence, he spoke. "You don't know," he said. "I'll stay. I like sleeping in a bed."

She was quiet for a moment, and then she replied in a quiet voice. "When you get tired, you'll come back. But right now, you aren't tired, so yeah, I do actually know that you won't really stay."

After that, they sat in silence again for a while, and then Sarah stood up and went into the kitchen. Billy stayed sitting on the couch, scowling. She folded some tea cloths and moved some glasses from one cupboard to another, but the whole time she was looking over at him and wondering what he was thinking. Despite her busy work, she wasn't actually getting anything done, so she decided that instead of puttering uselessly around the kitchen, she would just go upstairs. She took one more look at him, but he was still looking angry and he didn't look back at her, so she decided to leave.

He stayed on the couch for a few more hours, until the sun was well up in the sky and heading down towards the mountains at the back of the house. Since Sarah had gone upstairs, both of them had been absolutely silent. She'd gone to the bedroom to lie down, and she was still there, on top of the covers, staring at the ceiling, and wondering what she should do next.

Down below, she heard the patio door open and close. In a rush, she got up and went downstairs, but Billy Boy was already gone from the couch. Looking out the back window, she could see his back as he walked away. She wanted to follow him and catch him. After all, this wasn't how she had planned for this parting to happen. But then she decided that there was no point in forcing him to come back and do it the "right" way. She was just happy that he'd been able to do it so soon. She had worried that he would stick around and be miserable about it for a while. So she wasn't exactly happy that he'd left, but she definitely felt relieved. Instead of following him, she sat down in one of the big couches and continued to watch his back as he walked away. Even though she was feeling very sad, she was still happy to be at rest in the house.

Sam

As he walked, Billy wasn't happy at all. He had thought that he'd get his revenge for the way Sarah had treated him by the way he left. But when she didn't follow him, it made him even angrier, and so he just kept walking. He didn't want her thinking that he was desperate, and so even though he felt like going back to the house, he couldn't because he was sure that she would gloat over his return.

Eventually, he had walked far enough to get away from the flat area and then he returned to the railroad tracks. The sun was beginning to go down, and it was shining on the highway running on the other side of the river. That was one advantage of not travelling with Sarah anymore. He wouldn't have to be afraid of the highway. He resolved that when the river became narrow enough he would cross it and get back to the road, instead of following the tracks or forest trails.

In the meantime, the tracks were still passing through a wide area, so there was no need for him to worry about it immediately. He continued walking for a few more hours, but when the light was getting dim, he decided that it was time to stop.

That first night alone made him a little bit nervous. He wasn't able to sleep much, and he was quite cold. He hadn't been able to get much sleep, but he still felt good in the morning when he woke up. He figured that if that was as bad as a night without Sarah would get, then he really was going to be fine without her.

He kept following the tracks, which continued to get closer and closer to the river on the left side, until the water was flowing past the bottom of the ridge that the tracks were on. The river had narrowed from the mile wide basin that it had been flowing through. It was narrower, but it was still more than a hundred yards across and he knew it still wouldn't be easy to get across.

Billy saw a tree trunk washed up at the bottom of the ridge. Even though the river kept getting narrower, he would still need something to help him get across it. He had been watching for it, but he hadn't seen much driftwood go by. What little he had seen were just little sticks and nothing big enough for him to float on. So, while the tree trunk didn't look great, he didn't think that he would be able to find a better piece of wood anywhere further along. He went down to where the tree trunk was resting against the bank of the river.

Despite how it looked, it was a decent piece of wood. It was just covered in mud that made it look rough. It had broken off a few feet above the roots, and so it was a clean log and he wouldn't have to worry about the tangle of roots at the bottom. Also, it hadn't been in the water for very long, so the wood wasn't bleached or waterlogged yet and Billy knew that it would float.

He draped himself over the log, putting it in front of him and clinging to it with both his arms. He gripped it in a way that if it tried to roll out from under him, it wouldn't be able to. He stepped away from the bank, and almost immediately the river got deep. He'd thought that he'd be able to go a little ways out before it dropped off, but he was only a few feet away from the shore when it became too deep for him to touch the bottom. He started paddling with his feet.

After paddling for a little while, the current caught him, and started taking him down the river rapidly. He was still able to slowly go through the water under his own power, but the current was pulling him back toward the flats a great deal faster than he was able to move across the river. The banks were already starting to slip past him, and he had only gone twenty feet from the shore. Though he didn't feel particularly nervous about it, he still clutched the log tighter. The log was slippery and kept trying to get away from him, but he held on tight, and trusted it to keep him above the water.

He still kept trying to paddle forward, but in spite of his best efforts, he was being pulled downstream toward the flats. Eventually, he just gave up and let himself get pulled along. He kept slipping under the log, and he thought he might drown, but he wrestled with it, and eventually he managed to get it in a secure grip. He had adjusted his hold on the log in a way that was more comfortable, but that had let it move around a little under him. He returned to his original grip, and he was sort of giving the log a bear hug.

When the flats came in sight again, he resumed paddling, this time toward them. As he was passing, he saw the poplars and Sarah's house. However, he didn't care much about his pride at that moment. He was out in the middle of the river and the current was carrying him past the flats at a rapid pace. So, even though it would mean a humiliating reunion, he tried to get back to the house. But as much as he struggled, the river made the decision for him, and he didn't seem to be able to get any closer to the shore by the flats. In fact, the river was pulling him in the opposite direction.

The flats caused a huge curve in the river. It bent around the poplars and Sarah's house and then came back to the railroad tracks. The outside of the bend was against the highway, which was where Billy Boy had been trying to get to. The current still held him, but when the river curved, he got pushed to the edge of the fast flowing water. Paddling with all his might, Billy managed to break free of the current as the river went around the bend.

The river was still wide, so there was still quite a distance to swim to get to the highway. However, once he was out of the current, it quickly became quite shallow and it wasn't long before Billy was able to actually put his feet down again and start walking toward the shore. He walked for quite a while, remembering to drop the log into the water when he got to knee depth. The walk to the water's edge was long enough that it felt like he wasn't getting any closer. However, all of a sudden the shore was right in front of him.

Billy waded out of the water and scrambled up a low ridge to the highway. Like the railroad tracks, the road was built on a ridge of dirt. However, the ridge that the highway was built on was lower than the bed that the tracks were on. When he got to the top, there was a bundle of blood and fur sitting on the shoulder, and Billy was immediately reminded of what they'd disliked about the highway in the first place. He just wanted to rest, but he forced himself to get away from the roadkill. Then, when he'd gotten far enough away, he collapsed onto the grass beside the road.

He was feeling a little relieved to be alive. He hadn't let himself think about it very much when he had actually been in the water, but he'd known that he had been in real danger. As it was, he was alive and safely on solid ground, but he had still gone a long way back from where he had been at Sarah's house. At least he had made it to the highway, and so one part of the plan had worked, even if not in the way that he had thought it would.

After he rested for a while, he got up and started walking along the highway. There were even more dead animals on the highway than there had been before. There was a crow pecking at one of the bloody heaps as Billy walked by. After he had passed, there was a sound behind him, and it took him a moment to figure out that it had come from the crow.

Billy looked back, and the crow was cocking its head so that it could look straight at Billy with its right eye. "I think I know you," it said, and hopped toward him.

Billy shook his head, but the crow insisted. "I knew a fellow who looked like you. I guess it wasn't you, but he sure looked like you," it said. At that, Billy Boy's interest was piqued, so he asked the crow to go on.

"It was my uncle, actually, that knew him," said the crow. "He introduced us. I only met him a few times. My uncle had made some sort of deal with him."

"My father?" said Billy.

"I don't know, but he sure looked like you. Anyway, my uncle spied a little for him. Some of the bears were after this guy, and my uncle helped him stay away from them."

"Is he still alive?"

"My uncle?" asked the crow.

"No. My father," said Billy.

"I'm not sure. I know my uncle died a few years back. It was a heart thing. We all kind of figured it was coming. Still a shock though."

"But you don't know about my father."

"Nope. Like I say, it was really my uncle that knew him, I only met him a couple of times."

Billy glanced across the river and saw Sarah's house sitting on the flats, between the trees. Between her abandonment, his adventure in the river and hearing news of his father, the boy was feeling a little overwhelmed. Sight of the house had been making him angry, but that time it made Billy feel very lonely, instead. He had gotten used to having Sarah with him. He and his mother hadn't travelled. In fact, other than his exploring around Cadomin, the only real travelling he'd ever done alone was the walk to Father John's house. For company, even Father John had been better than nothing.

In his loneliness, Billy wanted to tell the crow the whole thing, about the bike and his mother and everything else. He had almost forgotten that this had all started because of the bike, but now it came back to him. It seemed really silly. If he could do it again, he would never have left home for a bike. There'd be no way.

Billy did tell the crow that he was looking for his mother, on the chance that he might have seen her. By this point the crow was standing at Billy's feet. He rubbed a wing over his eye a couple of times, and then turned back to Billy and said, "I might have seen her."

Billy couldn't believe his luck. "Really?"

"I think so. She was further along the highway. About a month ago, I think. I wondered what she was doing out here. It's usually just cars and corpses on the road."

"Did you talk to her?"

"I didn't. I figured we both had our own business, and if she minded hers, I'd mind mine."

"Do you know where she was going?"

"Not exactly, but the road only goes one way. It keeps going west, through the mountains, so I assume that that's also where she was heading."

While he was happy to hear about his mother, Billy was disappointed to find out how far ahead she was. If she'd been further along the road a month earlier, then, by that point, she must have been really far ahead of him.

"You want to catch up to her, I imagine," said the crow, and then hopped a couple of times in place. "I know a shortcut. There's a trail through the woods that cuts off a big curve in the road. It's a bit hard to follow, but you should be able to cut her lead by going that way."

Billy thought about it, and while he wasn't thrilled about leaving the highway again, he also knew that he'd never catch up with his mother unless he found a way to make up some time and distance on her. So eventually he asked the crow if it would show Billy the shortcut.

"It's about a half mile up the road, and then the trail starts on the other side of the highway. I'll show you where it is. You'll never find it on your own."

So with that, they started walking down the highway. At first the crow just hopped along beside him, but soon the bird took flight and glided over Billy's head. Sometimes it came low and hovered beside Billy, and other times it soared high above him.

The highway wasn't very busy, but there were still occasional vehicles zooming past. There weren't many big trucks, but there were still a few. Billy still jumped a little when one went by, and so it was good that it didn't happen very often.

When they arrived at the trailhead, the crow landed and told the boy. Billy looked around at the forest on the other side of the highway, and decided that the crow had been right, and that he'd never have been able to find it on his own. The trailhead looked like the rest of the forest, but he took the crow's word for it that it was there. He looked both ways to see if there were any cars coming, and when he was sure that there weren't, he ran across the highway to the other side.

On the other side, he could see where the trail started. It just looked like a slightly thinner spot in the trees. There was a wide ditch beside the highway, with a little bit of a puddle in it, and on the other side the forest started. The forest on that side was very thick, and the only thing to mark it was where it thinned out for the trailhead.

"Now I'll warn you," said the crow, "this trail has some steep parts and parts where it's hard to follow. Be careful."

Billy thanked the crow, and then started walking on the trail. It was like he'd plunged headfirst into the forest. The trees grew really close together, and while he knew that they didn't mean any harm, the pines still scratched him as he walked past. The visibility was terrible as well. He was only twenty feet in, but when he looked back, he couldn't see the road anymore. It was disheartening, but he forced himself to turn back to the trail and continue going forward.

The crow hadn't lied about the steepness. Almost immediately the trail started going uphill. Also, as the trail went up it didn't seem like a trail anymore. At first, it seemed to disintegrate as all sorts of little paths branched out from it, and soon after that, it disappeared completely, and the boy felt like he was just forcing his way through brush. After a while, Billy had a hard time even finding a clear spot between the trees that would allow him to continue. He found himself clutching a pine bough, looking up into deep forest, and backward into equally deep forest.

He was angry. "This isn't even a trail!" he shouted to no one in particular. He struggled upward for a few more feet, but was forced to stop again when another tree blocked his path.

From above him the crow spoke to him again. "No, it's not a trail." Billy looked up and saw the crow sitting on a bough ten feet above him.

"You left the trail back there," said the crow. "You've been trying to break a new trail for a couple of hundred feet. No wonder you're angry." He sounded vaguely irritated, but also smug.

Billy just scowled at the crow, and then turned around and started heading back down the hill. It wasn't easy, but he'd already come that way, so he knew that he would be able to get back down again. The crow stayed with him this time. When the boy thought he had found the spot where he'd left the trail, he started going back uphill again, but the crow stopped him.

"Not that way. You've got about another twenty feet to go back down the hill. I'll fly there and then you can just follow me."

The crow took off for a moment, and then landed on another tree further down the hill. Billy sighed, shrugged his shoulders and then followed the crow. When he got to the tree that the bird was sitting on, it was obvious where the trail was. He couldn't figure out why he'd ever gone in the other direction in the first place. He started walking up the proper trail. It still looked pretty rough, but he was hopeful that it would be easier than trying to crash through the bush.

As he struggled up the trail, the crow was still hanging around, flitting easily from tree to tree and providing useless directions every few minutes. He would say things like, "Watch out for that root," when Billy had already stepped over it, or, "it gets steep here," when Billy could just look up and see for himself that the trail was getting steep.

Finally, the boy arrived at a little clear space at the top of the ridge. He looked back down to his right, and saw the highway winding along below him. He was a little shocked and disappointed by how close the highway looked and realized that in spite of his all his efforts, he hadn't actually gone very far.

He sat down, and the crow came and landed beside him on a rock that was sticking out of the ground. It had continued to follow Billy ever since the boy had first gotten lost. It could tell that Billy was upset. The bird didn't usually concern itself much with other people's problems, but decided that perhaps it would be worth it to concern itself with Billy. Also, the crow felt a little bad about the way the shortcut had turned out. So even though it wasn't sure whether it should or not, it took a deep breath and introduced itself.

"My name is Sam," said the crow softly, trying to sound gentle. "I'll come with you if you want. Just to make sure you don't go off track and get lost again." He was trying to be kind, but Billy thought he heard a note of triumph in the crow's voice.

Billy wasn't sure that he wanted the crow to come. All the comments and the little passive aggressive ways of being right about things had made the boy quite tired. That was in addition to the exhaustion from climbing. He also didn't like feeling that he couldn't manage for himself, and so anyone who had offered to help would have caused offense. He especially didn't want to have to accept help from the crow. However, he knew that Sam was probably right, and that it would be much easier to follow the trail if the bird came with him.

However, Billy didn't want to actually tell Sam that, so he just shrugged his shoulders. The crow took this as an invitation, and immediately started chatting happily about the trees and the weather and anything else that came to mind.

The trail went along the top of the ridge for a while, and then started down the other side. Along the top, the trail was in good shape, but it started disappearing again as soon as Billy started walking down the slope. Even though Sam wouldn't stop talking, Billy was glad the crow was there, since he kept the boy on track more than once.

Billy decided that, if the crow hadn't spoken to his mother, he must have a shy streak that wasn't apparent. Sam didn't seem capable of being quiet, and it otherwise seemed very out of character that he didn't approach her. It seemed like the crow would have found someone to talk to whenever he was able to.

The trail continued being very difficult. It seemed to always go up and over the mountains and never around them, and so it was always either climbing steeply, or going steeply back down. As a result, Billy never felt like he was making much progress, since he felt like he had to walk twice as far as he should have had to.

Billy was beginning to wonder if Sam had lied to him and whether this could even count as a shortcut, since it went up and down hill so much. It didn't take him long to decide that the crow hadn't meant to mislead him. If Sam had deliberately lied, he wouldn't have been able to keep it a secret for very long. It would have spilled the beans before they even got to the trailhead, and so Billy knew that it must have been accidental.

The boy decided that Sam had gotten the idea that the trail was short by flying high over it, or by flitting from branch to branch. The crow knew that the trail was rough and steep, but he didn't really understand what rough or steep were like when you actually had to walk through them. Sam knew that he didn't have to fly as far as he had to go when he was just following the highway, so he had assumed that the trail must be a shortcut.

Billy had this impression confirmed when they met a friend of Sam's as they were walking. The crow's friend was a cougar that seemed a little irritated and definitely surly. The cougar definitely wasn't happy to see Sam, and it didn't even seem interested in trying to hide it.

The crow explained that Billy was taking a short-cut to the highway.

"And you brought him this way?" On hearing it, Billy realized that he had expected the cougar to have a low voice. It was much higher than he had been expecting. The cat looked like a natural bass. It was still a very smooth voice, however, and the cougar sounded like it would have been a good singer if it had wanted.

"This trail gets to the highway, doesn't it?" asked Sam. It was the first time Billy had heard any note of doubt in the crow's voice.

"It does. Eventually," said the cougar. "There's miles of hard going before you get there, though."

"Worse than back the other way?" asked Billy.

"I suppose not," said the cat. "Now that you've made it this far, you might as well keep going. You're closer to the end than you are to the beginning anyway."

It was obvious that Billy had worked harder than he had had to. He looked over at Sam angrily. The crow didn't say anything, but he hung his head a little, and wouldn't look up at the boy.

"Anyway, I have to get going," said the cougar.

"Oh, okay," said Sam. "I'll see you later."

"Not if I see you first."

And with that, the cougar leapt from the stump it'd been sitting on. It scrambled quickly through the bush and into the forest above them, soon disappearing from view. It was already getting dark, and Billy was about ready to stop for the night, but Sam insisted that they go on.

"Peter's a nice guy, but I wouldn't put it past him to try to eat you. It's what he does, so you can hardly blame him for it. Of course, if you were already dead, he'd definitely leave you alone. He doesn't like dead stuff at all. Anyway, he knows you're here now, and if he can't find anything else to kill tonight, he might be back for you. So it'll be best if we're not here."

So they kept walking even after the sun had gone down and the stars had come out. Eventually they stopped, but only because Billy insisted that he was too tired to keep going. And even then, the crow said he was going to act as lookout to make sure the cougar didn't come back for the boy.

In the morning, Sam told Billy to just stay put, and then the crow flew high above the forest so he could look down on it and get a clear view. It was a few more hard miles back to the highway, but they actually weren't far, so Sam felt vindicated. He came back down and told the boy, who still wasn't happy about the hike in front of him, but also felt glad that they were close to the road.

The trail was really hard, and Billy figured that the crow had been seeing the trail with his wings again, because it took Billy quite a while to get back to the highway. Like before, instead of going around, which would have made the whole thing a lot easier, the trail went up a mountain and then back down it.

Finally, he made it down. Waiting for him on the highway, there was the flattened corpse of a mountain goat. He moved away from the goat, and then he motioned for Sam to come down to him so that they could talk. Or rather, so Billy could talk. He knew he'd have to talk over the crow to get Sam to listen, so he turned off his politeness and prepared himself to interrupt whenever he needed to.

Sam came down and stood beside him on the road. As Billy had expected, the crow immediately began talking. "Looks like it's getting cloudy up ahead, so you might want to hunker down and wait it out. Of course, it doesn't look so bad. I mean, maybe it could be fine. Then hunkering down would be dumb. You could probably walk a little bit more."

"So where did you see you my mother?" asked Billy.

"It was close to here, I think." Sam looked around to get his bearings. He turned his head from left to right and hopped around in a circle, so that he'd be able to see where he was. "She was back that way," he said, pointing with his beak back along the highway.

"But that was a month ago, right?" asked Billy.

"Yes." Sam heard the urgency of Billy's questions, so he forced himself to keep his answer succinct even though it went against his instincts.

"I need you to do me a favour," said Billy. "I need you to go on ahead and see if you can find my mother."

"Hold on, hold on..." said Sam, backing away from Billy.

"I need you to do this. You're the only one who's seen her."

"I was just going to show you to the trail," said Sam. "Then I showed you the way back to the highway, 'cause I worried you might get lost. But I didn't know I'd be helping you after you got back to the road."

"I know, but I need you to do this," said Billy.

Sam thought about it for minute. He was quiet, and he turned away from Billy so that he could look thoughtfully out over the river flowing beside the highway.

"I really didn't sign up for this," said Sam quietly after a few moments. "I don't think I can."

After hesitating for a moment, Billy said, "I'll give you something in return."

The crow turned back to Billy at that. "What are you going to give me? Look at you. You don't have anything."

"I was trying to find my bike before. When I find it, you can have it."

"What would I do with a bike?" Sam asked. Billy knew it was a fair question, and he didn't have an answer. The crow obviously couldn't ride it or even move it. He could perch on it for a while, but soon he'd have to leave it behind. However, Sam thought about it for a minute, and then cocked his head to one side and asked hopefully if the bike had a bell on it.

Billy thought for a second about whether he wanted to tell the crow about the bell. He was sad that it had even come up, because he quite liked the bell, even though he almost never used it when he was riding around the forest. Other than trees there wasn't anything to get out of the way, and the trees had never listened to the bell anyways. Nevertheless, Billy had been hoping that Sam would feel bad and help him for free, and Billy wouldn't have to give up anything at all.

However, he decided that he needed help more than he needed the bell, so he told Sam that the bike did, in fact, have a bell. Giving up the bell that he hardly used was much better than giving up the whole bike. If he could find the bike that is, and there didn't seem much hope of that happening, so Sam would probably get nothing. Billy thought, out of a sense of fairness, about mentioning this to the crow. However, he decided that finding his mother was the most important thing, not finding the bike and certainly not making sure Sam got his reward.

So after they had agreed that Sam would get the bell, the crow flew off to scout ahead for Billy's mother. Billy kept walking while there was still light. As Sam had said, there actually were a few clouds ahead, but nothing too threatening, and the boy wasn't worried about it.

Just after sunset, Billy sat down on the grass at the side of the road. Sam wouldn't be back for a week or so. That was the arrangement they'd made. The crow would fly ahead and see what he could find, and if he came across Billy's mother, then he'd stop her and talk to her, so that she'd know Billy was behind her. Every week Sam would come back to give Billy a report.

However, it was only a few days later that Billy saw Sam flying toward him. At first he felt excited, thinking that maybe Sam had already found his mother. But then he realized that she couldn't possibly be that close, so he knew that the crow's return could only mean that something was wrong.

Pilgrimage

Sam landed in front of Billy, and told him that his mother had left the highway up ahead and was travelling on another trail through the mountains. Sam had met another crow who had seen Billy's mother and had seen her wandering off into the woods.

"Do you know which trail she's on?" Billy asked.

"I do," said Sam. "I'll go on ahead and mark it so that you know where it is when you get there. I'll go to the trailhead now. I'll rest there tonight, and then, tomorrow, I'll head up the trail to see if I can find her."

"How far is it?" asked Billy.

"You'll get there tomorrow, probably."

"Just make sure I can see where the trail starts. I don't want to walk right past it."

"Don't worry. I'll make sure it's obvious," and with that, Sam flew away.

It was near sunset the next day that Billy came to what was clearly the head of the trail. He had been keeping an eye out all day, and a couple of times he'd thought he'd found the trailhead, but after a little investigation he had decided that they weren't the trails he was looking for. He hoped that Sam had made it clear where the trail really was.

As it turned out, when Billy finally got there, the beginning of the trail had been marked very obviously. Sam had lifted the corpses of a couple of squirrels from the highway and draped them over the boughs of some pines at the head of the trail. Billy thought that although it was pretty gruesome, it did make an effective marker.

The boy went between the two hanging squirrel corpses, careful not to actually touch either one. Once he was actually on the trail, it was much wider and more obvious than the other trail had been, and he didn't have any trouble following along, even when it got steep. The trees were growing further apart, so the existence of the trail was even more obvious than it had been initially.

He did wonder how Sam would go about finding him again underneath the trees. The trees were widely spaced, but they still formed a canopy above him, and he wasn't sure that the crow would be able to see through it. However, Sam seemed like he had pretty good eyesight, and since the forest was thin where Billy was walking, and he hoped that he was worrying for no reason. Besides, he didn't have much choice, regardless of whether Sam could find him again or not. If his mother had gone this way, he had to follow. So he hoped for the best and just kept going.

Evening came on with no sight of the crow or anyone else for that matter. He was still on a steep part of the trail, so he settled down for the night by nestling against a tree for protection and stability.

In the morning, Billy woke to find himself surrounded by a flow of people, all of whom seemed to be heading west, up over the mountain. Most of the people seemed to be in family groups of some sort, a mother, father and some children. The younger parents had

young children or infants that they were carrying, while the older parents
had children Billy's age and a few teenagers. The men all had white shirts
and suspenders, and the women all wore cotton dresses. The dresses
were long and hadn't been made for hiking, and so there was a fair
amount of dirt at the hems. The children were dressed in miniature
versions of the same outfits that their parents were wearing.

All of them were heading up the mountain in total silence. Well,
it wasn't total, since their feet made crunching sounds as they passed,
but none of them spoke as they walked. Billy stood and looked around,
unsure of what to do. They seemed to be going the same way as him, so
after a minute of hesitation, he started walking with them, trying to
blend in. It wasn't any problem to keep quiet, since there was no one to
talk to, but he knew he stood out because he wasn't wearing the
uniform, and he was by himself. No one said anything, though, so he
just kept going.

Walking not far from him was a younger couple with an infant.
He walked along for a while before he decided to approach the couple,
but then he sidled up to them, and they greeted him with pleasant
smiles. He asked what was going on.

"We're on a pilgrimage," said the mother. "On the other side of
this mountain is a holy place where our prophet first got his message
from God."

"We go there every year," added the father.

"Is there a church or a temple or something?" asked Billy.

"No. There's just a clearing that we always go to," said the
father, "but we don't know for sure that that was even the spot. We just

know that it's on the other side of that mountain somewhere. But we always go to the same clearing. Even though we don't know for sure if it's right, it's still better than planting ourselves in the brush somewhere."

Billy told them he was going the same way, looking for his mother, and the young couple invited the boy to travel with them. Roy and Jessica were their names, and their baby was Henry. The baby was only a few months old. The couple hadn't been planning on coming on this pilgrimage at all, since they had thought that Jessica was going to be very pregnant. But Jessica had decided that she wanted to go no matter what. So they steeled themselves for a hard hike, and then Henry had arrived early. After that, there was no problem at all in coming. Billy got the impression that if they'd had to wait another year to come, it would have been really hard on them. On Jessica anyway.

Roy seemed like the casual one. He seemed cheerful enough, but he definitely wasn't as driven as Jessica. She told Billy about all the good things she was doing for little Henry to make sure his brain grew properly, but also to make sure that God knew him and kept track of him. Jessica's hope was that little Henry would grow up and be able to use his huge brain in a Godly way.

They were going to reach the clearing on the next day. They figured they'd have to camp near the top of the mountain that night, and then go up and over the ridge the next morning.

Roy and Jessica were really nice to Billy. They expressed an interest in helping him find his mother and his bike. They nodded empathetically as Billy tried to explain why he had really liked the bike, and gone off looking for it. They also expressed dismay and anger that anyone could have been cold and heartless enough to steal it in the first place.

Billy didn't tell them about Father John and Sarah. He wasn't sure why he held it back, but, even without knowing why, he felt that they wouldn't really understand what had happened at the cabin. They'd try to understand, and even when they couldn't, they would probably try to look like they got it anyway. But the boy didn't feel like watching them try to fake understanding, so he just kept it to himself instead. He told them that he wasn't able to find the bike, so he had just returned home. By the time he had gotten back, his mother had left.

He immediately regretted even telling them that much. Jessica looked very angry and said she would never have left if she thought there was a chance that her son might return. He tried to explain that his mother hadn't thought he was coming back, and she softened a little bit, However, when Billy admitted that he'd basically given up on the bike, and was actually mostly looking for his mother, Jessica looked irritated again. She didn't say anything, but she frowned and shook her head.

They kept walking up the mountain all that day. Most of the time, no one ever said anything, but there didn't seem to be a hard and fast rule about it. Every once in a while, a kid in one of the other families would say something, and they were never shushed. There just wasn't much to say, he guessed. Roy and Jessica were quiet as well, so Billy kept his mouth shut and just kept trudging along. They weren't actually going as fast as he was used to, so he wound up leading the way most of the time.

The forest became closer, and the pilgrims were forced to walk in single file on the trail. They couldn't spread out over the side of the mountain like they had in the morning. Henry started to whimper, and then cry loudly. Jessica bounced him up and down and sang in a low voice to him. Jessica wasn't worried about what the other families would think. No one turned and looked at them or anything at the sound of Henry crying. She tried to quiet him down just because she didn't want to have to listen to a screaming baby.

Eventually she fed him, and he calmed down. She put a blanket over her shoulder and Roy draped it over the front of her while she walked and fed Henry. Billy looked away nervously.

Soon they stopped for the night, and the boy got confused and irritable. He thought it was still quite early for it. The sun was still up and it was still fairly warm. However, he didn't feel like arguing about it, so when Roy and Jessica sat down, he just sat down with them.

All the families had gathered together, and one of the fathers managed to start a fire. The teenagers were sent out to gather more wood. Billy stood up ready to join them, but Roy put a hand on the boy's arm. Billy was a guest and Roy said that he didn't need to help. Billy looked at the teens, and then back at Roy and figured that even though he was perfectly capable of gathering wood, if Roy didn't want him to, then he wouldn't. So the boy sat down again.

Henry was sated, so Jessica pulled him away from her breast and laid him on her lap. Roy took the blanket off of her and folded it up. Then he placed it under the baby by lifting Henry up and sliding it underneath him.

Soon some of the teens returned with wood which they placed on the fire. It had been a very small fire, just the twigs and moss that could be gathered growing around the campsite. Once it had more wood to burn, the fire leapt up happily and gave off quite a bit of light. By the time they got back, the sun was starting to go down, and so the extra light was welcome.

Most of the wood that they'd found was just small twigs and branches that burned quickly, but they had also managed to find a few bigger logs that would feed the fire for a while. Not long after the logs had been put in, Billy could hear them begin to sizzle and pop as the heat started to push the moisture out of the logs.

Around the fire, a number of low conversations sprang up. The quiet of the day was broken, and Billy heard children whining about how tired they were, and adults either trying to comfort them, or else telling them to buck up and stop complaining.

Billy hadn't noticed them during the day, but there were a few older couples as well. Unlike the rest of the group, they remained quiet as they crowded in around the fire. Obviously they weren't too old to make the hike. However, they still looked more exhausted than the younger people around them. There was one older woman rubbing vigorously at her knees while her husband fiddled with some blankets that she was sitting on.

The rest of the teens returned carrying more bundles of wood. They had brought enough fuel to keep the fire going through the night. They had already put a good deal of fuel on the fire, but they had also gathered extra wood that they put in a pile nearby. After they were satisfied that there would be enough, they sat down with their families. When it seemed like everyone was comfortable, a large, bearded man stood up and started talking to the whole group.

"This is a struggle for many of us, I know. And for some of us more than others," he said, gesturing across the fire to where the older couples had congregated. "But I think such a thing makes our prophet very happy to see. As you know, the prophet was laughed at in the streets when he came and proclaimed his vision. So having his followers return back to the scene of his revelation reminds him that at least some of us took it seriously. And so I think it's worth it, no matter how much difficulty we have in getting here."

"Many of us know the story of how our prophet was ridiculed and taunted in those first years, but there are some of the younger folk who have never heard it before, and probably some of us older folk who could stand to hear it again."

"When our prophet came out of the mountains, he went first to the town of Hinton to proclaim his vision and tell people what he'd seen. He went to the valley shopping area and the people left off their shopping and gathered around him to listen. He told them what he had seen."

"He told them how he had stayed out in the forest for a month, and had the revelation. As he lay there, his skin began to grow sores which were very painful. Slowly the centers became hard and then these sores became diamonds as they burst out of his skin, trailing blood on the ground. Then God sent angels down to gather the diamonds, and the archangel Barachiel came and told the prophet that God would collect all the diamonds and place them in a special case, so that when the prophet died he would be able to see them all collected in Heaven."

"And after the angels left, the prophet woke from the dream, but it hadn't been just a dream. He knew that he'd had a vision and he sat still for a while until he was sure that he understood. He decided that what it meant is that we don't know we're doing it, but we constantly shed these diamonds. And God sends down angels to collect the diamonds, and keep track of them for us. And this is the way that judgement is done on us when we die. God looks to see how many diamonds he's gotten from us, and then decides whether to let us into heaven or not."

"The people of Hinton laughed at him. They didn't want to hear any more about his vision. They thought he had lost his mind. He couldn't take their ridicule, so he retired to a hotel where he drank many strong drinks. In the middle of the night, he woke up and went away from the town of Hinton that wouldn't believe him. He wandered through several more towns, preaching his revelation, and they all laughed at him. But then he came to our town of Entrance and when he told us of what had happened to him, many of us believed him and took him seriously."

"Of course, there were many unbelievers even in Entrance, who resisted the prophet at first, but soon they either moved away or began to believe. We built a church and even after the prophet was taken from us, we have kept the faith, and now we make this pilgrimage."

"So our mission in life is to create as many diamonds as possible for God to collect. And our diamonds will be spiritual, and we can create them any time, though we rarely do. And, as it was for the prophet, the creation of these diamonds will be terribly painful."

"The question, then, is how are we to make these diamonds? Do they come from the way we feel? Is it enough to feel kindness and forgiveness for our fellow men? It isn't. Feeling without action is worthless. What we feel inside doesn't help the outside world, and another person who feels that you are cruel and unforgiving will continue to do so, unless you at least talk to them about it."

"So is it by acts alone that diamonds are made? Some would have you believe that. They feel that because acts affect the world, they must be the most important thing."

"But acts can be done without any feeling or kindness, and those acts surely can't create diamonds. No one does good by accident. Or rather, they might, but it isn't really good if you didn't mean it. There has to be effort. And you can only make an effort for something that you intended and felt."

"So the truth of the matter is that we need feeling but it needs to be in the form of effort and then action. And effort requires pain. I know that it seems harsh to require pain, and the prophet wasn't a harsh man. Perhaps he never intended for pain to be part of this. But things done without pain are those things that are easy to do. And things that are easy don't require an effort, so they won't do it. There has to be effort involved to create diamonds."

"Be happy then. If we are honest with ourselves, we recognize that we spend very little time and energy creating diamonds for God.

Probably far less than we should. But look back at the way we have come up the mountain, and see that the ground is littered with diamonds that we have left there. For there is no doubt that this pilgrimage is a significant act. Nor is there any doubt that many of us experience some pain in accomplishing it. And we perform this pilgrimage with good and happy feelings, knowing that we do this in order to honour our prophet, honour which he was denied."

"So this is another reason why we perform the pilgrimage. Not only does it make our prophet happy to see it, but it helps us generate diamonds, and reminds us of what we ought to be doing all year long."

After he had finished speaking, the bearded man smiled at everyone around the fire and then sat down. Slow murmuring started up around the fire as the families began talking again. Billy Boy had very rough elbows, and looked at them and wondered if they were going to turn into diamonds. They just looked like dried up, wrinkled skin to him. He wondered if Father John had made any diamonds without knowing it. He also thought that if he'd actually made any diamonds himself, it might be nice to actually have one in hand, instead of handing them all over to God and angels.

It was fully dark by that point in time, so Billy curled up facing the fire. He found the low hum of conversation comforting, and he was soon dozing off. Roy pulled a blanket out of his pack and tossed it over to the boy. Billy wrapped it around himself and fell asleep.

The next morning, they were all up again bright and early. There were a few clouds to the east of them, but otherwise the sky looked promising. It took a little while to get them all organized and moving again, but it was less work than might have been expected with that large a group. Even the little kids allowed themselves to be corralled fairly easily. Some families left independently, to be followed by some of the other families later. Perhaps that was another reason why they could get going fairly quickly, they didn't seem to actually require much organization. They all knew which direction to head in, so when each family was ready, they just started walking.

By noon they had reached the top of the mountain, which was still low enough that they hadn't passed the tree-line. Though the forest was quite thin at that altitude, there were still pines around them. They rested at the top for an hour or so, and then started down the other side. Again, there didn't seem to be an official time-keeper or anything. The group of old folks just rose to their feet spontaneously and started walking. Everyone else just followed behind them.

It was only two in the afternoon when they got to their destination. It was a large clearing with no sign that it was terribly important. Immediately the man with the beard went into the center of the clearing and turned to face all the other pilgrims. Billy thought he was about to make another speech, but instead he just opened his arms wide and smiled at each of them as they entered the clearing.

All the pilgrims moved around the edge until they formed a large circle with the bearded man in the center. He remained standing while the rest of the pilgrims found seats. It took a minute, because the ground was rough, and while a few people found a fallen tree or a rock to sit on, most of them had to make do with just spreading a blanket on the ground.

Billy remained standing for a minute, but then Roy put a hand on his shoulder and indicated that he should sit down. There wasn't anything to sit down on, but that didn't bother Billy Boy. He just sat in the dirt and crossed his legs. He also leaned forward, so his elbows were on his knees, and his chin was resting on his fists. He sat like that as he watched the bearded man speak.

"Well, we've made it. I know, no one needs that pointed out. But we made it. Again." He paused and bent down to pick up a stick at his feet. When he stood again, he started twirling the stick around in the air while he spoke.

"There are things I've been meaning to say, but I've been keeping my mouth shut until we got here. Now that we've made it, I figure that I can speak freely. Folks, the truth is that very few other people know or care about what we're doing. That sounds mean, but it's just realistic, that's all. And it doesn't mean that it's not worth doing. But we're not going to change the world. We're not trying to change the world. Changing the world is for other people. I sometimes wonder whether the desire to change the world is the first clue that you're on the wrong track, but I won't go into that." He paused again. He let the stick drop from his hand, and then pinched the bridge of his nose. He was still smiling, but it was kind of a sad smile.

"We come here every year knowing that for most of the people out there it won't make any difference. And that's something we accept. Actually, if people knew we were doing this, they would think we were crazy, like they thought about our prophet."

"We've been told that the meek will inherit the earth. Folks like to take that literally, and then they like to think that they're one of the meek. Or they figure that it's not true anyway, and then they imagine that they're one of the bold. Neither side seems to realize that it's more of a wish than anything else."

"The meek aren't going to inherit the earth. The bold aren't going to let them. And it's the bold who would think we're crazy for coming up here every year, and it's the bold who would think we're crazy for following the prophet, and it's the bold who would think we're crazy for living out in the woods in the first place. The bold think we're nuts. And if we wanted to actually inherit the earth, we're going about it all wrong."

"So there better be something else that we're trying to get by acting so crazy. And there is. There's a reward, and it would be tempting to think about that reward and brag about it. We would try to convince everyone else that the reward is worth it, and that we would be bold if it weren't for the great reward we're going to get for being meek."

"That would defeat the purpose though, and we wouldn't really be meek anymore. We have to try to keep doing what we do without thinking too much about the reward. And we're not going to try to tell other people about the reward."

"So then if we're really meek, then we should hope that the meek don't inherit the earth. And we'll hope that the meek don't inherit heaven either. Some of the bold will no doubt wind up there, and they'll talk too much, and tell everyone else what to do, and because we're meek we'll go along with it, and keep our mouths shut. And sooner or later, there'll be some bold person in charge of everything."

"So we're doing this for nothing, and that's what makes it worthwhile. I know that sounds kind of crazy, or cynical, or... well... something. And I also know that it's not anything that you folks want to hear. That we came here for nothing. But that's what makes it worth doing. If you were here to get something, even if it's something worth getting, then this pilgrimage is defeating the purpose."

"I talked last night about making diamonds. I still think that's true, and I'm not trying to convince you otherwise. I said there were two things that we needed before we could make them. Feeling, or effort, and action. But there's also a third thing. I didn't want to say anything about it last night, because we still had a long climb ahead of us, and if I had told you about it last night, then you might have gotten discouraged."

"The thing is we need to be selfless. I know that we can't make diamonds unless we're selfless. And being selfless is the hardest thing to do. Being selfless, really selfless, makes you look crazy. Other people always expect you to get some reward for things that you do. So doing a thing that doesn't have any reward... it'll look nuts."

"So if you think you might be crazy, then you're on the right track. And it's up to each of us to decide if we're crazy and selfless enough. I can't tell you. You have to decide for yourself. So the truth is, you know what you've done here, and why, and that's going to have to be enough reassurance for you, because I can't, in honesty, provide anything more."

"Forgive me if I sound harsh. You all just had a long, hard journey, and probably the last things you want to hear are the things that

I've just been saying. But I need to be honest and true. Otherwise, why would you trust me? No reason."

"But here we all are. We can hope that the forest won't want anything more from us tonight, and in the meantime we'll just sit with our thoughts and be happy that we've done the right thing. Hopefully, that'll be enough."

With that, the speech was over. The bearded man walked over to an older woman and sat down next to her. A slight buzz started up around the circle again. No one seemed shocked, so it was clear that they were all familiar with the ideas, and had heard the speech in some form before. Most of it hadn't made much sense to Billy. He found it vaguely disturbing, but he couldn't have said why that was. He couldn't tell if he was supposed to be meek or bold or something else. He often thought of himself as pretty bold, and he also thought that even if he tried to be meek, he might accidentally be bold anyway. It definitely seemed like it was kind of bad to be bold, but he was pretty sure that he couldn't help himself.

The only part of the speech that Billy Boy really understood was the ending, when the bearded man had said that the forest might want something else from them. He didn't want to let on that he didn't get the rest of it, but he was curious what else the forest might want. He decided that there was no shame in wondering about that part, at least, so he asked Roy and Jessica what had been meant by it.

"Sometimes the forest takes one of us during the night," Roy said. "We tried to fight the forest the first few years we came out here, but we always lost. Then Roger said..."

"That's the guy with the beard?" asked Billy.

"It is. He said that we shouldn't fight. Since we were out in the forest, we were just there by its permission. It has a right to take what it wants from us. That's what he said. There was some argument, but since we'd been losing anyway, and we never managed to save anyone, there didn't seem to be much point in fighting anyway. So we stopped. It still doesn't sit well with many of us, but we have to endure it, that's all."

Billy wasn't very happy with that answer. He asked what it meant that the forest sometimes took someone. Roy told him that they would wake up in the morning and someone would be gone, but he didn't know what the forest did with them. The taken were never seen again. There was usually some blood, but they hadn't ever found a body, and they'd never found any other clues about what had happened. And since they didn't even look for the taken anymore, they still hadn't found anything.

"So you just forget about them?" asked Billy.

"We don't forget," said Roy sadly, "but we don't try to find them either." He paused when he saw the unhappy look on Billy's face. "I know it's hard to understand, but this is just part of the sacrifice."

Billy wasn't satisfied with the pilgrims just sitting around in a circle either. He had expected some type of ceremony or something, but Roger's speech seemed to be all they were going to do. The whole thing seemed a little anti-climactic. Also, if they were waiting to see if one of them would get taken, then they seemed too calm. Even if they weren't going to fight about it, Billy still thought they should at least be nervous or upset about it. They just seemed resigned.

"Do we just wait around 'til tomorrow morning?" he asked, and Roy replied in the affirmative.

Billy decided that it was time for him to leave. He had planned to stick around for the night so that he could see what happened, but since nothing seemed likely to occur, other than the forest kidnapping someone, it didn't seem like it would be worthwhile for him to wait around. He stood up and tried to say his farewells to Roy and Jessica. However, as soon as he started, they immediately asked him to just stay and wait for them.

"Stay 'til tomorrow at least," said Jessica. "Then we'll be able to help you find your mother and your bike. We can't leave now, but tomorrow will be no problem."

Billy tried to protest, but he was over-ruled, and since he was feeling guilty about leaving them, he sat down again to wait for night to fall. In the meantime, Jessica started asking him questions about his life and his family. Roy had gone off to talk to another family, so it was just Billy, Jessica and Henry.

She asked him more questions about what he was doing out in the forest. He began telling her the whole story. This time he didn't leave anything out. He still wasn't sure how much he could trust her, but she seemed so earnest and interested in his life, that he felt like it would be wrong not to tell her everything. Against his better judgement, he wound up telling her all about Sarah and Father John.

When he was done, she said that it seemed like he'd been through a lot to find his mother. "You're a very independent boy," she said. "Your mother will be very proud of you."

"Well, she might be, but she doesn't know about it, yet," said Billy, looking away from Jessica. He wasn't entirely comfortable with being complimented even at the best of times, and there was something about this exchange that felt wrong to him, even while it was going on. He liked Jessica, and he liked Roy, and he even liked little Henry, but they were a part of this weird religion, and he just couldn't shake the feeling that there was something kind of sinister about them. He began wishing that he hadn't stayed. He wished he'd left earlier when he'd first decided that he wanted to, and never had the conversation with Jessica.

"She'll know soon enough," said Jessica, and then started coddling Henry a little. He was making slightly irritated sounding gurgling noises, and she was pre-emptively trying to placate him.

"So, Billy," she said after Henry had become quiet again. "What do you think of what Roger had to say?"

Billy tried to be tactful, but it wasn't in his nature, so he just blurted it out instead. "Seems pretty crazy to walk all the way up here for nothing. Though it sounds like maybe it was supposed to be crazy. I don't know what Roger was saying. Maybe I just didn't get it. But it still seems crazy. Especially if someone's going to get taken."

"It is kind of crazy, but that's the point Billy," said Jessica calmly. "If it weren't crazy, then it wouldn't honour the prophet or be worth doing at all."

Billy furrowed his brow, and tried to understand, but after a moment he gave up and told Jessica that it still didn't make any sense.

"It's only by doing crazy stuff that we are selfless, like Roger was saying."

"All right," said Billy. He decided that even though it didn't make any sense, he wasn't going to bother arguing about it. He decided not to talk about it anymore.

Jessica smiled at him, then picked up a blanket and draped it over her shoulder while she started feeding Henry. The baby had started making noises again, which Billy was happy about since he hoped that it meant they didn't have to talk about crazy religious stuff anymore.

"I don't think it really is all right," said Jessica. "If you want, we can stop talking about it, but sooner or later I'd like to help you understand."

Billy said nothing, but he didn't really want to understand. By that time, all he really wanted was to get out of there. He didn't want to face Roy and Jessica's disappointment, so he figured he could wait through the night, and leave in the morning, but he was still anxious to get going. He knew that even in the morning, it might be hard to leave them behind, since it sounded like Roy and Jessica were planning to go with him. He also knew that he was too tired to face it right then, so he tried not to worry about it.

Peter

The night was quiet. Billy Boy couldn't sleep. He was awake and staring at the stars. He was nervous about trying to leave the next day. He didn't want to hurt anyone's feelings, but he really wanted to be by himself again.

Billy stood up, threw off his blanket and stretched his arms up to the sky. Then he looked around at the sleeping mass of pilgrims that surrounded what was left of the fire. It didn't send up sparks anymore, but it was still glowing and warm. There was an orange glow peeking out from beneath the grey ashes.

He walked over and put his hands toward it. There was definitely still heat coming off of it. The night itself was cold, however, and so he picked up the blanket that he'd tossed away when he stood up and wrapped it around himself again. Then he got as close to the fire as he could. He picked up a small log and placed it on the embers, hoping that it would catch without making too much noise. He wanted to be warmer, but he also didn't want to wake up the other people.

As he sat there, he saw on the other side of the fire the glow of a cougar's eyes approaching the outside of the circle. He wanted to shout out a warning, but he was frightened. He froze where he was, unable to do anything. Flames started spouting from the log he'd put on the fire, and it gave off enough light for him to get a better look at the cat that was approaching.

It was Peter, Sam's friend. The cat looked up at the fire for a moment and snarled at Billy. He wasn't too happy about the sudden burst of light, and he didn't seem to recognize the boy.

Billy wondered if he should just go up to Peter and say hello, but then he remembered Sam's warning, and thought that the cougar might just eat him, so he just stayed frozen by the fire. Peter crept to the edge of the circle where a small boy was sleeping. Anticipating the worst, Billy Boy looked away. Peter quickly sunk his teeth into the little boy's neck, so that he wouldn't wake up and make noise. When he was sure that the boy was dead, Peter used his mouth to grasp the boy's body by the shoulder and pulled away it from the circle and into the forest.

All this was done very quietly. The crackling of the log in the fire made more noise than the cat did as he took his prey. Billy wanted to follow the cougar and make him promise not to take any more. Billy also wanted to ask Peter if it had always been him that had been taking pilgrims.

There had always been blood left on the ground, so the pilgrims must have had a pretty good idea that it was an animal taking one of them year after year. If they'd known, then why hadn't they done more to protect themselves? It seemed like more of Roger's requirement that they be humble visitors in the forest, and so more of their kooky religion that the boy couldn't understand.

But he had also gotten an idea from Peter's little escapade. The pilgrims were expecting disappearances during the night. Now they would definitely have one, but why couldn't there be two disappearances? Billy thought about it for a minute. He didn't know if they'd ever had two disappearances in one night, but even if it was unprecedented, it didn't seem like they'd look for him. And if he just disappeared, he wouldn't have to deal with Jessica and Roy in the morning and talk them into letting him go on without them. He quickly decided that that was what he would do.

He knew that to be convincing, he'd have to leave the blanket in the camp. When he stood up and took the blanket off he could feel how cold the night had become. Winter was coming on, and he realized that he would have to pick up the pace if he was going to find his mother before the snow started falling. He hesitated for a moment, but despite the cold, he was determined, and so he left the blanket behind, even though it was really cold without it.

He put the blanket on the ground beside Jessica, and then went into the forest. He figured he would only go a little way in the darkness and so wouldn't get totally lost in the dark forest. He was hopeful that he would be able to go far enough into the trees that the pilgrims wouldn't look around for him. He went downhill from the clearing so that he could still just barely see the fire, then he stopped and curled up.

He dozed a little, but between how cold he was and the nervousness he felt about the morning, he wasn't able to get much sleep. The log he had put on the fire was almost burnt out before he was able to get any decent sleep, and then he only slept because he was so exhausted, not because he was relaxed.

In the morning, Billy woke up not long after the pilgrims, so he was able to watch their reaction to his disappearance. Jessica and Roy were voicing their dismay that Billy had vanished, but soon they were drowned out by the sounds of shock over the loss of the little boy, and the bloodstains that had been left behind. There didn't seem to be much risk of being found, but Billy stayed low in the forest, crouched down behind a fallen tree. In fact, there was a lot of wailing and crying, but none of the pilgrims actually went searching for either Billy or the little boy that Peter had taken.

After the wailing was done with, the pilgrims got themselves up, packed and ready to go. Roger went around making sure everyone had everything, and he went to the family of the little boy more than he went to the others. Billy could tell he was trying to comfort them, but from their faces it was clear that he wasn't doing any good. As they started walking back up the hill, the little boy's family was at the back. There were two older children, a son and a daughter, and the parents, and they all walked sadly at the back of the cavalcade of pilgrims.

Roy stayed behind as the rest of the pilgrims left, so they were at the back except for Roy. He stood for a minute looking out into the forest. He wasn't anywhere near where the little boy had disappeared. Instead, he was facing into the forest where Billy was hiding. His mouth moved, but whatever he said, he didn't say it loudly enough for Billy to hear. He looked sad but also curious, and his face had a quizzical expression. His mouth moved again, and then Jessica came back to him. The rest of the pilgrims had started moving away from the clearing, and Roy was holding them up. She tugged at his sleeve a couple of times, and then he turned around and joined them as they walked.

After the pilgrims left, Billy stood and went back to the clearing. It was still early, but the sun was already bright and the day was warming up already. Nothing had been left behind. Everything had been packed up and taken away. He started getting angry at the ease with which they had left without looking for either himself or the other boy. He felt like shouting because he was mad, but he refrained since he didn't really want them to hear and come back. He didn't know if they'd have returned even for something so obvious, but he didn't want to risk it.

So instead of shouting, he picked up a stick, moved to the edge of the clearing, and started whacking the stick against a tree trunk. He felt a little silly, but he was angry, and it was the only thing he could think of to do that wasn't loud or painful. So he kept doing it until the stick broke. He thought about getting another stick but decided that that would be going too far, and if he got a second stick, instead of just feeling a little silly, he would start feeling downright ridiculous.

After the stick broke, he went into the forest at the spot where he'd seen Peter the night before. Billy went in about forty feet or so, not even as far he'd gone to get away from the camp, and he found the boy's body.

There was blood everywhere, and the corpse itself was in terrible shape. The cougar had eaten most of one of the legs, and eviscerated the boy. Billy looked away, wondering why he'd even come looking for the body. He'd known what he'd find, and that it wouldn't be pleasant. Billy vomited and then turned away from the body. He felt very sad and also kept retching a little bit as he walked back to the campsite.

After he'd gone ten feet or so, he stopped and stood in the forest looking back toward the body. He was thinking that he should bury the boy, otherwise scavengers would nibble at him and make things even worse. But Billy figured that if the pilgrims themselves hadn't even been bothered about it, then it definitely wasn't his responsibility. So after a moment of hesitation, he continued walking back to the clearing.

When he got back, he sat down for a minute, and again he looked behind him in the direction of the boy's corpse. The feeling that he should go back and bury the boy had returned. Even though he knew that taking care of the body shouldn't have been left for him to deal with, but he still felt guilty that he had to leave. But the boy had no shovel, and no time. Besides, he was profoundly disturbed by the body, and wasn't sure that even if he'd had tools, he would have been able to deal with it. He wanted to get going from the clearing and find his mother, not spend his day disposing of the dead boy.

So after sitting by the remains of the fire for a few more minutes, in spite of his feelings, he stood up and started walking away. The trail started again on the opposite side of the clearing from where the pilgrims had gone. The trail was wide and easy to follow. By evening he'd gotten down into another valley, and the trail turned to follow it. Billy was happy about that, since he was tired of climbing over mountains, and was happy to be walking on the flat for a little while. He stopped by a little stream that was coming down off the mountain. He washed his face and had a little drink before he settled down for the night.

Relief

When Billy Boy woke up the next morning, he was shivering. The nights were getting quite cold, and, even if it might have given him away, he wished that he'd kept the pilgrims' blanket to wrap himself in. He knew that he couldn't stay out there in the cold weather much longer, so he needed to find his mother soon. If he didn't, he'd have to go back at least as far as Sarah's place to rest for the winter, and he knew it wouldn't do any good to go looking for his mother again in the spring. She'd either be dead or long gone over the mountains by that time, and Billy either wouldn't want to find her, or he wouldn't be able to.

He gave himself a shake and rubbed his arms, and then he started walking again. He was still cold, but he hoped that the walking would warm him up. He'd only gone a few miles when Sam flew down between the trees and landed on the ground in front of him.

"You're looking a bit worse for wear, buddy," said Sam, cocking his head to look at Billy.

"It's getting cold."

"I suppose. What are you going to do?"

"I don't know," said Billy. "Did you find anything?"

Sam turned his back to Billy so he could look down the trail. "There's a fork in the path up ahead. One trail goes back to the highway, and the other keeps going along this valley."

"Which one should I take?"

"I'm not sure. I didn't find any sign of your mom, so I don't know which way she went."

Billy sat down and started trying to puzzle it out.

"I have an idea, though," said Sam.

Billy looked up at him. "Let's hear it," he said.

"I'd guess she'd stay in the woods and that she wouldn't be heading for the highway."

"Why do you think that?"

"Because if she was on the highway, I would have been able to see her. It's not hard to spot a woman walking along the road, but I didn't see anything. So I figure she must have stayed on the forest path. I tried to find her, but I couldn't. But I still figure she's there, we just have to keep going."

"All right," said Billy. "Is the trail up ahead still in good shape?"

"The trail to the highway is good. The trail along the valley isn't as good, but still not bad. It won't be muddy or anything, and, from what I can see, it seems to keep going through this valley, so at least you won't have to climb."

"I guess I don't have much choice."

"You don't, actually. Unless you want to go back to the highway. But like I say, I'm pretty sure she didn't go that way, so there wouldn't be much point. I don't think there would be, anyway."

"I'll take your word for it," said Billy. "I guess I'll keep going through this valley. How far is the fork?"

"Less than a mile, I'd say."

"All right. I'm going to keep going. You try to find her on the trail in the valley."

Sam bobbed his head a little in what looked like a kind of salute, and then he jumped into the air and took off. Billy started walking again and it wasn't long before he came to the fork that Sam had told him about. Both paths looked the same to the boy, but even though the other trail looked just as inviting, he took the left fork that continued through the forest. He would have liked to be back on the highway again, but he trusted Sam's opinion that his mother wasn't on the road.

The forest trail wasn't bad. Billy had been worried that despite what Sam had said, it would be a mess, but it was fine. It got narrower and a little more difficult to see than it had been coming over the mountain, but Billy still had no problem following it.

Near the end of the day, the trail started climbing again. It gradually began to angle up the mountainside on his left. However, it was still a very gentle slope, and so it wasn't hard for Billy to follow.

After another mile or so, it stopped climbing altogether and began following a level shelf in the mountainside. Once it had levelled off, Billy decided he would stop for the night. He lay down under a tree and tried to make himself as cosy as possible.

Even though he was comfortable, he didn't fall asleep quickly, and the night seemed long. He dozed for a while, but then he woke up again in the cold. He opened his eyes and it looked like everything around him had disappeared. He couldn't tell for certain, though, because it was dark, so it might just have looked like everything was gone, but things were there, just hidden in the dark. Nonetheless, the trees were gone, and so were the mountains, and all he could see were the stars speckling the sky above him. He knew that he was seeing the blank slate again.

He was glad, because he felt like he could use the soothing feeling that it gave. He had tried not to think about it, but he had started feeling very sad since the pilgrims. He had already been feeling bad about his mom and angry about Sarah, but after the pilgrims, he was also sad and angry about everything that had happened with them, especially the little boy and disappearing on Roy and Jessica.

It was good to get those feeling taken away by the blank slate, but the experience wasn't nearly as pleasant as it had been the first time. It was dark and all he could see were the stars and he felt a little disturbed by it.

Soon, however, he started feeling relaxed and happy in spite of the darkness. He knew it was coming, so he could recognize the feeling that things didn't really matter and even the void around him began to seem friendly instead of frightening. Though he had been trying to ignore his bad feelings, they had been creating more of a burden for him than he had thought. Once they were gone, it was quite a relief to have them off his conscience.

It felt like an hour passed while he was lying there, but, in fact, it was only a few minutes before the forest and mountains rose around him again. As soon as he could see them again, he started getting sleepy and dozy. And so, in spite of the cold, he managed to fall asleep.

However, he woke up again in the middle of the night when he heard loud sounds of singing coming from further down the trail. Everything seemed to have gone quiet by the time he was thoroughly awake, but, nonetheless, he stood up and started walking toward where the noise had been coming from.

Vince and Noel

After he had walked a little, he could see that a fire was burning further down the trail. His feeling of warmth and comfort had worn off quickly and he was cold again. Also the pleasant indifference of the blank slate was already starting to disappear, and the beginnings of the bad feelings seemed to add more chill to the already cold air. The fire looked warm and happy and he felt drawn to it even though he wasn't sure that he should approach. After the experience with the pilgrims he decided that he had to be more careful about meeting people in the woods, but he really wanted to get warm, so against his better judgement, he walked down the trail toward the fire.

It was a few hundred yards away, and when he got closer, Billy saw that the fire was at the edge of a hollow in the side of the mountain. It had been built close to where the trail ran, and that was why he had been able to see it. To the right of the trail, there was a wide clearing, nestled between folds of the mountain behind it. If the fire had been built inside the hollow instead of beside the trail, the sides of the mountain would have hidden it, and, unless he walked right up to it, the boy would never have seen it.

The fire itself was much bigger than it needed to be. When the flames leapt up, it was taller than Billy. Around the fire there were a dozen people sitting or lying down. They were messy looking, but they were all wearing warm clothes. Only a couple of them seemed to be awake. The rest of them had their eyes closed.

Billy felt a little shy about getting close, but soon his coldness overwhelmed his shyness, and he sat down beside the warmth of the fire. There wasn't any wind, and the smoke and ash were going straight up. Billy thought it might be the best fire he'd ever seen. He could still see his breath, but the warmth was washing over him. There were blankets around the fire as well, and he took one and wrapped it around his shoulders.

The two people who were still awake didn't seem to care about Billy's arrival. In fact, it didn't seem like they had noticed him at all. The fellow who was awake was heavily bearded, and even though his eyes were open, they were definitely bleary and he stared blankly into the fire. He started singing, and Billy recognized the same voice that had woken him up. The man's voice was kind of thin and very raspy. It sounded like he'd been shouting all night before he started singing. Also, he was off key, but he didn't seem to care.

As he stared at the fire, he sang what sounded like an old sea shanty. He paused to take a drink of beer, and light a cigarette, and then he continued singing. As he sang, he moved his feet away from the fire, by pulling his knees up under his blanket. Billy was tempted to join his singing, but he wasn't sure if his participation would be appreciated, and he didn't know the words anyway, so he kept quiet.

The other person who was awake was a woman. Unlike the man, she was very alert looking. After Billy sat down, she looked over at him. When he looked back at her she smiled, and looked like she was about to say something to him before she looked away. The boy, the singing man and the woman made a triangle around the fire.

She was also bundled in a blanket. She had blue eyes and thin lips, and if he'd known it, Billy would have realized that she looked a lot like him. As it was, he didn't know it, but he still found himself feeling a little protective of her. She looked fragile as she stared at the fire.

With the sudden warmth from the fire, Billy suddenly felt very tired again. In spite of feeling worried about the wakeful people around him and whether they would welcome him, he soon dozed off.

When he woke the next morning, the fire had died down, but it was a substantial heap of embers, and it was still very warm. Everyone around the fire was asleep, even the singing man and the fragile looking woman.

After a few minutes, Billy realized that it couldn't be very cold because he couldn't even see his breath. He stood up, shrugged off the blanket and started wandering around the camp. He looked up at where the sun was, and saw that the reason it was warm already was that it was well into the morning. It might even have already been noon.

Billy had been getting up early for so long that he was a little surprised that he had managed to sleep in. But he was even more surprised that no one else was awake. The boy looked around for some water, but he couldn't find anything besides beer. Eventually, one of the campers woke up. He stood up and stretched. He was a tall, lanky looking man. The man didn't have a beard, but there were a few days of growth on his face. When he turned around, he saw Billy. He seemed a little bit surprised, but then he smiled.

"Hey, little man. Where did you come from?" he asked.

"I was just up the trail a little. Back there," said Billy and pointed back along the trail.

"Well, good to see you. Were you cold out there?"

"Very. That's why I came to the fire."

"That's good. No point in freezing when there's a fire nearby." He pulled out a pack of cigarettes and lit one. Then he picked up a blue, ceramic coffee maker from amongst the debris beside the fire and looked inside. He pulled out the basket and dumped the old coffee grounds on the hot embers. They hissed and steamed while he handed Billy the coffee flask.

"There's a little stream back past that rock over there," he said gesturing behind him. "Can you go fill this up for me?"

Billy took the flask, and went to the back of the clearing where the tall man had indicated. There was a huge rock sticking out of the ground. Billy went behind it, and between the rock and the side of the mountain, there was a tiny stream pushing over the rocks toward the ground. Billy placed the flask under the flow of water and filled it up, then returned to the campsite.

The tall man had put new coffee grounds into the basket and was waiting for Billy to return with the water. Billy handed him the flask, the tall man said thanks and placed the basket inside the top of the percolator. Then he placed the whole thing on a flat spot in the embers left from the fire.

"My name is Vince," the tall man said after he had put down the coffee maker, and he held out his hand to Billy.

"I'm Billy," said Billy and took Vince's hand. He had never shaken anyone's hand before, but he'd heard about it, and he hoped that he was doing it right. He wasn't sure how hard he was supposed to grip. Vince gave his hand a little bit of a squeeze, so Billy squeezed back.

"So what are you doing out here, Billy?"

So Billy told Vince the whole story. He wasn't sure why, but he trusted Vince implicitly. He included everything about Father John and Sarah and the pilgrims. He knew he probably shouldn't. He'd only just met the guy, after all, but somehow Vince seemed trustworthy.

"Those religious crazies come out here every year," said Vince. "We stay away from them. They don't like us, and we don't like them."

"They let a little boy get eaten."

"What?"

"There was a cougar and he took the little boy. They didn't even look for him. They lose people every time they come out here, and they don't look for people who go missing. They figure they just owe it to the forest."

"There was a cougar?"

"Yeah. Peter is his name. They didn't even look for the little boy."

Vince tossed the butt of his cigarette in the fire. He picked up a cloth to protect his hand, and then moved the percolator on the fire. It had started bubbling over a little bit, so Vince put it in a colder spot so that it would just perk without boiling over.

"We have folks disappear sometimes too," he said to Billy. "Not all the time, but sometimes. There used to be more of us." He motioned around the circle. "But whenever someone disappears, we at least look for them. Can't say that it does much good, but at least we look."

Vince pulled out his cigarettes and lit another one. "A cougar, eh? We figured it was probably animals, though we also hoped we were making enough noise to keep them away. It's gotten worse in the past couple years. The fewer there are of us, the more they take us. And the more they take, the fewer there are of us."

A woman on the other side of the fire had woken up. She yawned, then she stood up and came around the fire to where Vince was sitting. She kept her blanket wrapped around her. She sat down and immediately put her head on Vince's shoulder. As soon as she sat down, Vince gave her a puff from the cigarette.

"This is Billy," Vince said to her, nodding toward Billy while he did so. "He was staying with those religious freaks up the hill."

Billy didn't like him calling them freaks. He wanted to say that, even though they had made him nervous, Jessica and Roy were really nice. But he kept his mouth shut, because he liked Vince and didn't want to contradict him.

"Hi Billy," the woman held out her hand to him. "I'm Rose."

Billy shook her hand and said hello. Vince gave her a short version of Billy's story. Rose looked over at Billy and raised her eyebrows at him.

"You've been through a lot," she said. She had to sit up as Vince leaned forward to take the coffee out of the fire. He set the pot down on a rock beside the fire, and then grabbed a couple of mugs from the ground. He looked inside quickly to make sure they were clean enough.

Apparently they were, so he poured coffee into them and handed a mug to Rose.

He was taking a sip of his own before he remembered Billy. "Sorry, did you want some?" he asked. Billy nodded. He hadn't had coffee very much, but when he had had it, he had liked it because of the heat. It didn't taste good. He didn't like how bitter it was. But bad taste or no, he could really use some warmth going down his throat. Vince grabbed another cup off the ground, gave it quick inspection, and then poured a cup for Billy.

The first sip that Billy took was unpleasant, but as he'd known he would, he enjoyed the warmth of it. As the three of them drank coffee, the rest of the camp woke up. As people woke up, Billy was introduced to everyone.

There was Jason, who was a young and strong looking fellow. He looked more nervous and energetic than the rest of the campers. He had dark hair and didn't seem to smile much.

Then there was Prue, who was Australian and very tall. She gave Billy a hug instead of shaking his hand. He got a little flustered by that.

The bearded man was named Noel. He looked much more clear-eyed than he'd seemed the night before, though his voice was still trashed when he spoke to say hello to Billy. "I saw you get here," he said.

"I didn't think you noticed," said Billy.

"Don't let him fool you," said Vince. "He notices everything. Even when he's singing."

The last camper still asleep was the woman who'd been awake

the night before when Billy arrived. Her name was Jill, and she was still slouched over, unconscious by the remains of the fire. Once everyone else was up, Rose went over and shook her until she was awake.

Even after she was up, Jill still looked kind of rough. Her eyes were a little bloodshot and her skin was pale. She took a cup of coffee, but it didn't seem to do much to revive her. After a little while, she started looking more awake, but she still seemed delicate.

Billy asked what they were doing out there. He'd been thinking about asking for a while, but he hadn't wanted to pry. Vince was obviously the leader of the group, and so it was no surprise that he answered. "We're kind of like those religious freaks, I guess. We come out here for the summer every year and just rough it for a couple of months. Most of the time we all live in town, or in the city, but during the summer we come out here, and just spend a couple months relaxing in the bush."

"Why?"

"Just because we need it," said Noel. "The world is getting us down, and the only way to recharge is to get away to the woods. I think we all would live out here permanently if we could."

"As it is, we'll have to head back soon," said Vince. "It's getting cold, and we all have to get back to work soon."

Noel looked a little disgruntled at that statement, but he didn't say anything about it.

"In the meantime," Vince continued, "you're free to stay with us for a little while. Until we have to leave for the winter. It won't be long, I guess, but you're welcome to rest for a few days, anyway."

"But I have to keep trying to find my mom," said Billy.

"You look like you could use a break. And you won't get far without some better cold weather gear."

The rest of the day didn't take very long. By the time everyone had woken up, there wasn't really that much daylight left, so they didn't have any problem waiting it out. And that's what it seemed like the campers were doing. Waiting for the light to disappear. Billy had been used to wishing the light would last longer, but the campers seemed to relish the sun's disappearance.

After the sun had set, Vince built up the fire again and opened a two-four of beer. He started handing out beers to everyone around the fire. He even offered one to Billy. The boy wasn't really sure if he wanted it, but he decided to take it anyway. He didn't know what needed to happen, so he watched as the others opened theirs. The caps didn't look like they'd twist off, which is what had gotten Billy confused in the first place. He wasn't sure if he'd need a bottle opener or something. But they were, in fact, twist-off caps, so once Billy saw that everyone was just twisting them, it wasn't very hard for him to get the bottle open.

He had a sip. It wasn't very good, but everyone else seemed to be enjoying theirs, so Billy tried to like it. It was a little bit like water, but it tasted stale or mouldy.

As he sat there, Noel came over and sat beside him. "You've heard about our problem," he said. "The animal problem."

"Yeah," said Billy. "Vince mentioned it this morning."

"Vince says you know the cat that's been doing it."

"I think I do. He stole a little boy from the pilgrims, so I think it's probably the same cat. His name is Peter."

Noel lit a cigarette and leaned close to Billy confidentially. "Maybe you could talk to Peter for us. Get him to leave us alone."

"I could try," said Billy. "I don't really know him very well. We only met the one time. I don't even know if he'd remember me."

"Still. You could try. For us."

"Sure, I'll try. But it wouldn't be too hard to stop him. Build a cabin or something."

"That's what Vince wants to do." Noel sat back, looking faintly disgusted. Then he remembered himself, and smiled and leaned forward again. "I think that would ruin everything," he said.

"We try to get out here to get away from it all. Vince wants to start bringing it all here with us, so that we can keep the cougar away."

"Really?" asked Billy. "He doesn't seem like he'd want that."

"He doesn't say it out loud. I don't guess Vince even knows it himself yet, but once we start building a cabin, it'll be no time before we have a rifle and cars and everything else. We might as well just get an RV right now, and get it over with."

Billy looked at his beer, and then took another sip. He decided he didn't like Noel as well as Vince, and he wasn't sure about Noel's logic. Father John had been kind of crazy, but he'd still managed to build a cabin without bringing everything else with him. Of course, maybe he had been able to do it because he was crazy. Maybe the campers wouldn't be able to stop themselves once they got going. He wasn't sure, but no matter what else happened, Billy wanted to help the campers avoid getting eaten by Peter, so if that meant he would have to go and talk to the cougar, then that's what he would do.

"We've lost one person this year already," said Noel. "Poor Rob. We need to do something, I know. But it just seems like a bad idea to start building things. So if you'd go talk to the cougar, that'd be great."

"All right. I'll do it. If he comes around, I'll see if I can talk him out of taking anyone."

Noel smiled and then stood up. He walked to the other side of the circle to sit with Jill. She had definitely perked up from the morning, but she was still looking a little worse for wear.

Billy hadn't noticed Vince approaching, and so he was a little surprised when the man came up and sat down beside him.

"What did Noel have to say?" he asked.

Billy looked over at him. Vince was smiling sadly, and looking at the fire while he spoke.

"He asked me to talk to the cougar and get him to stop taking campers."

"Can you do that?"

"I don't know. I only talked to Peter once, so I'm not sure he'll even listen to me."

"I know Noel is against us building anything out here, but I think we'll have to. Even if you convince this particular cougar to stop taking us, there'll be another cougar, or a bear or something. Whatever happens we have to build a cabin or something, just to protect ourselves."

"But if you can get this cougar off our back for now, that'll be really good," said Vince. "Do you trust Noel?"

"I think he's kind of weird," said Billy.

"So do I," said Vince. "And the truth is, that if you get this cougar to leave us alone, it'll be good for him. He'll say that we don't need to build anything. And even when the next animal comes along to start hunting us, he'll say maybe we should just talk to it."

"But I still want you to succeed," he said. "We can't lose any more people. So do what you can, little man. That's all I can say."

Billy looked away from him, feeling kind of bad. The blank slate had worn off completely and the guilt had returned. It seemed worse when it came back. Billy didn't want any more campers to die, but he also didn't want to hurt Vince. Vince put his arm around him, and clinked his beer bottle against Billy's. He smiled at Billy, and said again, "Do what you can."

Then Vince stood up and went back to sit beside Rose. Billy stared into the fire. He knew what he was going to try to do, but he didn't feel entirely happy about it. He was trying to think of some way to save the campers and help Vince at the same time.

As it got later and later, the campers started falling asleep one by one. Soon, the only people still awake were Noel and Jill. They were both looking the same as they had the night before. Noel didn't start singing again, but he still looked more intense than he should have. Billy thought he might burst into a lusty song himself just to break the tension that he was feeling himself.

Jill was looking nervous and delicate again. She smiled over at Billy and then came over and sat down beside him. They both felt nervous, and they both sat quietly for a minute. After a minute, however, Jill started talking.

"Noel says you're going to fix things with the cougar," she said.

Billy was instantly angry. The boy wasn't sure if he was going to be able to do anything at all, and Noel had had no right to start telling people about it. While he knew he had to set Jill straight, she seemed very easy to break and let down. And he was going to feel really bad when he let her down.

"I'll try," he said, "if the cougar comes around. And if he'll listen to me. I don't know if he will."

"Oh."

"Noel shouldn't have said anything," said Billy.

"No, he shouldn't have," she said. She also looked irritable. That was a reaction that Billy hadn't expected. He'd thought she'd be forlorn and sad, not angry. She wasn't smiling when she looked at him, though it was clear that she was trying to be friendly.

"Don't put yourself in danger," she said. "This is our problem, you don't need to be involved if you don't want to."

"I want to help," said Billy.

"I know," she said, "and both Noel and Vince are taking advantage of that. You don't really have to help us at all. I mean, obviously I want this solved too. But we don't seem to be able to solve it on our own, so now we're using a little boy to get it done. And both these guys have their own reasons why they want it solved. Those reasons are separate from keeping us safe, and neither of them really know how to solve it themselves, even though it's really their own agenda. Anyway, all I'm saying is be careful."

"What do you think I should do?" asked Billy.

"I think you should leave," she said. "I'd leave us to solve this for ourselves."

Billy thought about this for a minute. She had made some good points, but he still felt that if there was a chance he might be able to do something, he should at least try. "I'm not sure that I could just leave," he said. "I want to help Vince. I like Vince better."

"I like Vince better too," she said, "but I think Noel has a point. I'm not sure which one of them is right. What I do know, is that it really shouldn't be your problem, especially if you don't want it to be."

"I think it might be my problem already," said Billy.

She smiled at him and gave him a hug. When she did, she reminded him of his mother more than she already had. She had a kind look and she made him feel protective. Billy curled into her, and he got comfortable, but he knew he couldn't fall asleep if he wanted to watch for Peter.

Negotiation

On the other side of the fire, Noel had fallen asleep. Jill had lain back to make herself comfortable, and it wasn't long before she fell asleep as well. So when Peter finally appeared at the edge of the fire, only Billy was still awake.

He looked like he was creeping up on Noel. Almost everyone else had paired off, which made them more difficult to get. So instead of trying to get half of a pair, Peter was going after Noel. When Billy saw the cougar, he sat up and stared at the cat. Peter noticed, and recognizing Billy from the pilgrims' camp, he assumed that Billy wasn't going to do anything this time either, so he kept advancing cautiously on Noel.

However, this time Billy stood up and pulled a burning stick from the fire. The boy was shaking and terrified, but he did it anyway. And he started advancing around the fire, toward where Peter was creeping up on Noel. When the cougar got close enough, Billy said quietly, "I'll wake everybody up."

The cougar gave no indication that he would leave, but he did sit back on his haunches and he stopped moving toward Noel. "Then I'll run away and come back tomorrow," said Peter calmly. He was watching Billy intently for any sign of what the boy planned on doing. The cougar's eyes reflected the light from the burning stick in Billy's hand.

"Do you know who I am?" asked Billy.

"I remember you from the pilgrims' camp," said Peter. "You were awake, but you didn't do anything."

"I met you before that. I'm Sam's friend."

"Oh, right. The one who was taking the wrong trail. I guess you made it through all right. What are you doing here?" He looked briefly from side to side, and then said before Billy was able to respond to his question, "Actually, can we move away from the fire to talk? I don't want to wake these people up with our talking."

Billy nodded and they walked a little way into the forest so that they were out of earshot of the camp. Peter seemed to be scared of the burning stick, so, even though Billy was nervous, seeing that the cat was also frightened allowed the boy to manage his fear well enough to walk along beside the cougar. When they had gone twenty feet into the forest, Peter turned to him and indicated that it was all right to start talking again.

"I promised I would talk to you and get you to stop taking these campers."

Peter snickered a little at this. "Why would I stop?"

"Didn't you just get the little boy from the pilgrims' camp?"

"Yeah, but I'm hungry again. Also, it's hard to resist. They're just so exposed and easy to take. They hang out in these woods all summer and do nothing to keep me from taking them. They aren't really very tasty, but I can't resist. They just sit around the fire, doped and drunk, and I can just grab them. They're just as easy as the pilgrims. I don't know why these people have decided that they have to make it so easy, but they do, and I'd kick myself if I didn't take advantage."

"Is there any way I can get you to stop taking them?"

"I don't think so. Why are you out here, anyway? This isn't your problem. I'm not going to eat you, though. I'm not really that crazy about Sam, but I still wouldn't eat one of his friends."

"Even if it's not my problem, I still feel like I should try and do something."

Peter looked around a little irritated, and then said, "Look, I won't take any more this year. I'm not that hungry right now, anyway. But that's all I can promise. That I won't take another one this year."

"You'll start again next year though?"

"If they come back next year, then yeah, I'll start taking them again."

"Is there any way I can get you to leave them alone for good?"

"Only if you can tell me where else I can get such easy prey. Besides the pilgrims. They'll come back every year, too."

The only thing Billy could think of was the road kill on the highway, and he figured the cougar wouldn't be interested in that, since he wasn't a scavenger. He remembered there were a few ranches around Hinton, and he figured the animals there might be pretty easy to capture, so he suggested it.

"Those places have nothing but horses. Horses are hard to get. They run really fast, and they know how to use their hooves. Never mind the ranchers with rifles. Believe me, I tried already, and it was a disaster. I barely got away, I was really tired and I still hadn't gotten anything to eat. I got so hungry that I actually thought about eating one of the deer corpses by the highway. I didn't, but it was a close thing. I would have felt really ashamed if it had come to that."

Billy thought and thought, but he couldn't think of anything else. Then he realized that if the cougar left them alone for the rest of the year, but came back the year after, then that might actually be helpful to Vince. It wasn't a great solution, obviously, but it was still better than nothing, which is all he'd thought he'd accomplish.

So he brought up the agreement again, just to make sure that Peter would still go for it. "Like I said, I can hold off for the rest of this year," said the cougar. "I doubt if they'll be here much longer in any case. But if they come back next year, then I won't have any choice but to take a couple of them. And you owe me. Remember that." With that, Peter turned around and disappeared into the forest.

Billy went back to the circle, thinking that even though he hadn't been able to do as much as he'd been hoped, at least he'd been able to buy the campers some time. He nestled in beside Jill, bundled up in some of the spare blankets and fell asleep.

In the morning, he told Vince and Noel what had happened with Peter the night before, and what Peter had agreed to. Noel wasn't happy, but Vince nodded knowingly. "Now are you ready to build a cabin?" he asked Noel. "If we want to come back next year, we have to build something. The little man here has bought us some time to do that, but we can't wait any longer." Billy was a little disturbed by how smug Vince seemed about being right, but it was too late to change his mind by that point even if he'd wanted to.

Noel said he still wasn't sure, and he wandered away from the fire and the camp. He seemed very unhappy. Vince watched Noel for a while after the other man had walked away, then shrugged his shoulders and began organizing the remaining campers into work groups. It seemed like Vince had been planning this for a while. He went back to the stream and brought out some saws and axes that he'd been hiding there. Then he pulled some blue prints out of the bundle of clothes and blankets near the fire, and spread them out on the ground. Looking at the plans, he tallied up how many of each kind of board he would need, and then he handed out an axe or a saw to each of the campers. He told the people with the axes what kind of tree they would need to cut down for him, and told the people with the saws how long the boards would need to be. After all the campers had been given assignments, they disappeared into the forest, and only Vince and Billy were left in the clearing by the fire pit.

Billy smiled and looked like he was about to volunteer, but Vince told him that he didn't have to help build the cabin. Instead, he gave Billy a few blankets and told him he should probably head off to find his mother before winter really started.

Billy knew that Vince was right, but he wanted to say goodbye to Jill before he left. He asked Vince where she was, and Vince pointed above him into the forest on the mountain above them. Billy went into the forest, but he couldn't find her. He found a few of the campers starting to cut down a tree, and he asked them. They pointed further into the forest, and so Billy went in that direction. However, after a few minutes he was lost and there was still no sign of Jill. He called her name, but there was no response, so he turned around and found his way back to the other campers. He went back down past them to the fire where Vince was still standing.

Billy said goodbye to the man, and then the boy started heading down the trail again. He felt sad that he hadn't been able to find Jill, and he also wasn't sure he liked the change that had come over Vince. Once Vince had started barking orders, all the sad resignation had slipped away, and Vince seemed happy to be chopping down the trees. Or ordering other people to do it, actually. That was even more disturbing. The ease and happiness with which Vince organized the campers was upsetting to Billy. So the boy was happy to leave the camp behind him, even though he wished that he'd been able to say goodbye to Jill.

When he had walked for twenty minutes into the forest, he saw Noel off to his right standing between the trees. He stopped for a moment wondering whether he should bother the man, but then Noel saw him and came over.

"Sorry I couldn't get a better deal," said Billy. And he was genuinely sorry since he had begun to feel like he had misjudged Noel.

"Don't worry, Billy," Noel said. When he got close, he knelt down to Billy's level and tousled his hair. He was awkward about it, but Billy knew that he meant well.

"Sorry I put you at risk."

"There wasn't much risk," said Billy. "Peter said he wouldn't have eaten me, so I was safe the whole time."

"That's good. Still though, we didn't know that. I should have been more careful."

"Don't worry about it," said Billy, and then asked Noel what he was going to do now that the building had begun.

"I don't know what I'll do," said Noel. "I guess you know that this didn't turn out how I'd hoped."

"You can go back and help build the cabin. They've already started." Billy gestured behind him.

"I don't know if I want to."

"What else could you do?"

"I haven't figured it out yet. You're on your way?"

"I am. I have to find my mother before it gets really cold."

"Good for you. I guess I should also be figuring out what I'm going to do before the weather gets too cold."

"I think you should go back and build the cabin," said Billy. "I'm not sure how it'll work out, but I'm not sure what else you could do."

"That's probably the best idea. But I really don't know. I've thought I might start a new group, and go out even further next year. Anyway, you don't have to worry about it. Good luck finding your mom," he said and walked away, back into the bush again. Billy watched him for a moment, thinking that starting a new group might actually be the best idea. The boy was still wondering what Noel would do as he started on his way down the trail.

Pursuit

The trail stayed flat for a few miles, and then started climbing again. It wasn't as gentle as it had been, though at least Billy was able to stay upright. It wasn't so steep that the boy had to bend over and use his hands.

At the end of the day, Sam came back again, fluttering down between the trees to land at Billy's feet.

"She crossed the highway up ahead, and went up into the woods on the other side," he said.

Billy looked confused for a minute before he questioned Sam about it. "How did she get back to the highway? Isn't there just the river on the other side, and do I have to cross it again to follow her? How do you know this, anyway?"

Sam took a breath, and then launched into an explanation. "This trail joins the highway again in a few miles. On the highway, there's a bridge over the river. She used that to get across the river, and then she started up another trail into the forest on the opposite side of the highway. I heard it from some elk that have been hanging around near the bridge. Elk are usually pretty reliable. They said it was only a couple of weeks ago that they saw her cross the bridge, so you're definitely catching up."

Billy took a minute to absorb this news, and then gave Sam his orders. "You need to go back and see if you can find her. I'll keep going.

I'm going to walk at night as much as I can 'til I catch up with her."

"You'll get lost," said Sam, shaking his head.

"If I think I'm getting lost, then I'll stop walking 'til the sun comes up. But if I want to catch up with her, I need to keep going as much as I can."

"You're already catching up with her."

"Not fast enough," said Billy. "Winter's coming soon, and I don't have time to waste. So you go on ahead, and know that I'm coming behind you as quick as I'm able. And make sure you come back and tell me if you manage to talk to her. If I know she's waiting for me, then I can at least take it a little bit easier. Not much, but a little."

"All right," said Sam and flapping his wings he lifted off and turned west.

Billy took a bit of a rest, and then continued walking. He kept going even after the sun went down. He didn't mind walking in the dark, actually. It was getting cold, but the walking kept him warm. He knew that there was a distinct possibility that he would miss things in the dark, but, most of the time, he was able to see all right. He had been worried that he would lose his way, and he might have if the trail had been narrower or more overgrown. However, the trail was wide and clear, so even in the darkness, he didn't have any trouble following it.

However, after a couple more hours of walking, he was getting sleepy, and he decided he needed to stop. He found a small hollow at the base of a tree to nestle into, and so he settled in and bundled up with the blankets. After he stopped moving, he got cold right away. He thought that for the next night he might just bundle up even before he stopped. It would probably be too warm while he was walking, but hopefully, he'd build up some heat to hold onto for a while during the night.

When he woke up the next morning he wondered how far he was from the highway. He packed up his blankets and tossed them over his shoulder to rest on his back. In the late afternoon, the trail started going steeply down to the right. He almost jogged, but he forced himself to stay under control, and so even though the hill wanted him to run down it, he held himself back and kept walking at as close to a regular pace as he could. It levelled off, and soon he arrived back at the highway.

The sun was starting to go down, but he could see the bridge up ahead, and he decided he wouldn't stop until he'd crossed it. At least then, he'd be close to the trailhead on the opposite side. He didn't want to keep going too much further in the dark, though, since even though he was able to see most things all right, he would almost certainly miss the trailhead.

The bridge was deceptively far away. He had thought he would reach it in about a half an hour, but it took him almost two hours to get up to and over it. Once he was on the other side, it was completely dark, so he took refuge in the ditch and covered himself up with the blankets. He'd forgotten about the early bundling idea, only remembering too late. Even covered up, his face was still quite cold. He buried his face in the blankets like he was having a nightmare, and that seemed to do the trick. His nose still ran a lot from the cold, but at least the rest of him was warm.

In the morning, he looked up and saw that Sam was returning again. He was happy, because it hadn't been anywhere near a week, and so he was hopeful that the crow would have good news.

It turned out he was right. "Your mom is a few miles ahead. I spoke to her, and let her know that you were following, but I don't think she was planning on going any further anyway. She's holed up in a cave, and I don't think she was planning on moving again until spring."

"How is she?" asked Billy.

Sam cocked his head a little, then flew up and perched on Billy's shoulder. The crow was trying to be friendly and compassionate, like when someone puts an arm around a shoulder. Even though he didn't mean to cause any pain, the crow's claws hurt as they sunk in.

"She's looking a little rough, I have to say. I think she's had a hard time." Sam could see that, despite what he'd intended, his claws were hurting Billy, so he fluttered off his shoulder and landed back on the ground again.

"Go back and stay with her. I just have to follow this trail, right?" He pointed to the trailhead twenty yards ahead of him on the right. It was obvious in the daylight, but he would have walked right past it in the darkness. He had thought it was further along, so he wouldn't have been expecting it.

"Yeah, that's the one," said Sam. "I'll go and check on her, but then I'll come back and make sure you know where you're going."

"I'll be all right."

"Let's just make sure, okay? I know you've been fine so far, but there's no point in getting lost now, is there?"

"All right," said Billy as the crow took off.

Billy started walking up the trail. It climbed steeply, and he had to bend over a couple of times to use his hands. After a few miles, the trail disappeared entirely into the face of a cliff. It wasn't sheer, there were many outcroppings and tumbled rocks on the face of the cliff, but it still went almost straight up. Billy hadn't had to do any actual rock climbing before. He'd had to go up steep hills, but the climbing he'd done had consisted mainly of scrambling briefly over fallen trees or boulders, and not the sustained effort required to get up a cliff. It didn't look impossible, but Billy still wasn't sure whether he'd be able to handle it. There was a long way to climb, but it was between the tumbled rocks, so there would at least be plenty of places to hold on.

Sam came back a few hours after Billy had started. It was a good thing that the crow returned when he did. Billy had gotten stuck amongst some rocks, and wasn't sure how he was going to go any further. The boy was wedged in under an overhang and he couldn't see anything more that he could hang onto. He was sure that he couldn't climb any further. The rock above him looked smooth. He thought he could probably climb down again, but going further up looked impossible.

"How am I supposed to get up to the top of this cliff?" asked Billy in frustration before the crow had even landed.

"Your mom is coming with a rope."

"How did she manage to get up here?"

"She must have climbed it."

Billy looked up and still didn't see how anyone could climb up without having some skills that he didn't have. He hadn't thought that his mother had those skills, but she must have had them if she'd found a way to get up the cliff.

Billy's Mother

It wasn't long before Billy's mother arrived at the top of the cliff. He hadn't been sure that he'd be able to find her at all, so it was very good to see her again. Billy was choked up when he first saw her. He was still stranded amongst the rocks, and so the situation was still pretty bad, but, nonetheless, he felt a huge sense of relief when he saw her.

Even from where he was, however, he could see that she was looking a little rough, as Sam had said. Her hair was tangled and knotted, and she looked terribly gaunt. When he saw her, he was even more amazed that she'd been able to climb up the cliff. She was looking like she'd have trouble climbing anything at all. Her clothes were ragged and her favourite red sweater, which she was wearing, had developed large holes.

She covered her mouth for a moment when she saw Billy, and he saw her shoulders hunch with a sob for a moment. But she pulled herself together quickly, and when she had recovered, she lowered a rope down toward him. When the end of the rope came to him, he grabbed it and tied the end around his middle. She pulled and with her help he was able to climb up to the top of the ragged cliff.

When he got there, the two of them hugged for a long time. Sam flew up, but he perched off to one side. He was watching, but he didn't get involved or say anything. She kissed Billy a bunch of times and then cupped his head between her hands like it was a crystal ball.

"Why did you follow me?" she asked.

"I didn't want to stay in Cadomin by myself. Besides, I thought I could find you," he said. "And I was right."

She picked him up and carried him a few steps, but he was too heavy and even though she was ecstatic, she was still too weak from pulling him up the cliff to be able to carry him far. So she put him on his feet, and they walked holding hands back to the cave that she was living in.

He introduced Sam and told her how the crow had been very helpful in finding her. Then he told her all about the adventures he'd had since leaving home. She expressed amazement about Father John and the poplars. She was surprised that such an intense feud could have been going on so close to Cadomin and she hadn't had a clue. She also expressed relief that she'd gone west and so hadn't had to deal with the poplars at all. She praised Billy's bravery and good sense in escaping both the poplars and Father John. She seemed particularly interested in Sarah, and in the house that she'd found.

She already seemed to know something about the pilgrims. "I'm glad you didn't get too involved with those people, Billy," she said. "That 'prophet' that they talk about, was nothing but a drunk. That's why everyone ran him out of town whenever he showed up. Those people are crazy."

Billy tried to explain that being crazy was part of their religion, but he decided that he didn't care or understand enough to try to make her understand. He had liked Roy and Jessica, but it didn't seem likely that he would ever see them again, and so it didn't matter whether he or his mother understood their crazy religion.

She felt bad for Noel. Like Billy, she didn't know whether he was right about the cabin, but she understood his point of view and knew that he would be pretty sad about it. She also thought he sounded like kind of an awkward underdog type, and so she naturally felt that he deserved her sympathy.

When they arrived back at the cave, they went inside and sat down. She had made it as cozy as possible with blankets and things, but it was still a cave. It was a good thing that Billy had brought more blankets, because it was terribly dank and got cold at night. It wasn't very good shelter, but it was all that she'd been able to find.

Sam fluttered in after them and landed on an outcropping of rock. Billy Boy and his mother took seats amongst the blankets. When they had all settled themselves, Billy asked her quietly if she'd had any luck finding his father. He assumed that she hadn't, but he didn't want to be a downer, and since he didn't know for sure, he thought it would just be right to ask about it.

Her face told him that he had, actually, been right. She explained that she'd heard a few rumours, but she still didn't have any concrete information. He was living on this mountain, or that mountain, or he'd gone over the mountains entirely, and so she'd have to go to the coast if she wanted to find him. She pursued a couple of these rumours, but soon realized that it wasn't worth the effort she had to go through to follow them up. She had wound up climbing various different mountains, just to find that there was no one up there. The views were spectacular, but not what she was looking for. After she had had to climb back down to the highway a few times, she decided that she would need to make sure she had better information before going in pursuit.

Then she had heard from some other crows that Sam's uncle had died and she knew that no one was looking out for her husband anymore. At first, this news really threw her for a loop. She told Billy that she had sat down and cried beside the highway for most of a day when she had heard about it. She knew that without anyone looking out for him, her husband had probably gotten himself into bad trouble. Her chances of finding him alive were suddenly a great deal slimmer.

Since she didn't think she'd be able to find him alive anymore, she thought about turning back right then. However, when she woke up the next morning, it was so beautiful out that it put her in a different mood. She decided that she wanted to find him regardless of whether he was alive or not. Also, she started feeling angry and determined. Even if he wasn't alive anymore, she wanted to find out what had happened to him. So she decided that she would keep going.

It wasn't long before she had cause to wonder if she'd made the right decision. She got what seemed like a good lead from a deer, so she climbed up to the top of the mountain. She couldn't find any sign of her husband and she had nowhere to go, so she hunkered down in the dank cave. It was in the cave that she finally saw some sign of her husband, as there were some scraps of rotten blankets left. However, that hardly seemed worth the climb, and she wondered if she should have just turned back when she was still down below. It was obviously too late to worry about it by that time, however, so she didn't spend much time thinking about it. Instead, she just hoped the cave would be enough shelter to get her through the winter.

Billy wasn't surprised that she hadn't been able to find his father. He hadn't expected her to have any luck. But while she hadn't been able to find any trace of his father, she had managed to find his bike. He was very surprised about that, since he'd almost forgotten that he'd been looking for it. Sam was very happy, since, with the bike found, the crow figured he'd be able to get his reward soon. Billy had almost forgotten about the crow. Since his introduction, Sam had been doing a good job of making himself unobtrusive, which Billy knew must have been really hard for him to do. When he heard about the bike, though, Sam couldn't help but speak up.

"Where is it?" asked the crow.

Billy's mother turned to look at Sam and said, "A bear has it."

Both Sam and Billy were a little crestfallen at that. They didn't think they'd be able to get it back from a bear. For one thing, as everyone knows, bears are enormously strong. For another, they're terribly smart. Well, not smart exactly, but very sceptical and so hard to trick or con.

"He lives up the hill," she said. "He's generally pretty nice, actually, but he has the bike and I don't know how open he'd be to giving it up. He'd heard about bears riding bikes in the circus, so when he was passing through Cadomin and saw the bike, he decided to take it to see if he could ride it. He's been practicing a lot, but I still don't think he's very good."

"Do you think we can convince him to give it back?" asked Billy.

"Maybe," said his mother. "We can try, anyway. Like I say, he seems pretty attached to it, but maybe because he's not that good at riding it, he'll be happy to just get rid of it. We'll go up tomorrow, and see if we can't get it back."

They rested up. There wasn't as much talking as you'd think. His mother told her story in more detail, but it was a lot simpler than his had been. She had stuck to the highway as much as possible, so she hadn't had nearly as many adventures as Billy. She had done some climbing to follow up some of her leads, but she hadn't been looking for adventures as she climbed. She had just wanted to get to the top and see if she could find her husband. After she decided not to act on anymore rumors, she stuck mostly to the highway, hoping she could pick up some good information from the deer and sheep that grazed beside the road. Like Sarah, she was also disturbed by the number of corpses, but she had just looked away and gone past them. The accident between the car and the moose hadn't happened yet when she passed along that part of the road, so she hadn't had to deal with it.

Trying to get news of her husband, she had talked to more animals than Billy had done. However, except for the wild rumours, she hadn't been able to find out much of anything. In fact, even though he hadn't actually spoken to that many animals, Billy had had more luck than she had, just by talking to Sam, who was at least related to the crow that had been watching his father. Even when she had finally been able to talk to some crows, they'd just heard about the deal, but they didn't really have any new information.

In any case, she had only left the highway again because it was becoming clear that if she stuck to the road, she'd never be able to find out much of anything at all. When she started taking the trails, she met more animals, but none of them had had any news for her about Billy's father.

By that point, she was starting to feel pretty ragged. Never mind that she was quite lonely as well. At least Billy had had Sarah and Sam for companions. She'd gone the whole way without any help from anyone. It made Billy think of Jacob again, and how he spent most of his time alone. He had also gone crazy and talked to himself. The boy wondered if there was a connection. He didn't like to think of his own mother going crazy too.

She'd already told him how she got to the cave. The front cave where she was staying wasn't sheltered or anything, but there were more caves further back that she hoped would be warmer in the winter. In any case, she knew she couldn't have made it back to the house in Cadomin before the snow started falling, and it seemed unlikely that she'd find anything better than the cave. So, despite her concerns, she hoped that it would do, and she had settled down for the winter.

She had met the bear by accident. There were supposed to be some goats nearby, so she figured that she'd go and look for them before it got too cold. She didn't have much hope that they'd be able to tell her anything. She was feeling pretty disheartened anyway, and besides, sheep very rarely knew about anything going on in the wide world. They concentrate on their feet and the rocks around them. That's why they're so sure footed, because that's all they think about. But as a result, they know very little about the rest of the world.

However, she never found the sheep. She went around a large

rock in the middle of the trail, and came upon the bear. She froze, but her fear was unfounded since the bear didn't even seem to notice her. He was desperately concentrating on trying to balance on the bike. However, the seat was way too small for him, and he kept falling off. He tried valiantly for a while, but then he fell off again and growled at it. It was only at that point that he noticed her watching. He didn't look particularly happy to see her, but he didn't actually growl at her or make any other kind of menacing gesture.

All he did was ask how much of his attempt to ride the bike she'd seen. So that he wouldn't be too embarrassed, she lied and said that she'd only seen a little bit. She then explained that lots of people have trouble with bikes and he really shouldn't feel too bad. She told him that little kids even have special wheels to hold the bike upright.

The bear was very interested in this last bit. He wondered if there was anywhere close by where he could get these special wheels. She assured him that, unless he wanted to go wandering into Hinton and go to the hardware store, he'd just have to make do without them.

Right from the start, she recognized it as Billy's missing bike. However, she didn't think that there was anything she could do about it. Even if she could have done something, she wasn't sure what the point would be. She didn't really expect to see Billy again, so even if she was able to get it back, she wouldn't be able to give it back to her son.

She was curious and asked the bear what he was doing with a bike anyway, and then he explained about the circus and his desire to see if he could ride.

"Do you want to join the circus?" she asked.

"Not really," he said. "It just seems like I should be able to do this. I mean, if a circus bear can do it, so can I."

She explained that in the circus, they force the bears to do it. The animals don't have a choice about it. He thought this was interesting as well. She had thought he would be outraged that bears could be enslaved like that, but mostly he just thought that between the lack of training wheels and without any slave-drivers forcing him to ride, it was no wonder that he couldn't do it.

She found out that his name was Jerry and he'd been hanging around at the top of the mountain for a while. She didn't figure he'd know anything, but she asked him about Billy's father. It seemed she was right. Or, at least, he didn't seem to want to talk about it. She didn't want to press the issue, so she couldn't be sure. It was possible that he was hiding something. If he'd been smaller and she'd been less afraid of him, then Billy's mother might have interrogated the bear further. But as it was, she couldn't see that there was any way to get him to talk. Besides, she wasn't even sure that he was hiding anything. It was also possible that he was only interested in the bike, and what she took for signs of devious behaviour were just signs that he wanted her to leave.

So she decided not to push it. She wasn't going to force him to talk about things that he didn't want to talk about. If she got him angry, he could maul her pretty badly, so she decided that she'd just leave it alone. She was feeling nervous, but she stuck around to be polite, and she didn't leave until they'd had a chat. They didn't talk about her that much, focussing mostly on the bear's frustrations, instead. Of course, there was his irritation with the bike, but he also told her that what he really wanted was to live by a lake. However, all the spots were already taken, and he hadn't been able to find anything. When she stood up to leave, he told her that she could come back anytime she felt like it. She had gone back to visit him a few more times, but he'd never talked about Billy's father, and so she hadn't seen any point in keeping up the visits. It had been a while since she'd gone to see him, but they hadn't had a fight or anything, so she figured there would be no problem with her and Billy going to visit him the next day.

Jerry

The three of them went to bed early and the next morning they got up bright and early to go see the bear. His camp was a couple hours hike up the trail from the cave. The day was sunny, but cold. Even though the trail wasn't used much, it was still easy to follow. Around noon they made it to Jerry's camp.

But there wasn't any bear to be seen. They looked around, and from the mess it was clear that he was still living there, but they couldn't see any sign of Jerry. They were beginning to wonder if they should just turn around and head back to their cave, when the bear came whizzing in on the bike and skidded to a stop in front of them.

All three of them were shocked, but Billy's mother expressed the most surprise. She'd seen how much trouble the bike had been giving Jerry, so she was the most astonished at his newfound ability to ride it. She had expected to find him struggling with it, like she had before.

"I just kept at it, and kept at it, and once I was able to balance, the rest just came easily. Now I love it," he said and then he took off again and made a large circle around them.

Billy knew this didn't bode well. If Jerry still hadn't figured out how to ride the bike, then the bear would have been more likely to give it back. But now that he knew what he was doing, it seemed unlikely that he'd let it go. The bear really seemed to be enjoying himself.

Once Jerry had come back and gotten off the bike, Billy's

mother introduced Billy and Sam. She expressed admiration for Jerry's ability to learn how to ride the bike, and told him that he looked good on it.

"But isn't it faster for you to just run?" she asked.

"It is," admitted Jerry, "I can run pretty fast. But it's not as much fun as riding. If I was going on a big trek then I'd walk or run. But for booting around the mountain top, the bike is great."

"Sooner or later you'll have to leave it, though, right?"

"Sometime, maybe, but not anytime soon. I like it up here. If I could get a place near a lake, I'd go right away, but those spots are all taken. I doubt if I'll be getting in there anytime soon. That's the only thing I'd move for. So, for now, I won't be going anywhere."

Billy's mother looked over at Billy and shook her head sadly. Like Billy, she was thinking that the bear wasn't likely to give up the bike if he'd actually learned how to ride it. Nonetheless, she told Jerry that she was pretty sure that it was actually Billy's bike.

"You got it in Cadomin? That's where we're from. And Billy had a bike just like that that disappeared."

"Maybe it's another bike."

"In Cadomin? That's hard to believe."

First Jerry turned a little away from them and looked at the ground guiltily. Then he rallied and turned to face them looking angry and defensive.

"I think it's a different bike," he said unconvincingly.

"Jerry..." said Billy's mom, but Jerry interrupted her.

"There could be dozens of bikes out here. It wouldn't be hard to find another bike. So nobody can know for sure that this is the same one."

"Can I just get the bell off of it?" said Sam. He said it quietly. He didn't want to make the bear any angrier than he already was, but he desperately wanted his reward, so he decided to take the risk.

"Why would I give you the bell?" asked Jerry.

"I promised him the bell if we found my bike," said Billy, "and since we found the bike, it's only fair for him to get his bell."

"It's not your bike," said Jerry.

"Jerry," said Billy's mother gently.

Jerry got up and got back onto the bike. "Jerry what? You know how much trouble I had learning how to ride this thing. I'm not going to give it away now, just because your son lost his bike. I'm sorry you lost your bike, Billy, but I'm not giving you mine."

"It's not yours!" said Billy.

The bear growled at him and said, "Yes, it is. Now all of you, go away. I'm going for a ride, and I don't want you to be here when I get back."

With that, Jerry rode away. The three others stood up and slowly started walking back down the trail feeling defeated. They hadn't known exactly what was going to happen, but they had all thought that there was at least a chance that the bear might be willing to part with the bike. They hadn't been counting on his learning how to ride.

"So what do we do now?" asked Billy.

After thinking for a minute, his mother replied. "We'll have to find some way to trick him so we can get the bike back."

"How'll we do that?"

"I don't know. We'll have to think on it a bit."

"We could just steal it back from him," said Billy.

"I don't know," said his mother. "I bet he watches it pretty closely when he's not riding it. Besides, now he knows that we want it, so if we take it, he'll know it was us. Even if we can get it away from him, he'll come after us as soon as he figures out that its missing."

They were all quiet for a while, then Sam spoke up. "He said something about wanting a spot on a lake."

"He does. Maybe we could use that," said Billy's mother. She thought for a moment, and then said, "We could tell him that there's an opening at a lake and then he'll probably go and leave the bike behind. Then we can take it and disappear before he realizes there's no spot and comes back. He'll probably still come after us, but at least we'd have a good head start."

"But we can't tell him about the lake ourselves," said Sam. "He won't believe us, so we'll need someone else to actually tell him."

"You're right. Everybody likes him, though. I don't know who would tell him, unless we fool them as well."

"We could do that. Didn't you say that there's a herd of goats up here somewhere? If I tell them, they'll probably believe it. They don't know any better. And then they'll tell Jerry."

"That might work, but I don't know if I can get them to tell Jerry."

"Don't worry," said Sam. "I'll take care of it tomorrow. The sheep will think that they're doing him a favour."

Deception

Their spirits picked up again once they had a new plan and soon they were laughing as they walked. Sam had become his old self again, talking volubly.

He told them a funny story about a bighorn sheep that he'd known. It had been so completely oblivious to the outside world that Sam had been able to convince it that there weren't going to be any people coming by anymore. Sheep usually know more than goats, but this one had made itself very isolated, and so Sam was able to convince it that the mountains had been closed for business. Sam told it that the highway was being torn up, and all the animals were going to have to fend for themselves. The sheep had been depending on getting fed by tourists during the summer. When it heard that the road was being torn up, it knew that it wouldn't be able to do that anymore, and so it panicked. It began thinking that hibernation would maybe be a good idea since it wouldn't have to eat as much. It started hoarding food.

Sam decided that his joke had gone far enough when the sheep had been talking about hibernating for a while, and seemed resolved to try it. The animal had been trying to find out how the squirrels found so much food for the winter and how they picked a place to hide it. Sam told the sheep that there was nothing for it to worry about, the crow was joking, and, of course, the people were still coming to the mountains. After being told how it'd been fooled, the sheep was angry, and it had a negative view of crows after that. However, Sam figured that it was worth having the sheep mad at him. When he told other animals that the sheep had been trying to figure out how hibernate, they got a good laugh about it, and Sam was happy to let them. Sam knew that many animals already had a bad opinion of crows, so he didn't have to worry about ruining his reputation with them. It might have confirmed their notions, but Sam thought it was hilarious, so he had to tell other animals about it.

When the three of them got back to the cave, they sat down and Sam was quiet. He seemed to be planning what he would say to the goats the next day. "Where did you say they were?" he asked.

"I just heard about them but I never actually found them. After I met Jerry, I never went back to find the goats," said Billy's mother. "I didn't think they'd be any help, anyway, so I never bothered. They were supposed to be somewhere on the mountain above the trail. They might not even be there anymore, for all I know, but they'll be around here somewhere. I heard that they've been up there for years, so I doubt if they would move now."

"If they're around, I'll find them."

The next day, Sam took off early after saying goodbye to Billy and his mother. "Wish me luck," he said before he flew away. Silently, they both actually did wish him luck. Things depended on him, and they really needed him to succeed.

Sam had no trouble finding the goats. They were a few miles past Jerry's camp, above the tree-line, and on the top of the bald mountain. They were eating the few strands of grass that were poking out from among the rocks. The crow flew up to where they were grazing and then settled down on one of the rocks himself.

At first the goats just ignored him and kept eating. He was tempted to say something, but he kept quiet, and pretended he was there on other business. He started preening, which seemed like kind of an odd activity for a crow, but he needed to do something to keep himself busy and not look suspicious.

After a few minutes he noticed that the oldest goat was glancing over at him every few minutes. It tried to pretend that it wasn't looking, and whenever Sam looked over, it would quickly put its head back down and start eating again. Then it stopped, walked onto an outcrop, and looked out over the valley below him. A little below them lay Jerry's camp and far down below were the highway and the river.

Sam flew over and landed on a rock that was standing beside the old goat. It gave him another glance and then looked back out over the scene below.

"Highway looks quiet today," said Sam.

"Is it?" said the goat, irritably. "I can't see that far."

"Been flying over that highway for quite a while. Just came east over the mountains."

The goat looked up at him. "That so?" He was desperately trying to sound like he didn't care, but one thing Sam knew about goats is that no matter how disconnected they are, they also desperately like to hear news of the outside world. That's why they're so gullible, because not only do they not know anything about anything, they also really want to hear and desperately want to believe everything that they do hear.

Crows don't generally bother much with goats, even though they're about the only ones left who will still listen to crows. Goats rarely have anything worth taking, and they never have any interesting news, so even though they'll probably listen, aside from the satisfaction of tricking someone, there isn't much of anything to get. And that isn't really all that satisfying because goats are so gullible that it's no challenge.

Sam was feeling a little nervous because the other jokes that he'd pulled were just for kicks or something shiny. In this case, the stakes were higher. He still stood to get something shiny out of it, but it was much more important than usual. With an effort, Sam forced himself to put his doubts aside, and started feeling confident that he could get these goats to believe him. He even hoped that he might be more convincing than usual, since this was the only time he'd ever talked to a goat with such a specific goal in mind.

"Great trip," said Sam. "Wore me out, so I probably wouldn't do it again, but still a really great trip."

"How was it great?" asked the goat, giving up the charade that it didn't care. It turned and looked directly at Sam.

"There were some beautiful spots," said the crow. "Not far from here there's this little lake. High up, close to the top of one of the mountains, but not so high that there aren't trees around it. There's a full forest. So you'd expect someone would be using it. But other than a few squirrels and some other birds, no one seems to even know about it. I was there for a few days, and I didn't see anyone."

"Really?"

The eagerness in the goat's eyes made Sam think that maybe it would want to claim the lake for itself. For a moment, Sam wondered if the herd was looking for another place. If that was the case, then, of course, the goats wouldn't tell Jerry about it, and the whole trick would be pointless.

"Are you looking for somewhere to go?" asked Sam casually.

"No, not for us. We're happy here, and, besides, forests don't do much for us. Nothing much to eat. But our friend the bear is looking for a place."

Sam was relieved but tried not to give any outward sign of it. "Then I'd say he'd better get to that lake pretty quick. I don't know how it's stayed hidden, but it won't stay that way for much longer. Its prime real estate, and I haven't been keeping my mouth shut about it. Told a cougar about it for one thing. He didn't seem too interested, but I'm sure he's told other people."

He made up a few more things to tell the sheep about his travels. It didn't seem believable that, from an extensive trip, he would just have the lake to talk about. He told the goat about the milky looking river and about forest fires on the other side of the mountains. When he felt like he'd given the goat enough details to make his story believable, he took his leave.

"Well, I've got to get going. I hope your friend finds that lake all right." After he left, he flew back to the cave and let Billy and his mother know that he'd told the goats about the fictional lake. Then he went up to Jerry's camp and perched on a tree with a good view. He watched the bear ride around the camp on the bike for a while before the old goat appeared. The bear stopped riding and put the bike down so that he could talk to it.

Now everyone knows that goats don't lie. They're very honest creatures, and while they may repeat things that they've heard, they never knowingly tell untruths. So unless they know for certain that the goats have themselves been lied to, creatures tend to take what they say seriously. Sam was hoping that Jerry would be too excited about the lake to spend much time interrogating the goat about where it had gotten its information.

Sam's hopes were well grounded. Near the end of the conversation, the crow got nervous when the goat voluntarily mentioned that it'd gotten its news from a crow. However, the bear didn't seem to pay much attention. Jerry figured he wasn't going to get a better chance to live by a lake, and so he was determined to get there as quickly as possible. He was so excited that he didn't let his natural bearish scepticism alter his views. The bear was already imagining himself beside the lake. In his mind, he already had it all mapped out, and knew exactly where his territory would be. He got the goat to give him directions.

Obviously the goat didn't have a precise idea where the imaginary lake was supposed to be, but it was as clear as it could be, and Jerry seemed satisfied. Even with the vague directions, the bear was eager to get going. After quickly getting himself ready to go, he thanked the goat and said goodbye. Before he went, the bear gave a long, wistful look at the bike, which was lying on the ground. He took it gently and leaned it upright against a rock. Then the bear took off at a run, lumbering into the forest to the west of his camp.

Sam saw the bear leaving, as he had been watching from above as all of this was going on. He watched as Jerry disappeared into the bush below the camp before the crow flew back to the cave to let Billy and his mother know that the plan had worked.

When Sam told them the news, they started for Jerry's camp right away. The crow flew back to watch and make sure that the bear didn't change his mind and return. He was feeling triumphant and eager, so he also flew down to the bike and pecked at the bell a few times. It made a pleasing ringing sound, but Sam couldn't see any way that he'd be able to remove it himself. The bell was just attached with wing-nuts, which might have been simple enough. However, the crow couldn't get a grip on them with his beak no matter how hard he tried. After fiddling with them for a while, he gave up and flew back up to his perch in the tree above the lair, and waited for Billy and his mother.

It was almost nightfall before they arrived, but even though it was getting dark, they didn't stop, even for a quick rest. They just grabbed the bike and immediately started heading back to their own cave. They knew that they were probably safe, since if the bear was going to come back, he would probably have done it already. Nevertheless, if Jerry did happen to return, they didn't want to risk getting caught at his camp.

It was quite late by the time they got back to the cave, so they lay down and got some sleep. They were worried about the bear, but they also knew they couldn't climb down from the cave in the dark. In the morning they set out again, back along the trail toward the cliffs. As Sam flew along beside them, he desperately wanted to ask about getting the bell, but he decided that he'd wait until they had at least gotten back to the highway.

They weren't sure of where they were going, but they knew they couldn't stick around. Sooner or later, Jerry would give up trying to find the lake, and then he would come back to his camp near the mountain top. When he came back and found the bike missing, he would figure out that he'd been tricked. So as soon as it was light the next morning, they left the cave and headed back down the trail toward the highway.

But before they got to the highway, they had to get down the cliffs. Billy's mother had brought the rope again, and when they got to the cliffs, they tied it around a small tree that was growing near the top and let the rest of it dangle over the edge of the cliff. First they lowered the bike down, and then Billy climbed down. When he got to the bottom, he had a bit of trouble getting around the bike so he could put his feet on the ground, but eventually he made it. When he was standing on solid ground, he untied the bike and held the rope for his mother.

Billy's mother then climbed down, though she seemed a great deal more confident than the boy, and she only had to use the rope for occasional support. Sam just fluttered around and called out encouragement occasionally. When it became clear that his exhortations weren't necessary or welcome, he stopped, and just let her climb down in peace.

After they had gotten down the cliff, it wasn't long before they managed to get back to the highway. Though being at the bottom of the cliffs made them feel safer, they still hadn't really made a plan and so they had to stop and figure out where they were going. Sam figured he'd waited long enough and so he asked about the bell. The wing-nuts were a little rusty, but not really difficult. Billy took them off, and then gave the bell to Sam.

The crow stood on the asphalt in front of them. Billy knelt down beside him, and he looked like he was going to try to hug him, even though he didn't really know how to hug a crow. Eventually he decided to just pat the crow on the head instead. Sam turned away for a moment, and if he could have sniffed, he would have. Instead he just hopped up and down, then turned back to Billy and his mother.

"If I hear anything about your father, I'll let you know. Do you know where you're going?"

They hadn't yet made a plan and so neither of them really knew where they would wind up going. Without a better idea, Billy told the crow that they'd probably head back along the highway, and so if Sam wanted to find them, that's where they'd be.

"We need to have a better plan than that," said Billy's mother. Her brows came together and she looked concerned. "At least the cave was something, but it's getting really cold out here, and we need to figure out where we're going to go for the winter."

Billy remembered Sarah's house. Sarah had said that he was welcome anytime. It seemed like this would be a good time to visit, so he convinced his mother that they should go there. Billy was still hurt that Sarah had abandoned him, but he couldn't see a better option. He imagined that the house would be very cozy over the winter. In the spring, they could return to Cadomin. Billy's mother didn't know anything about the house, but she was willing to take the boy's word for it, so they decided that they would go to Sarah's house for the winter.

"Do you remember where we met?" Billy asked Sam.

"I do. On the highway at the wide part of the river."

"Well, Sarah's house is just across from there. If you get any news, that's where we're heading."

Both Billy and Sam looked awkward. "Thanks for all your help," the boy said.

"Hey, no problem. I got paid, after all," said the crow, and held up the bell in one of his claws.

After a few more minutes, Billy's mother spoke up. "Come and visit us, Sam, even if you don't have any news."

That seemed to make it possible for Sam to leave. He shuffled around for a moment, then flapped his wings and took off. The bell hung awkwardly beneath him, grasped tightly in his claws. Once the crow was high enough that he just looked like a speck, Billy looked back at his mother and they tried to figure out how they would get to Sarah's house.

Sarah's House

Billy figured they shouldn't cross the bridge, since that would put them on the wrong side of the river. He didn't want to risk having to cross the water again when they got to the flats. Swimming hadn't worked very well the first time, so instead, he tried to get his mother to remember where the train tracks were so that they could walk along them back to Sarah's house.

Since she'd followed the highway, she hadn't really thought about the tracks. She imagined that the tracks were quite a ways away, and she didn't know of any trail that would take them there. She tried to convince Billy that they should just follow the highway back and deal with the river when they had to, but he really didn't want to have to worry about getting across again, so they sat down and tried to figure out where the train tracks might be.

It took them a while, but eventually they thought that they'd figured it out. They believed the tracks were on the far side of a ridge that ran along beside the highway. There wasn't any trail, so they had to push through the forest until they got to the tracks. It took them several hours, and it was even harder with Billy trying to manoeuvre the bike through the brush, so they didn't make much progress. After a few hours, however, they managed to make it up and over, and found that they had been right.

The tracks were nestled between two tall ridges of the

mountains. When they finally reached them, they were exhausted and they needed a little rest. After they'd gotten their breath back, they headed east. They were glad to be heading out of the mountains. Even the days were starting to get nippy by that time. The cave would never have been warm enough to see them through the winter. Even if they hadn't been fleeing from the bear, and they'd been able to stick around, they'd have had to leave the cave in any case.

The tracks were uneventful. They didn't run through the valley for very long. A few trains came, but it was always at wide points, and they had no trouble getting off the tracks and out of the way. There were a few narrower parts that made them nervous, but they ran at those points, and they didn't have any close calls.

They wondered if Jerry had given up on finding the lake yet, and wondered if he had returned to find the bike missing. Had he decided to come after them? And if he had, had he found the right trail? Was he following along behind them? No matter what the bear was doing, they knew that there wasn't much they could do about it. They wouldn't be hard to find on the tracks, but they were going as fast as they could, and they just had to hope that they were free and clear.

After a few weeks they arrived back at the wide part of the river and not long after that they came to the flats. They descended from the tracks and not long after they saw Sarah's house. Most of the leaves on the trees had already fallen and the grass was yellow. As they walked toward the house, the dead grass swished around their knees, and the leaves crunched under their feet. When they got to the door, Billy rang the bell.

Sarah opened it, wondering who could be calling. She was glad to see Billy. She bent down a little so she could hug him. She'd been worried about him ever since he had left in such a huff, and she was happy that he'd come back. She was also happy to meet Billy's mother and she gave a little clap when she saw the bike. She let him bring it inside so that it wouldn't get stolen again, and so that if Jerry came by, the bear wouldn't see it and know they were there.

Once they were inside and sitting down, Sarah brought them tea. The house was the same as Billy had remembered, nice and warm and comfortable. After they had both had some tea, first Billy, and then his mother went upstairs to the bathroom and had showers.

In the weeks that followed it got very cold, and only a few weeks after they'd arrived, the snow started coming down. There had been no sign of Jerry the bear, and Billy's mother guessed that maybe he was just too tired and disappointed by not finding the lake that he hadn't even bothered trying to find them.

Jerry had returned and figured out that Billy and his mother had taken that bike, but he didn't know for certain that the lake was imaginary. Maybe the three of them had just been waiting for their chance, and when he had left to find the lake, they'd come and taken the bike. That didn't mean the lake wasn't real. After all, it had been a sheep that had told him about it. He'd completely forgotten about the crow, and so even if he couldn't find it, there was still a chance that the lake was out there, and maybe in the spring he would go on another trek to try to find it. In the meantime, he really did have to hibernate.

In any case, Billy and his mother were glad they'd made it back to Sarah's house before winter came. It was very cold outside, but the house was warm. However, it didn't seem very long before spring arrived. The snow started melting and it started getting warmer. After things had been melting slowly for close to a month, there was a really warm week that melted the remaining snow really quickly. The river got higher, and they worried that the flats and the house might flood. But in spite of their fears, they were safe and the water never got above the banks.

Sam came for a visit when spring arrived. The crow had many stories about what he was doing with the bell. He'd used it to confuse a guy in the forest enough that he could steal his keys. Sam couldn't use them, and he didn't know what they opened, so he gave them back right away, but he was still proud of himself. He had also often used the bell to trick animals into running away and leaving food behind. He made it seem like some hikers were coming, and at least some of the animals would run away, leaving behind whatever they were eating.

Also, he'd noticed that there was a new town going up on the south side of the highway. It had just started out as a cabin, but people from all over were flocking to it. People who wanted to get away, but not get too far away, were arriving in droves. It was close to their pilgrimage site, so even the religious people were moving to the new town. It was getting big enough to be an eyesore.

Sarah wasn't crazy for Sam. She didn't really like crows at the best of times, and he was too talkative for her. However, she was polite enough not to say anything and let Billy and his mother talk to Sam without causing any commotion.

After Sam left, it was time for Billy and his mother to get going back to Cadomin. It had been the plan all winter that they would leave after the snow melted, but they were really at home in Sarah's house. They took their time packing up, and then Billy's mother asked him if he really wanted to get back.

Billy looked up at her and shook his head. He liked Sarah's house better than the house in Cadomin. Since the weather was warming up, he'd started riding the bike again. He hadn't gotten very far, and he was still a little worried about running into Jerry while he was out riding. Nevertheless, he was happy riding around, and his mother seemed happy with Sarah and with the house. Besides settling down to wait for his father to return, there didn't seem to be any point in returning to Cadomin.

It felt like the very last day of winter or the first of spring when there was an unexpected knock on the door. When the three of them heard it, they all started and then immediately froze, not knowing what to do. After a moment, Sarah stood up and hesitantly went to the door. She looked through the front window to see who was on her step. There were a man and a woman talking quietly to each other. They didn't look dangerous, so she went and opened the door.

The visitors stopped talking to each other and immediately turned, smiling, toward Sarah. The woman started talking.

"Hello. Don't mean to bother you or anything. My name is Nancy and this is Brandon. We're with a small religious group on our way to the new town on the other side of the highway."

"All right," said Sarah. She was feeling skeptical and wasn't sure what they wanted. They seemed harmless enough, but without knowing what they really wanted, it was impossible for her to be sure that they didn't pose a threat.

"We just hoped that it would be okay with you if we spent a few days camped out near here," said Nancy. "These flats are the best place we've found for resting up since we left Entrance, and so we were just hoping it'd be all right with you if we stopped a while."

"Of course," said Sarah. She was still a little bewildered. It didn't seem like that could be all that they wanted, but, at that moment, that was all that they were asking and she couldn't see that there was any good reason to refuse them.

After that very brief conversation, the two visitors turned and left. Sarah closed the door behind them and went back to the sitting area. She told Billy and his mother who the visitors were and that they would be staying near the house for a few days. On hearing, Billy was fairly certain he knew who they were and what they actually wanted. However, he didn't want to arouse anyone's interest, so he didn't say anything. He hoped that the visitors would just stay for a few days, and then be on their way without incident.

The first day was fine. They didn't have any contact with them that day at all. It was bright and sunny and the visitors had set up camp a fair ways from the house, near the river. For a while, Billy watched them from the front window. But he couldn't see what they were doing, so he soon got bored.

Sarah wondered if she should take them some tea or something.

She had accepted that they had really just wanted to ask her permission before they camped on her land. Now that she'd accepted that they really were actually harmless, she'd begun thinking that she should be finding ways to be more welcoming. There were too many of them to stay in the house, but she figured that she could at least take some hot drinks out to them.

Billy talked her out of it, however. He was still hoping that the religious visitors would just leave without having any contact with the three of them. He worried that if Sarah went out to bring them drinks, she'd get involved in a conversation and wind up joining them or something. He actually wasn't sure what they might do, but he still didn't think she should talk to them.

However, by the next day, Sarah was feeling determined to be kind to the visitors, and so she was going to take them some tea whether Billy liked it or not. When it became clear that it was happening regardless of his opinion, the boy volunteered to take the tea out himself. He wasn't happy about it, but it seemed better to do it himself than let Sarah do it. After all, at least he'd already been exposed and he knew what to expect and also how to resist it.

So Sarah made tea and put it in a large thermos. Then she loaded a tray with some milk, sugar and mugs for the visitors to use. She only had six mugs, but she was sure that they'd share and there wouldn't be a problem.

Billy took everything out to the visitor's camp. There was a circle of tents around a central space with a blackened fire pit. There was also a stump that had obviously been used for chopping wood, and he put the tray and thermos down on it.

The visitors quickly gathered around him and the tea. There were Nancy and Brandon as well as three other men and two women. They were all happy to take some tea. The last to join them was a fourth man, who appeared from behind one of the tents and came over, smiling. He had platinum blond hair and blue eyes. If Billy had known, he would have seen that the man looked exactly like a blond version of himself. However, Billy didn't see it. Some of the other visitors noticed, but only Nancy actually commented on it.

"You and David look related, Billy. Don't you all think?"

The other visitors mostly kept quiet, though one or two agreed with her unenthusiastically. They knew that David had a checkered past, and didn't want to make too much of his resemblance to Billy. Neither the man nor the boy seemed that interested in the similarity, so it wasn't brought up again, and the conversation quickly progressed on other lines.

The visitors were on their way to the new town that Sam had told the three of them about. Not only was the town closer for their pilgrimage, but they felt that it might be fertile ground for religious conversion. Billy didn't want to be discouraging, so he didn't bring up the founder's comments about them. If Vince had anything to say about it, it didn't seem likely that they would have much luck spreading their religion in the new town. The boy started feeling bad for them. They really weren't that bad, and, ever since they'd first arrived, Billy had been judging them very harshly. However, there wasn't anything he could do about how they'd fare in the new town, so the boy just nodded along with their ambitious plans.

When the tea was finished, Billy headed back to the house, carrying the thermos and platter with him. When he got back, he went inside and put everything in the sink to wash later. Sarah asked him how it had gone, and Billy replied that everything had gone just fine.

It wasn't until he was asleep that night that Billy recognized what his similarity to David must mean. Both Sarah and his mother were asleep when Billy sat bolt upright in bed. While he slept, he had remembered that his father had also been called David, and at two in the morning he was woken by his sudden understanding. He didn't scream, and instead he just sat there with a confused and surprised expression on his face.

He wanted to go back out to the camp immediately to look at David again. However, he knew that that wasn't a good idea, so he just lay awake feeling stressed most of the night. He didn't fall asleep again until five in the morning, and when he woke up again at eight, he was still feeling tired. After breakfast, his mom disappeared upstairs to do some mending, and so he found himself alone to tell Sarah what was going on.

She didn't know what to do. On one hand, she thought that Billy's mother really needed to know regardless of how much it might upset her. On the other hand, the boy had filled her in on how long his mother had spent waiting for her husband, and Sarah didn't want to be responsible for causing that to start again. So she wasn't sure what she needed to do. She pondered a while, but eventually her sense of fairness won out, and she decided that the boy's mother needed to be told no matter what.

It wasn't what Billy had wanted to hear. He wasn't sure what to do either, but he was already leaning toward keeping it a secret. He hadn't expected Sarah to come out in favour of saying something, and it forced him to make up his mind right away. Sarah's decision made him more determined not to tell his mother. She had nearly killed herself searching for his father, so no one could claim that she hadn't tried hard enough. She was finally getting over things, and the boy didn't want the two of them being pulled back to Cadomin or anywhere else. He figured that she'd follow her husband, and who knows where they'd wind up. He'd end up wishing they'd just gone back to Cadomin. At least if they just went home, he wouldn't have to deal with either the pilgrims or the campers again.

So he decided that he wouldn't tell her, and he got Sarah to promise to keep quiet as well. It was bothering him a little, but he was sure that it was for the best, and he was just keeping secrets, not actually lying. So when his mother came down from doing some mending, Sarah and Billy just exchanged significant glances but didn't actually say anything.

The next day, however, Billy's mom was out in the backyard clearing some dead leaves from the garden. Sarah wasn't much for gardening, and she hadn't raked when the leaves had fallen the previous year. Billy's mom still had the gardening bug, however, so when the snow had started melting, and the leaves started appearing, she had begun itching to get outside and clear them away. She knew that she wouldn't be able to get any new plants to put in the gardens around the house, but she was hopeful that there would still be at least a few hardy perennials that would come back and give her something to tend in the mounds of dirt near the house.

When she was out raking, David had left the visitors camp and was out walking down by the river. He sometimes felt the need to get away and go walking by himself. The other visitors thought secretly that he was pretty intense, and they were pretty intense themselves, so David was actually very intense. He was often against doing anything that might make things easier at all. He felt that doing things the easy way, even when it made sense, was a disservice to God and the prophet. When the boy had brought out tea, David had been a little scandalized, in fact, but when he saw all his compatriots drinking, he decided he'd join in. He'd been against resting on the flats at all, but he'd been overruled. He tried to put a good face on it, but he was agitating fairly regularly for them to leave. He'd just been rebuffed again, so he decided that he needed to go for a walk.

The camp was out the front of the house, but he was walking beside the water, which curved around until he was behind the house. That was how he'd gotten to a spot where Billy's mom could see him. If he'd stayed in the camp, she would never have seen him. The water was far away, and so was he, but, even from a distance, she was still sure it was him. The look of him had been burned on her mind for a long time.

Her first instinct was to start shouting and waving, but now that she'd actually found her husband, she also found herself frozen and unexpectedly confused. She just stood in the yard, clutching the handle of the rake and staring at the man by the river. Finding him had been her goal, but, like Billy, she knew that getting her husband back would mean that they would probably have to travel again. She had gotten comfortable at Sarah's house, and didn't want to have to leave again. Besides, while she didn't know anything about the new town, she had been to Entrance before and didn't like it. Also, it seemed certain that her husband was now a very religious person and she wasn't sure how that would work.

So when she started moving again, she just went back through the patio doors and into the kitchen area. She was still clutching the rake when Sarah found her. She told Sarah about her husband, and Sarah pretended that it was news to her. However, she was secretly relieved, since now that the boy's mother knew, and so she no longer had to keep secrets. And she knew that both Billy and herself were in agreement about the other aspects of the situation. Namely, that Billy's mother shouldn't get involved with his father again. Whether they should tell his mother or not had been the only question.

By the time that Billy got home, Sarah and his mother had been talking for a long time. He'd been out biking and exploring. When he got home, both women looked over at him with serious looks on their faces. His mother was concerned how he'd react to hearing that his father was outside, and Sarah tried to convey with her look that she hadn't said anything. Billy understood and so he acted surprised and upset when his mother told him the news.

In fact, Billy hadn't been feeling nearly as upset as he thought he should. He knew that his father being outside should have sent him for a loop. However, all Billy had been able to think about was how to keep his mother from finding out. Now all he could think about was how to keep her from joining his father. He didn't know much, but he knew that he should have been feeling upset for both himself and his mom, not just for her.

But when his mother asked him about what she ought to do, he discouraged her from going out to David. At this point, his mom went upstairs, leaving Sarah and Billy alone to talk about the situation. However, once the major points had been discussed, there really wasn't much else to say. Sarah explained the raking and David's walk, and it wasn't long before Billy drifted away. They were all inside, but all three of them had isolated themselves in different rooms of the house.

Sarah knew that she wasn't as affected as the other two. She wasn't actually involved, in that she'd never even met Billy's dad, let alone developed an emotional relationship with him. So what she felt worst about was that the two of them were sitting alone in different rooms when it seemed like they really should have been together. The two of them had a great deal to talk about, but Billy was still downstairs in the sitting area, and his mother had retired to her bedroom upstairs. Sarah wasn't actually sure what they might need to say, but she was sure that the two should be talking.

She had no idea how to approach either of them, however, and when the visitors were packing up the next day, she wanted to tell them, but wasn't sure how she should go about it. Maybe they'd notice on their own, but she wasn't sure if they would. Neither seemed very attentive at the moment, so the visitors could easily leave without even drawing attention.

Nancy came to the door again, to say thank you and to let Sarah know that they were going. Sarah was in an odd mood, and though she tried to at least be civil, she knew she probably came off as distracted. She was hoping that this would make things better, but she wasn't sure that it would.

When Nancy came to the door, she was tempted to ask them to stay. She was also tempted to go upstairs and find out for sure whether Billy's mom had made a decision yet. As it was, she did nothing, and just tried to say goodbye properly. Nancy smiled quizzically, wondering what she was thinking about, but she stifled her curiosity, accepted Sarah's farewell and left.

Their leaving seemed like it should have been a relief, but the house was still filled with total silence. Sarah watched out the front window for a couple more hours until the visitors had packed up and left. Then she went upstairs to find Billy's mom. She was sitting in Sarah's bedroom at the front of the house, watching out the window. She still wasn't saying anything, but she must have seen the whole thing since she hadn't been able to pull herself away from the window. There wasn't any activity, but even during the night, she wasn't able to sleep, so she had kept watching the camp.

However, the visitors were now gone. She knew that it was crazy to keep watching, but she just kept looking out the window. She'd been waiting for her husband to come back for so long, and she had found him, and then not even gone to talk to him. She hadn't gone to talk to him, because she didn't want to follow him, and she knew that's what talk would lead to. Nevertheless, she felt like the bottom had fallen out of her. As she looked out at the empty spot by the river, she felt like her insides had collapsed.

Sarah asked her if she wanted to come down, but she just shook her head and continued watching out the window. Sarah went back downstairs to where Billy was still sitting near the back of the house. There was no chance that he'd seen them go, so she told him that the visitors had gone. He looked up at that and, having seen her come from upstairs, he asked what his mom was up to. Sarah told him she was asleep. She really didn't have any idea what she ought to be doing, but it didn't seem right for the boy knowing that his mother was up there staring into empty space.

When the two of them went upstairs to bed, Billy's mom had at least moved back into her bedroom. She had figured out how pointless it was to be staring out the window at nothing, so she'd left Sarah's room and gone across the hall to her own room. However, she'd also closed the door behind her, so when Sarah and Billy came upstairs, they still weren't able to talk to her. They each just went to bed and hoped that things would be better in the morning.

They didn't seem to be, however. Billy's mom had gotten up before either of them and gone outside for a walk. After breakfast, Billy stood at the patio doors watching his mother wander around aimlessly. Sarah sat down with a cup of tea and watched him watching her. Finally, he'd had enough, and, whether she liked it or not, he decided to go out and talk to his mom. He walked quickly, almost running through the grass toward her. It was very lush and green, mixed with the brown, rotting remnants of last year's grass. Sometimes it scratched his legs as he passed, but most of the time it felt soft and pleasant.

His mother had stopped walking and she was lying on her back looking up at the sky. She had an odd, happy expression on her face. She looked peaceful and Billy decided not to bother her, and so he sat down in the grass beside her. A few minutes later she seemed to wake up and then, slowly, she sat up. It was only then that she noticed him sitting beside her.

"Sorry, Billy, I didn't see you there," she said.

"That's okay," he said.

"I didn't see anything at all, actually," she said. "Everything went away."

"I know," he said. "It's happened to me as well. You should enjoy it right away. It doesn't last nearly as long as you'd like it to."

She lay back in the grass trying to recapture the feeling. Billy knew she wouldn't be able to entirely, but hoped that it would work the same for her that it had for him the first time. They sat beside each other in silence for a while. It felt comfortable and relaxed, and so it wasn't anything like the very tense silence that they'd been enduring for the previous couple of days.

Then she sat up again and looked over at him. After a long moment, she asked if he felt all right about the decision she'd made. She knew she probably should have asked sooner, but she really hadn't had the energy. The whole situation was hard enough without having to ask him. But she still wanted to know. She wasn't even sure that it would have made her change her mind, but she wanted to know what he thought.

Billy Boy smiled and said that everything was fine. Just fine.

26917148R00165

Made in the USA
Charleston, SC
24 February 2014